Praise for Nancy Thayer's
Hot Flash series

"Readers who loved the previous books as well as those new to the series will enjoy the adventures of these spirited women navigating family, love, and aging during the holidays."
—*Booklist,* on *Hot Flash Holidays*

"Who could fail to root for [these] five as they face aging with honesty, determination and a lot of help from their friends?"
—*Publishers Weekly,* on *Hot Flash Holidays*

"Women of a certain age . . . will chortle knowingly at her all-too-vivid [depictions] of the multiple tolls that age takes on the female face, form, sex life, and self-worth. Thayer lays it all out with perverse relish—aches, pains, incontinence, hormone surges, sagging this and bulging that."
—*The Boston Globe*

"Time after time, [Nancy Thayer] makes me laugh, makes me think, makes me appreciate that she understands what women want to express. Thayer's writing often reminds me of Elizabeth Berg, Jeanne Ray, and Anne Tyler. . . ."
—*Women's Lifestyle*

Also by Nancy Thayer

The Hot Flash Club Chills Out
The Hot Flash Club Strikes Again
The Hot Flash Club
An Act of Love
Belonging
Between Husbands and Friends
Bodies and Souls
Custody
Everlasting
Family Secrets
My Dearest Friend
Nell
Spirit Lost
Stepping
Three Women at the Water's Edge
Morning

Hot Flash Holidays

A Novel

NANCY THAYER

BALLANTINE BOOKS • NEW YORK

Hot Flash Holidays is a work of fiction. Names, characters, places, and incidents are the products of the author's imagination or are used fictitiously. Any resemblance to actual events, locales, or persons, living or dead, is entirely coincidental.

2006 Ballantine Books Mass Market Edition

Published in the United States by Ballantine Books, an imprint of The Random House Publishing Group, a division of Random House, Inc., New York.

BALLANTINE and colophon are registered trademarks of Random House, Inc.

Originally published in hardcover in the United States by Ballantine Books, an imprint of The Random House Publishing Group, a division of Random House, Inc., in 2005.

ISBN 0-345-48552-1

Cover photograph: © Tanya Constantine/Getty Images

Printed in the United States of America

www.ballantinebooks.com

OPM 9 8 7 6 5 4 3 2 1

THIS BOOK IS DEDICATED TO
Mary Lethbridge, Eileen McGrath,
Nina Murray, and Emma Rusch

AND IN MEMORY OF
Ethel Anastos, Barbara Andrews,
Grace Grossman, and Margherita Sutro

ACKNOWLEDGMENTS

Wisdom is hope and knows no age.

My gratitude is immense for the wisdom of my editor, Linda Marrow, and my agent, Meg Ruley.

I couldn't have written this book without the gifts of inspiration, anecdotes, humor, chocolate, wisdom, and oh, yes, an ankle bracelet, from my friends, younger and . . . older. Enormous thanks to Deborah Beale, Mimi Beman, Jill Burrill, Laurie Chatfield-Taylor, Jennifer Costanza, Martha Foshee, Tina Gessler, David Gillum, Kim Guarnaccia, Gilly Hailparn, Charlotte Maison, Joan Medlicott, Margrethe Mentes, Elena Murphy, Robyn North, Letitia Ord, Tricia Patterson, Jane Patton, Pam Pindell, Selma Rayfiel, Susan Sandler, Laura Simon, Josh Thayer, and Sam Wilde.

And Charley, thanks for being better than chocolate!

CHRISTMAS

1

On this early December day, snowflakes sparkled down to earth like granted wishes from a magic wand.

Inside the handsome lounge of The Haven, Yule logs blazed cheerfully in the fireplace, while Presley, Sinatra, and Springsteen sang Christmas carols. Near the long casement windows, five women were looping lights around a Norway spruce so tall they had to use a ladder to reach the highest branches.

"Okay, that's the end of the last string," Marilyn called from behind the fat tree.

"Plug them in," Shirley told her.

Marilyn knelt to fit the plug into the socket.

"Oooooooh!" Shirley, Faye, Alice, Marilyn, and Polly sighed with delight as dozens and dozens of multicolored miniature lights twinkled to life.

"Now," Shirley announced, "for the fun part. How shall we do this?" Shirley was the director of The Haven, but the four other women were her best friends, practically her family, and she wanted to please everyone.

"I think we should all hang the ornaments we brought where we want," Polly suggested.

"But keep in mind," Faye added, "it will look better if the heaviest, biggest ornaments go on the bottom boughs, with the smaller ones on the higher branches." She was an artist, with an artist's eye.

"Yes, but we don't want it to look too *perfect*," Alice insisted. "We want it to look real."

"Good point, Alice," Shirley agreed. "Perfection, as we all know, isn't real."

"Sometimes it is," Marilyn disagreed, in her thoughtful, vague way. "The horseshoe crab, genus *Limulus*, for example, is perfect. Its design hasn't changed since the Triassic period, that's two hundred forty-five million years."

"Lovely," Faye said gently, amused. "Still, we really don't want to hang a horseshoe crab on the Christmas tree."

"I suppose not. Although one year we did." Marilyn smiled at the memory. She was a paleobiologist—the others teasingly called her a pale old biologist—and her grown son and her ex-husband were molecular geneticists. "Teddy was nine, and fascinated with crustaceans and fossils, so we bored holes in lots of shells, slipped colored cords through, and hung the tree with crabs, mollusks, and gastropods."

Alice snorted with laughter. "You are so *weird*!"

"Oh, I don't know," Polly chimed in. "David told me that he and Amy are hanging *only* homemade decorations on their tree. And my daughter-in-law is such a purist, she'll use *only* vegetable dyes, natural wood, straw, and such. Afterwards, they'll probably carry the tree outside and feed the entire thing to the goat."

The others laughed. As they talked, they moved back and forth from the tables and couches where the boxes of decorations were set out. Occasionally Shirley dropped another log on the fire.

The spacious room, with its casement windows, high ceilings, and mahogany paneling, seemed to glow with contentment. Once built to house a private boarding school, this old stone lodge had been abandoned for a few years. Then Shirley, with the help of her friends and a few investors, had bought it and opened The Haven, a premier spa and wellness resort with a burgeoning membership and second-floor condos for staff or friends.

She had staff (she had *staff*! Shirley, who had struggled financially most of her life, got a thrill every time she remembered that). But she hadn't wanted her staff to decorate the Christmas tree, and neither had her friends. They'd wanted to do this together. They'd agreed to bring three boxes of decorations each, and they'd agreed to do it without advance discussion or collaboration, so their choices would be a surprise.

Now they worked quickly, climbing the ladder to adorn the top, stretching left and right, standing back to appraise, kneeling to the lowest branches, murmuring to themselves, exclaiming at what the others had chosen.

Shirley was a sucker for whimsical creatures with smiling faces: elves, snowmen, Santa Clauses, cherubs, fat angels with crooked smiles and tilted halos, fairies with freckles and yarn hair.

Faye had selected expensive glass ornaments: gorgeous faceted stars, elongated teardrops and iridescent icicles, extravagantly striped or translucent balls in gleaming gemstone colors.

Polly loved to cook. She'd baked dozens of gingerbread men and women, sugar-cookie stars, leaping reindeer, trumpets and drummer boys and crescent moons, the absorbing, familiar activity bringing back memories of Christmases when her son was little. She'd decorated them with colored icing, silver balls, and sprinkles of colored sugar, and glued ribbons firmly on the back, for hanging. She'd also strung cranberries and popcorn on fishing wire and bought boxes of candy canes.

Alice, less sentimental and more practical, had chosen thirty of the skin care, cosmetic, and aromatherapy prod-

ucts on sale at The Haven, and tied their lavender boxes
with glittering gold and silver bows.

Marilyn's contribution was a boxed set of antique ornaments from the Museum of Fine Arts, and a hand-
made collection of brass and enamel stars, sun, moon,
and planets purchased from an Asian gentleman selling
them from a rug on a sidewalk in Harvard Square.

When every ornament was hung, the five women
stepped back to admire their handiwork. The mixture
was eccentric, aesthetically enchanting, and wildly cheerful.

"It's fabulous," Shirley said. "Let me get my camera."

Alice said, "I'll pour the hot chocolate." She twisted
the cap off a large Thermos and poured the fragrant
liquid into Christmas mugs—little gifts from her to the
others. Then, without the slightest twinge of guilt, she
took out a can of Reddi wip, shook it, and topped
the drinks with snowy swirls of the white concoction.
After that, she opened a little plastic bag, dipped her
hand in, and sprinkled dark chocolate shavings on the
creamy peaks.

"I brought some Christmas cookies—without the
glue." Polly opened a red and green tin, and the sweet,
warm aroma of butter and sugar rose into the air.

Marilyn and Faye pushed two of the more comfortable wing chairs close to the sofa so they could all sit in
a half-circle, facing the tree. Shirley returned from her
office with the camera and began snapping shots of the
tree and its trimmers.

Shirley wore purple Tencel pants with an emerald top
that flattered her auburn hair. Her earrings and necklace
were miniature battery-operated Christmas lights that
blinked on and off.

Faye wore scarlet trousers in a silk-and-wool weave
with a matching jacket over a sleeveless white shell. A

chunky choker of garnet and jade circled her neck. Her white hair was held back with a matching barrette.

Plump, auburn-haired Polly wore jeans and a bright green sweater with white snowmen she'd designed and knit herself.

Alice looked majestic in a velvet tunic and pants of swirling crimson and indigo, embellished with lavish gold embroidery. Earrings, necklace, and bracelets of heavy, scrolled gold gleamed against her dark skin.

Marilyn wore brown wool trousers and a shapeless gray sweater. She wasn't color-blind; she just kept forgetting to think about her clothing.

The five curled up on the sofa and settled into the chairs.

Shirley raised her mug. "To the holidays!"

"To the holidays!" the others toasted.

They all sipped the rich hot chocolate, and sighed in unison.

Faye focused dreamily on the twinkling tree. "This is going to be the best Christmas ever!"

Alice chuckled. "Yes, and I'm Glinda, the Good Witch of the North."

"Did you know," Shirley informed them, "in the movie *The Wizard of Oz,* Glinda, the Good Witch of the North, was played by an actress named Billie Burke when she was *fifty-three* years old?"

"You're kidding!" Polly nearly spilled her cocoa. "She looked so young! All that blond hair. The sparkling pink dress. The tiara."

"I wish I had that dress," Faye mused.

"I wish I had her magic wand," Marilyn murmured.

Alice lazily turned her head toward Marilyn. "Really. What would you do with it?"

Marilyn didn't hesitate. "I'd turn my mother back into her normal, independent self. Oh, yes, and renovate Faraday's sexual abilities."

"He's still impotent?" A former hotshot executive, Alice didn't mince words. Besides, they'd helped solve one another's problems before, and were ready to do it again, if they could.

"Always." Marilyn's tone was rich with regret. She'd only discovered the joys of sex in her fifties, and she wanted to make up for lost time.

"You need a magic wand to make his wand magic," Polly joked.

"What's going on with your mother, Marilyn?" Shirley asked.

Marilyn sighed. "My sister says she's going downhill fast. Not physically, mentally. Sharon wants me to have Mother come here for Christmas and stay indefinitely, so I can watch for signs of senility and help her decide whether or not Mother should be 'persuaded' to go into an assisted care facility."

"Hard decision," Faye sympathized.

"I know." Marilyn pinched the bridge of her nose. "Sharon said she can't make this kind of decision herself, and she's absolutely right."

"How old is your mom?" Alice asked.

"Eighty-five. She lives in Ohio, in the same town where we grew up, only a short drive from my sister's home. I've always felt guilty that I haven't been able to help Mother as much as Sharon has. But I live so far away, and I don't want to give up my position at MIT."

"Not to mention," Alice teased, "you often have trouble keeping your thoughts in the same millennium, never mind on the same species."

"There is that," Marilyn agreed easily.

"Is Faraday spending the holidays with you?" Shirley asked.

Marilyn nodded. "He is. He's got two grown children and some grandchildren, but one lives in California and the other in Ohio."

"It's hard when your kids live so far away." Faye looked wistful. "Thank heavens, Laura and Megan and Lars are coming back east for Christmas. I can't wait to get my hands on my little granddaughter again. I hope she remembers me."

"Faye," Alice bossily reminded her, "you've chatted with her every day on your web-cam."

"Yes, but it's not the same. I want to hold her. Smell her. *Cuddle* her."

"I know exactly what you mean." Polly's son and his family lived only a short drive away geographically, but emotionally, they were on Pluto.

"Will you get to see your grandson for Christmas?" Faye asked.

"I've been invited for Christmas dinner." Polly made a face. "But it will be at Amy's parents' house, and they have piles of relatives, so I know I won't be able to hold Jehoshaphat much. Plus, they're so *virtuous*. I always feel like Mae West visiting the Amish."

"What about Hugh?" Alice, Marilyn, Shirley, and Faye all asked in chorus. Polly had been dating the handsome doctor since April, and their hopes for her were high. Polly deserved someone wonderful.

"Hugh's spending Christmas Day with his children and his ex-wife." Polly mimed pulling out her hair. "The size-six, perpetually dependent, helpless little Carol."

"Well, that sucks," Shirley said. "Come have Christmas with us."

"Thanks, but actually, I've been invited to Christmas dinner at Carolyn's, and I just might go there instead."

"Oh, do!" Faye told her, impulsively. "I'll be there, with Aubrey."

"Really?" Polly brightened. "I wonder whether Carolyn would mind if I brought Hugh."

Of course she would, Faye thought silently. Carolyn wants her father to marry *you*. She shifted uncomfortably on the sofa, then leaned forward to grab a cookie. Polly had helped Carolyn during a stressful time in her life, and Carolyn, whose mother had died when Carolyn was just a child, had pounced on Polly as a surrogate mom. Polly was so good-natured and sweet, she didn't seem aware of Carolyn's intentions to match her father up with her, and if she *were* aware, Polly would be so horrified, she'd probably move to Alaska. Faye really liked Polly, the newest member of the Hot Flash Club, and didn't want to cause her any embarrassment.

Alice looked puzzled. "Faye, I thought you said Lars and Laura and baby Megan were coming to have Christmas with you."

"They're coming east, yes," Faye explained. "They're spending Christmas Eve and Christmas morning and most of the day with me. They're going to Lars's family for Christmas dinner."

Alice groaned. "Christmas is so complicated!"

"Yeah, but the food's good," Polly pointed out cheerfully.

Simultaneously, everyone reached forward to grab a cookie. They all laughed.

"I always gain ten pounds over Christmas," Faye moaned, munching.

"It's impossible not to," Alice assured her as she chewed. "It's stress eating."

Polly giggled. "Last night I ate a pepperoni pizza, a pint of ice cream, and two bags of mega-butter popcorn."

"I can trump that," Alice said. "I bought a box of expensive chocolates to take to my bridge group, and last night I sat down and ate them all."

Shirley licked a curl of cream off her spoon. "Hey, Faye. You said you think this will be the best Christmas ever. Want to elaborate?"

"Well, I didn't mean *ever*," Faye corrected herself.

"The best Christmases I ever had were with Jack, when Laura was a little girl. Christmas is really about children. There's nothing like the joy on their faces, the surprise when they see all the gifts under the tree. This Christmas, Megan is three, old enough to really appreciate everything. Plus, I've moved into my darling, new little house—not that I didn't love living in my condo here at The Haven, Shirley," Faye hastened to assure her friend. "But it's so nice to have a little place all my own. I've got three bedrooms, you know, and one is for me, one is a guest bedroom, and one is for Megan! I painted the room myself—"

"—I saw it the other day," Polly told the others. "It's exquisite. A little girl's *dream* room."

"I can't wait for Megan to see it!" Faye beamed. "She's *so* clever! Do you know what she said? Laura told her to eat the crusts on her bread, and Megan said, 'Mommy, don't you know? They only put crusts on the bread so you won't get peanut butter on your fingers when you're eating the sandwich.' "

Alice was amused. "Sounds like she's going to be a lawyer like her father."

"I've bought so many presents I feel guilty." Faye searched the other women's faces. "But isn't this what Christmas is all about? Giving lots and lots of fabulous presents? Spoiling your family?"

"I think it's about making dreams come true." Shirley's voice was rich with longing.

"First of all, it's a religious holiday," Marilyn reminded them.

"And now it's become one gigantic gimmick for our consumer economy," Alice weighed in with a frown. "We're bombarded with ads and sentimental scenes of smiling families around the tree. We're brainwashed with syrupy Christmas music and completely unrealistic promises that our families will be happy if only little

Johnny gets a video game or little Mary gets the right doll."

"Are things okay with Gideon?" Faye asked gently.

"Why do you ask?" Alice demanded. "Christmas *sucks*, whether I'm happy or not!"

"I sort of agree with Alice," Polly cut in. "Well, I don't think Christmas *sucks*, but I do think it's gotten far too commercialized. And it does raise unrealistic expectations."

"But where's the joy in life, without unrealistic expectations?" Shirley cried.

Marilyn cocked her head, studying Shirley. "I'm surprised at you, Shirley. I would have thought you'd tell us that Christmas is a festival of light during the darkest days. That it's about hope for new life during the coldest season of the year."

Shirley blushed. "I *do* think all that. But you know, I never got to have children, and my three former husbands were all assholes, so I never had a really *happy* Christmas before. I was never with someone I loved, who loved me in return."

"So what dreams do you think will come true this Christmas?" Alice tried to sound casual. She knew it made Shirley unhappy, but Alice distrusted Shirley's beau, that jackal Justin. She just hoped that Shirley understood that this wariness came from her protective love of her friend.

Shirley gulped. She shouldn't be nervous, she told herself. When was she going to grow up? When was she going to stop being a coward? Hadn't she proven herself enough already? She'd been the creator of The Haven, and for two years now, she'd run the spa intelligently, just as if she were a clever person with good business sense. Her friends should trust her judgment. They should be *reasonable* about her forthcoming announcement.

Yeah, and pigs would fly out her butt.

This Christmas she was going to give Justin a gift that would change his life. She was *certain* that even though he was twelve years younger than she, Justin loved her, too, just as sincerely. Her Hot Flash friends had to stop fretting. Sure, Justin was handsome, but if he *had* looked at other women—and who could blame him, they were always looking at him!—that was *all* he'd done. He was in her bed every night.

"Well?" Alice prompted. It didn't take a psychic to know Shirley was feeling guilty. Something was up. "You're giving Justin a computer for Christmas, right?"

"Of course not." Shirley faked a laugh and sipped her cocoa, stalling. "He already has one." What she was giving Justin cost a lot more than a computer.

But that was nothing compared to what she suspected he was going to give her.

"Shir–ley," Alice wheedled, trying not to sound like a mother looking at a kid with a suspicious bulge in his backpack.

Shirley stalled. "I'm spending Christmas Day with Justin and his kids."

"He's got three kids, right?" Faye asked.

"Right." Shirley held up a finger as she munched another bite of cookie. "Spring's thirteen, her sister Angel is fifteen. Ben's ten; he has a different mother from Spring and Angel. The girls live in Stoneham with their mother and stepfather, and Ben lives on the Cape with his mother and grandmother. The girls don't like Ben and he doesn't like them, and Justin would prefer to have Ben on Christmas Eve and the girls on Christmas Day, but Ben's mother insists on having Ben on Christmas Eve and Christmas morning, and the girls' mother insists . . . Well, you get the picture."

"And you think this Christmas is going to be about making dreams come true?" Polly looked skeptical.

And Alice looked downright disbelieving.

Shirley decided not to tell them now. Why should she, after all? Justin was the recipient; he should know about it first. She could tell them later.

"But you see," she babbled evasively, "I finally have enough money to give really cool gifts! I've never had this kind of money before—"

Alice shook her head impatiently. "You're not rich, Shirley. You're just solvent, and you're working hard for every penny you make, and don't forget, you're getting older and you need to save for the future. You *are* sixty-two."

"Thank you, Mrs. Scrooge," Shirley sniffed.

Faye, playing peacemaker, changed the subject. "Alice, are you spending Christmas with Gideon?"

Alice knew she was being headed off at the pass. But why was she so worried for Shirley when the other three seemed to be perfectly comfortable with Justin? "Christmas Eve, we're having Alan and Jennifer to dinner. They're going down to the Cape for Christmas Day with her folks. Christmas Day we'll spend with Gideon's kids."

"You like them, don't you?" Polly asked.

"I like them all fine." Alice let out a big fat sigh. "I don't know why I'm so *cranky* these days."

"Hormones don't take holidays," Polly said.

"It's not just that," Alice admitted. "I've gotten cranky since I've retired." Seeing Shirley's mouth twitch, she said, "All right, I was probably cranky *before* I retired. That might be why I was such a dynamite executive at Trans-Continent." Alice shook her head in frustration. Her boiling energy, creative vigor, and, all right, slightly anal-compulsive need to get things done right and *soon* had carried her into the top echelons of a major insurance company during the days when most women, especially black women, were thrilled to stop scrubbing corporate floors and become secretaries. Alice had been *someone*. She'd been a *force*. And she missed that.

"You need to find something to do," Shirley advised. "Something more than playing bridge."

"You think I don't know that?" Alice snapped.

"You need a grandchild," Faye said in a dreamy voice.

"I already have grandchildren," Alice reminded her.

"But they live in Texas," Faye persisted, "and you seldom see them."

Alice gave Faye a level stare. "Faye, you know children are just not my thing. Oh, I loved my sons like a mother panther when they were young, and I took good care of them, even though I worked. I've got photo albums full of smiles. But babies in general aren't my thing."

"What will you do if Alan and Jennifer get married and have children?" Polly asked.

"Let's not go there." Alice still didn't like Jennifer. And it was *not* because Jennifer was white. After all, her four best friends were white. It was more that when Alice first became aware of Jennifer D'Annucio's existence, Jennifer had been having an affair with Faye's son-in-law, Lars.

Now, Alice, she told herself, don't be so judgmental. The best love she'd had in her life had been with a married man when she was thirty-five. She didn't consider herself less trustworthy because she'd had that affair, and she refused to let herself think less of Jennifer for her affair, either. Still, she was glad handsome Lars and his family had moved to California, even as she sympathized with Faye, who was *all about* grandchildren, that her family was so far away.

"Oh, *damn*!" Marilyn flew up out of her chair.

"What's wrong?" Polly asked, alarmed.

Marilyn's words were muffled as she tugged her sweater up over her head. She clasped it to her chest for modesty, her flushed face and chest clear evidence of the problem.

"I'm so *sick* of these hot flashes!" she cried.

"Me, too," Faye commiserated. "I don't understand the *point* of it."

Marilyn hurried to a window and pressed her burning face against the cold glass. "Nature's telling us we're past childbearing age."

"Hel-*lo*! I *know* that!" Alice grumbled. "I can look in the mirror and *see* that."

"Nature designed our reproductive systems before human beings had mirrors." Marilyn grabbed a magazine and fanned her face. "It's possible that in the evolutionary process, hot flashes once served a purpose which has become irrelevant. Perhaps in fifty years, or five hundred, women won't have hot flashes."

"I can't wait that long," Polly quipped.

"I know," Marilyn lamented. "It's not just the surge of heat I hate. It's the way it derails my mind. I'm making mistakes when I teach my classes, or I lose my place, or forget what I'm saying right in the middle of a sentence. It's embarrassing."

"At least you don't gain weight simply by breathing," Faye consoled her. "Aubrey's taking me out to wonderful restaurants so often, I'm ballooning up again."

"You look wonderful, Faye," Alice assured her. "I've decided to stop fussing about my weight. I enjoy eating, and so does Gideon, and he likes me the way I am, nice and squashable."

"That's fine, as long as your health isn't affected," Shirley warned. "Statistics show that the leanest people live the longest."

"Yeah, but do they have as much fun?" Rebelliously, Alice grabbed another cookie.

Marilyn was cooling down. She pulled her sweater back on and returned to her chair. "I've decided to take a sabbatical starting this June. I keep thinking perhaps my brain is just overloaded. I mean, in the past two years my husband left me for a younger woman, I had the most fabulous sex of my life with a guy who turned out to be a creep, I met all of you and joined the Hot Flash Club and the board of The Haven, I became a grandmother, and I started dating Faraday."

"That's enough to blow your fuses," Alice confirmed.

"What will you do?" Faye asked Marilyn. "Take a trip? Write a book?"

Marilyn shrugged. "Before I can plan anything, I've got to deal with my mother. I'll have a chance to see whether she needs assisted living when she's here over Christmas."

"*Christmas,*" Shirley crooned happily.

Alice rolled her eyes. "How can you be so perpetually hopeful?"

"It's a choice, I guess," Shirley told her.

Marilyn leaned forward to skewer Shirley with a look. "Um, you might also add that you have a lover who's good in bed, and no demented relatives."

Polly chuckled. "Remember 'Old Maid,' that card game we played when we were kids?"

"Oh, yes." Faye grinned. "There were all kinds of crazy characters who came in pairs. Like Greasy Grimes and Betty Bumps. But there was just one Old Maid. The point was to be the one at the end of the game who didn't hold the Old Maid."

"Now the goal is not to *be* the Old Maid," Alice joked.

Polly brushed cookie crumbs off her bosom. "I'm thinking 'Old Maid' was a rehearsal for real life. For example, my daughter-in-law is 'Princess Insanely Possessive Prig Pot.' "

Alice laughed. "Tell us how you really feel, Polly!"

Marilyn giggled. "Yeah, and Faraday's the 'Limp Lothario.' "

"Sure, they're flawed." Shirley spoke up before the others came up with an unflattering nickname for Justin. "But we still love them. We still want them to have a wonderful Christmas."

"We can't make other people happy," Alice pointed out sensibly.

"No," Polly agreed, "we can't. But we can do everything we can to set the stage for happiness."

Faye said, "You're right, Polly. That's what I'm going to do this Christmas, for my daughter and my granddaughter and my son-in-law."

"That's what we'll all do for those we love," Shirley said.

"I'll drink to that." Alice raised her mug.

"I'll drink to that, too," Polly said, "but first, can I have more Reddi wip?"

2

On the night before Christmas, all through the house, Faye wandered in her robe. It was two A.M. She was completely incapable of sleep. This afternoon, her daughter Laura, her son-in-law Lars, and her adorable baby granddaughter were arriving for the holidays. Faye was so excited she was nearly demented.

Megan was three years old now, and Faye was going to give the little girl a Christmas she'd remember always! In her exuberance, Faye had put up not one, but three Christmas trees.

The largest one was in front of the living room window. She loved the way the tree looked from outside, framed perfectly by the window, the lights shining with the radiance of home. She'd decorated it with all the ornaments she and Jack had used when Laura was a child.

The second tree was in the kitchen. Inspired by Polly's gingerbread ornaments for the tree at The Haven, Faye had rummaged around at the back of her utensil drawer and found her box of Christmas cookie cutters. All day, Faye had baked and decorated in a kind of domestic trance. She'd filled five bags of frosting with different colors and let her much-ignored artistic side go wild as she squeezed smiling faces and silly designs on sugar Santas and snickerdoodle stars for her kitchen tree.

But the *pièce de résistance* was in Megan's bedroom, where Faye had put a tiny Christmas tree in a pink pot with white bunnies. She'd decorated it with miniature lights and twenty-five fairies. There were twenty-five simply because Faye had made them all herself, out of pipe cleaners, yarn, papier-mâché, and fabric. It had been meticulous, intricate work, and by the time she'd finished the twenty-fifth fairy, her body refused to do more. Her back, arms, and eyes ached from concentrating on such minutiae. She felt as bent and twisted as an ancient Chinese peasant after years of embroidering silks. But the tree, when finished, was *magical,* a little girl's fantasy of fairies, sequins, tulle, beads, and bows.

Faye could not *wait* to see Megan's face when she saw the trees!

She hadn't ignored Laura and Lars, either. Piles of gorgeously wrapped presents surrounded the living room tree, and in the late afternoon, about twenty of Laura and Lars's closest friends were arriving for an informal holiday party. Faye was making her father's famous eggnog, which involved a sinful amount of vanilla ice cream and bourbon. The refrigerator was stuffed with cheeses and exotic olives, caviar and salmon. In the early afternoon, she'd start putting together little canapés for the party, just before she drove out to the airport.

For now, since she had insomnia, she might as well set up the dining room table for the party. Maybe that would tire her out and she'd be able to catch a few hours' sleep. She knew she was in a state of holiday hysteria. Perhaps finalizing a few more preparations would calm her down. Kneeling, she reached into the bottom of the kitchen cupboard to dig out the enormous crystal punch bowl. It hadn't been used for three years, not since her husband Jack died, and the sight of it released a flood of memories.

She and Jack had been married for thirty-five years.

His death had opened the floodgates of a dark ocean in her heart, with powerful tides beyond her control and waves that pulled her under and threatened to keep her there. Her ability to paint the beautiful still lifes and scenes that had once brought her joy and some small renown had drowned in grief, too. Nine months after his death, Faye had tried to paint again, only to discover that her work was accurate, but without soul, vibrancy, resonance. She gave it up. Another enormous loss.

Thank heavens for her daughter and granddaughter and for the love of her Hot Flash friends, her lifelines to the living world.

She rose, lifting the punch bowl to the counter. Had the damned thing always been so heavy? Yes, but she'd been younger, stronger, once. At times like this, her body made her age quite clear. Carrying it over to the sink was such an effort, it brought on a hot flash. She tore off her robe, ran a glass of cold water, and held it to her forehead, trying to cool down.

The gingerbread people smiled at her from the kitchen Christmas tree. Jack would have wanted Faye to go on with her life, to savor every moment of it, to be happy. And she wanted to provide a good role model for her daughter. So she had muddled on as cheerfully as she knew how.

It had been tough, selling the house where she and Jack had raised Laura. It had been like severing the line to a gleaming yacht whose cargo was the domestic reality of her younger life—favorite fabrics, familiar wood, comforting patterns of light falling through windows—and watching it float off into the mists, gone forever.

But the money she'd been able to give Laura and Lars had helped them buy their own home. More than that, it had served as a kind of bridge away from a rough patch in their marriage. Faye would have given up anything to help her daughter.

And this past year of living in the little condo at The Haven had been good for Faye in many ways. She'd learned to appreciate new spaces, new views, new possibilities. Now that she'd settled into her own new little house, she thought she might be able to enjoy quite a few years of contentment. Perhaps, even, of happiness.

She was doing work she loved, teaching courses in art and art therapy at The Haven. She had as full a social calendar as she wanted, cheerfully punctuated at least once a month with a Friday-night Hot Flash Club dinner at Legal Seafoods.

And now she was actually dating. *Seriously* dating. It was amusing, and terrifying, too.

"What would *you* have thought of Aubrey, Jack?" Faye asked, a little startled by the sound of her voice in the silence of the kitchen. "If you want me to stop dating him, you'd better give me a sign."

She had met Aubrey Sperry this April at The Haven's spring open house, and to her immense surprise, the attraction between them had been mutual, immediate, and intense. They'd kissed the first night they met, like a couple of hot-blooded teenagers, in the parking lot of The Haven, stretching toward one another over the gearshift of Aubrey's Jaguar. His mouth had tasted like peppermints, and his fine white hair had been soft as down. His fingers along her neck, his kisses on her throat, had been as delicate and tantalizing as the first drops of spring rain, and only because she didn't want to startle him did she refrain from shouting out, "Hallelujah!" for her body did feel born again.

But a sharp rapping on the window had startled them. They'd pulled apart to find Carolyn, Aubrey's only child and extraordinarily bossy daughter, glaring at them, as if she were Aubrey's mother and was about to yank him out of the car and spank him for misbehaving.

Faye could understand Carolyn's possessive concerns.

Carolyn and Aubrey shared the ownership and responsibility for the Sperry Paper Company, which had been handed down through the generations. No wonder Carolyn had freaked out when, the previous fall, Aubrey had, on a whim, married a much younger woman who had *appeared* naïve and sweet but turned out to be manipulative and mercenary.

In a way, Faye had been part of the chain of responsibility for this revelation. She, Alice, Marilyn, and Shirley, the founders of the Hot Flash Club and of The Haven, had followed their chosen life directive, which was, in a word, *Interfere.* They'd realized that four of The Haven's clients needed help, so they'd organized a special Jacuzzi/aromatherapy encounter for the women, who quickly became friends, and did what women friends have done since the beginning of time: plotted clever ways to solve one another's problems. Aubrey's wife's deceitful scheme was destroyed, and Aubrey's brief marriage was annulled.

And Aubrey's ego was crushed. He was seventy. He'd wanted to be youthful and virile. Instead, he'd been exposed as a fool.

In their most intimate, tender moments together, Aubrey had confessed his humiliation to Faye. He did not go so far as to say that he was anxious about his possible sexual performance, but their initial adolescent lust was cooled by the realities of life and aging. Faye let him know that she could be patient. After all, she was anxious, too.

They'd been dating for almost eight months now, and had not yet progressed past affectionate kisses and fraternal hugs. But that was all right. They'd both been so overwhelmed with moving houses.

Faye had done the lion's share of sorting through her possessions of over thirty years when, the year before, she'd sold her house and pared down to the bare necessities for her condo at The Haven. She'd sold some of her heirlooms, given stuff away, and rented a storage facility for furniture with which she couldn't bear to part.

It had been fun for a while, in a clean, crisp kind of way, to live in small rooms on the third floor of a building whose grounds were groomed by professional gardeners. But quickly she realized she wanted to have her own place, with her own yard, her own flowers, her own bird feeders.

So she'd bought this little Cape Cod located halfway between The Haven, where she taught part time, and Boston, with its theater, museums, and art galleries. During the past few months, in a kind of domestic ecstasy, she'd chosen new rugs, new wallpapers, new furniture, and unpacked her treasures from the storage units, rediscovering each beloved possession with a new delight. She'd hung her favorite still life, the painting Jack had loved the most, one she'd painted only a year before his death, above the mantel in the living room. She hoped it might inspire her to return to her work.

So far, she hadn't set up her easel or picked up a brush.

But in the fall, she'd planned and planted her garden with spring blooms. Digging into the ground, crumbling rich fertilizer into the dark earth, preparing healthy beds for the plump garlic-shaped bulbs, had been a satisfying and deeply sensual experience. She felt connected to the land, as if she'd planted part of her heart among the flowers. Afterward, she was too tired for much more than a microwave dinner and an evening with a book. She didn't miss the energetic demands of sexual passion, and she very much enjoyed the daily phone conversations with Aubrey.

Aubrey's relocation had been much more complicated. He, his daughter Carolyn, her husband Hank, and their baby had lived in a magnificent, if slightly Edward Gorey–esque, Victorian mansion riding high on a hill overlooking the town of Sperry. Big as an ark, the dwelling had been built by Aubrey's grandmother at the turn of the century, when servants as well as family were housed there. Aubrey had his own wing, and Carolyn had hers, and there were common rooms, and a plucky, though overwhelmed, housekeeper, who tried to keep the pantries full and the dust at least rearranged.

But the house was dark and inconvenient. Hank had been the one to suggest they move. He and Carolyn had bought a modern, sleek, practical new house near the mill, where Carolyn was executive vice president. Aubrey, officially president but eagerly easing out of the position, letting Carolyn take over the reins, had opted to buy a handsome apartment forty minutes to the east, in the middle of Boston, on Beacon Hill, near his various private clubs and the restaurants he loved to frequent.

The process of breaking up the Sperry home, which was practically a museum, and would actually become a museum for the town, was a staggeringly exhausting endeavor. The Sperrys had antiques and oil paintings needing expert appraisal, and it all required the services of several lawyers, which of course made the process even more time-consuming. Some weeks passed when Aubrey barely had the energy to phone Faye to say hello before he tumbled into bed.

So it was no wonder they hadn't yet tumbled into bed together.

It just might prove to be a problem, Faye thought, leaning against the kitchen counter, staring out her window at the moonlight on the snow, that she and Aubrey had not been able to consummate their relationship before they remembered how old, creaky, and saggy they were. Now that they had the time and the distance to regard the matter intelligently, they both had gotten shy about their aging bodies.

Aubrey was such an elegant man, with a luxurious

wardrobe and courtly manners, so meticulous about his grooming. He was actually shocked, Faye thought, to find that in spite of his rigorous personal hygiene, his body had betrayed him. Arthritis made him stoop and creak. He had to pop pills or suffer painful indigestion and even so, what he called "dyspepsia" called up embarrassing burps at inappropriate times and often, if he forgot his medicine, made him nearly double over in pain. His beautiful white hair was thinning, his pink scalp showing through, the few surviving strands at the front of his head crinkling and refusing to lie down, waving in the air like survivors from a sinking ship.

Still, he was head-turningly handsome. Faye enjoyed entering a party or the theater on his arm. More than that, she enjoyed looking at him, admiring his aristocratic profile, the way his face changed subtly when he was amused or aroused. Because she was thirteen years younger, she thought she'd be able to shut out the wailing Greek chorus of her own vanity when they ever did get around to making love—especially if they kept the lights off.

What would Laura think of Aubrey? Faye had told her daughter all about him, and Laura had assured her mother she was delighted to know Faye was dating. Aubrey was coming to the little Christmas Eve party tonight and would stay for a cozy family dinner afterward.

Faye imagined it: the four of them around the table, Aubrey charming Laura and Lars as they talked, and adorable little Megan on Faye's lap. It had been six months since Faye had flown out to California to visit her daughter's family. Yes, they had "talked" via their web-cams almost every day, but children took shy easily. Would Megan allow Faye to put her to bed? Faye had bought a rocking chair for Megan's room. Closing her eyes, she conjured up a vision of perfect holiday happiness: rocking her granddaughter to sleep, softly singing the same lullabies she'd once sung to Laura, gazing down at her grandchild's face, while downstairs the others got to know one another over coffee and Dutch apple pie, Laura's favorite dessert.

Her thoughts lulled her. The sweet, heavy brandy of sleepiness flowed through her blood, weighing down her limbs. Leaving the punch bowl on the counter, Faye left the kitchen and, flicking off the lights as she went, returned to the living room. She lay on her side on the sofa, pulling a woven tapestry throw over her for warmth. This familiar old trick had often allowed her to sink into sleep on nights when she tossed and turned in her own bed. She knew she would sleep now, and she was so grateful.

The lights of the Christmas tree shone in the room, like dozens of bright angels keeping watch.

Faye woke to find the sun streaming in. Great! No weather problems would keep Laura's plane from landing.

She stretched, feeling wonderfully rested. Glancing at the clock, she gave a little cry of terror—she'd slept almost until nine o'clock!

Racing into the kitchen, she started her coffee, then phoned American Airlines to see whether Laura's plane had left yet. A robotic voice presented "options," but of course the option to speak with a living human being wasn't one of them. Faye had to suffer through several minutes of pushing buttons and negotiating with a system that somehow, even though computerized, managed to be as smug and implacable as a high school principal. And it *was* like being back in school; it was like taking a test. The computer had all the power. She had to concentrate fiercely on what the robot said, and if, God forbid, she pressed the wrong number, she'd flunk and have to start all over again.

The whole process was so infuriating, it made her erupt in a Mount St. Helens of a hot flash. Really, Faye thought, there should be an option for menopausal women, who could scarcely remember their own names: "If you belong to the Hot Flash Club, press *1* for *Insane* and someone will be with you instantly."

Finally she keyed in the flight number and was connected to an information bank. Laura's flight had not yet departed.

Oh, no! The plane was due to leave at nine in the morning, and it was two minutes after nine! What had happened? Weren't they going to be able to make it? There couldn't be a blizzard in California—my God! What if there'd been an earthquake?

She raced into her tiny family room and turned on the television, quickly clicking the remote control to CNN. After a few minutes of watching the news, she calmed down. No earthquake reported. No disaster in L.A. All right. Fine. Everything was fine. The plane might be late—

—because while it was nine o'clock here, it was only six o'clock on the West Coast, she remembered, laughing out loud with relief. What an idiot she was! She had to *calm down*!

She finished her coffee, then went into the dining room, found the damask tablecloth, and flapped it out— she'd always liked the way the cloth *flew* out, exuberant, like a bird delighted to spread its white wings—over the long dining room table. As she drank her coffee, she nibbled on Christmas cookies and her homemade, salted, candied pecans. Perhaps not the healthiest breakfast, but it was the holidays, hardly time even to consider dieting.

She rinsed the punch bowl and set it on the table, then

brought out the punch cups, the ladle, the Christmas napkins, the pitchers for juice and sparkling water for those who didn't want punch, the plates, and the silver. She stacked Christmas CDs in her stereo player.

When the phone rang, she jumped so hard she nearly launched herself into space.

"Hello, my dear," Aubrey said. "I thought I'd check in to see if you need anything for tonight."

"Oh, thanks, Aubrey, that's so kind of you." His voice made her smile. "But I think I've got it under control. I'm just scurrying around, getting things ready for the little party."

"Then I won't keep you," Aubrey told her. "But you know I'm here if you need me. You've got my cell phone number."

She grinned like a schoolgirl. How sweet was that, to say *I'm here if you need me*! Oh, gosh, this really was going to be the best Christmas ever!

She unwrapped the twisted red, white, and green Christmas candles and put them in their tall silver holders. When the florist arrived with the flowers she'd ordered for the mantel, dining room table, and guest room, Faye was still in her robe, with so much left to do.

Hurriedly she showered and dressed, then drove off to pick up the turkey and the bluefish pâté from the health food store. She stopped at Wilson's Farm to buy apples, oranges, clementines, grapes, and several kinds of sweet rolls for tomorrow morning's breakfast. Her pantry and freezer were crammed with food already, but she wanted to have an abundance, wanted no one to be deprived of a thing.

It took her four trips to carry everything from the car to the house, and by the time she'd unpacked it all, she was drenched from a hot flash and trembling. Collapsing on a chair, she munched whatever was closest on the kitchen table. A few grapes. An onion bagel with a chunk of cheddar. She brewed a new pot of decaf with one hand while punching numbers in the phone handset with the other. Yes, the flight from L.A. had left on time, and was expected to arrive in Boston on time.

Her heart leapt with joy.

She'd better get busy! A huge pan of lasagna was in her refrigerator, dinner for tonight after the holiday cocktail party, so that was under control. It was the party itself she had to get ready for. She clicked on the radio to the classical station and heavenly Christmas music accompanied her as she chopped, diced, stirred, and spread.

Her hand was trembling. She needed something to calm her down—a glass of wine? No! She had to drive out to the airport in just—oh my God, in just one hour! She would not allow herself to impair her already excited senses. Chocolate. She needed chocolate.

From the freezer, she took a pint of Ben and Jerry's New York Super Fudge Chunk, which she'd always found worked better than a trip to the psychiatrist *and* a couple of Valium, and faster. So what if she automatically gained two pounds? It was the holidays; she had no time to worry about her weight.

She nuked the ice cream in the microwave for thirty seconds, just the perfect amount of time to get it to the perfect degree of melted richness. Digging a spoon in, she ate directly from the carton as she rushed upstairs to dress. Quickly, she removed her shirt and pulled on a Christmas sweater she'd ordered especially to please her granddaughter. Bright red, it was decorated with a scene of Santa in his sleigh, his sack bulging with presents, his white beard blowing back in the wind. The string of reindeer wrapped around the sweater, ending with Rudolph with his red nose on Faye's back shoulder.

Admiring the sweater, her eye fell on her clock. Oh, no! It was already one forty-five. Laura's plane landed at

Logan at three! It would take Faye a good hour to drive there, and that would be only if the traffic was not too congested.

Hurriedly, she kicked off the ancient loafers she wore to do housework, grabbed the half-eaten carton of ice cream, and started down the stairs in her thick wool socks. Her purse was on the hall table. She'd pull on her boots, coat, gloves, and just *go*. The car keys were in—

Suddenly, she slipped. Her body was sailing in the air.

"AAAH!" she cried, throwing out her hands to grab something, *anything*. In a flash, she hit the wood floor at the foot of the stairs. Her head hit *hard* on the last step. For a moment she actually saw stars. Then everything went black.

She was dreaming of Christmas when a car alarm sounded rudely in the distance. Why was she sprawled out on the cold, hard surface of a parking lot? And who had run over her? Why wasn't someone coming to help her?

Faye opened her eyes. She was collapsed in the front hall. Her ankle hurt. Her back hurt. Over in the corner, by the umbrella stand, lay an ice-cream carton in a puddle of brown liquid.

The noise wasn't a car alarm; it was the telephone. She'd been lying here long enough for the ice cream to melt—Laura!

Faye pushed herself up. A searing pain shot through her, beginning in her neck and radiating out to her shoulders and back.

The phone continued to ring. Carefully, Faye turned her arm so she could see her watch. Three thirty-seven. Laura's plane had landed, and here Faye was, on the floor.

"All right," she said to herself in the calm voice she'd used years ago when Laura was a child, "it's going to be all right. If you can't pick up Laura and Lars and Megan, they'll simply grab a cab. They're not helpless. You need to get yourself to the kitchen, swallow a couple of aspirin, and you'll be fine."

Slowly, sensibly, she tried to roll over.

Her left ankle exploded in fireworks.

She fell back against the newel post, eyes closed, gasping with pain.

"*Shit!*" she cursed. "This isn't right. This is terrible! It's *Christmas*!"

The phone continued to ring, a shrill, demanding, exasperating sound.

Well, if she couldn't walk to the phone, she'd damn well *crawl*.

Resting her left ankle on top of her right knee, she pushed with her right foot. Awkwardly, like a debilitated seal, she scooted on her back down the hall.

Someday, she knew, she would find this funny.

Right now, she felt only pain and frustration.

Tears ran down her cheeks. The phone rang and rang. After what seemed like a century, she bumped off the wood floor and onto the tile of the kitchen. A few more shoves, and she reached the alcove where she kept her phone book and phone. The demon clamped on her neck would not allow her to sit up, so she lifted her good leg and clumsily kicked at the ringing phone until it clunked to the floor.

"Mom?" a tinny voice said.

Grimacing in agony, Faye reached over and grabbed the handset.

"Laura!"

"Mom? I've been calling for ages. We're at the airport, we—"

"Laura, I've fallen and I can't get up."

Laura laughed. For a moment, Faye was horrified. How could Laura laugh at her? Then she remembered the television ad for an alarm button one could wear around one's neck. The actress who displayed it was a little old lady who quavered, "I've fallen and I can't get up." For some reason, which at the moment completely escaped Faye, she and Laura had always laughed maniacally at this ad, and so had everyone else she knew.

"I'm not joking, Laura." Faye strained to sound firm instead of frantic. "I fell down the stairs. I've twisted my ankle, and I've done something to my neck."

"Oh, poor Mommy!"

Laura's words were muffled. Faye could hear her repeating the information to Lars.

"Listen, Mommy," Laura said, clear once again. "We're going to grab a cab to the house. I want you to hang up now and phone your neighbors. Have someone get over there—"

"Darling, I can wait until you and Lars get here."

"No, Mommy," Laura insisted. "You need to get medical attention as soon as possible. I don't want you lying on the cold kitchen floor, and if you've injured yourself, you'll need to have it taken care of as soon as possible. Who knows how long it's going to take us to get a cab here at the airport the day before Christmas? You should absolutely *not* wait."

Faye was speechless. Who *was* this person ordering her around? Three years ago, Laura had been a neurotic mass of indecision. Obviously motherhood had opened up new pathways in her brain.

"I hate to bother people on Christmas Eve," Faye equivocated. "And I haven't really gotten to know anyone well enough—"

"Then phone 911."

Who are you and what have you done with the real Laura? Faye wanted to demand. "Oh, Laura, surely that's a little dramatic."

"Mom. Can you stand up? No, right? That's not dramatic. That's real. Your health is real. Why do you think there's a 911 in the first place? I'm going to hang up now. You phone 911. I'll phone you back in a few minutes." Decisively, she clicked off.

Faye felt like a giant tuna as she lay gasping on the kitchen floor. A really *pissed-off* giant tuna. She understood that Laura was trying to be helpful, but did she have to sound so bossy? Her daughter had been so officious! She'd made Faye feel like a child. A helpless, indecisive, pathetic little child! I'll be *damned,* Faye thought perversely, if I'm going to dial 911. She wasn't exactly old, feeble, and desolate! She had a gentleman friend— although she didn't want Aubrey to see her like this, a quivering pile of helpless blubber. Well, she had her Hot Flash friends—Polly! Polly was dating Hugh, who was a doctor!

She pressed the dial button for Polly.

The answering machine came on. Cheerful Polly had taped a few measures of Christmas carols before and after her message, and Faye nearly snarled with impatience as she waited for the beep.

"Polly? It's Faye, and I've done something really stupid. I've fallen, and I think I hurt my neck, and I was wondering whether Hugh might be there, perhaps he could suggest something . . ."

Faye clicked off. Who knew when Polly would get the message? Maybe she was better, now that she'd rested. She tried to sit up. Her neck made her literally scream with pain. *Fine!* She punched Alice's number.

"Hello?"

Thank God! Alice was home. She listened to Faye's appeal, and broke into a hearty laugh. "I told you Christmas sucks! I'll be right there."

Laura called again. "Mom, we're in line to get a cab. Looks like it will be a twenty-minute wait. Did you phone 911?"

"Help is on the way," Faye dissembled. "Now, darling, I'll probably be gone when you get here, so the spare key is under the porcupine boot-scraper on the front stoop—"

"Gee, Mom, why don't you just paint a sign: *Want to burgle me? Look in the most obvious place!*"

Faye swallowed a retort. "Your beds are all made up, and the food for the party is completely prepared." Without warning, an enormous wave of self-pity swept up through her chest. She burst into tears.

"Mommy?" Laura's voice softened.

"I won't be here to see Megan see her bedroom and her little tree!" Faye cried.

"Well, of course you will," Laura said sensibly. "Your injuries don't sound life-threatening. Look, Mommy, don't worry about anything. Just focus on taking care of yourself, okay?"

"Okay," Faye agreed. She knew Laura was being kind, but her words made her feel like some kind of decrepit old invalid.

But *damn*, she *was* some kind of decrepit old invalid, if she couldn't even get up off the floor!

Really, she couldn't believe this. Not this, now, on Christmas Eve. Not with her granddaughter coming. Faye couldn't help it. She broke into serious sobs of self-pity, boo-hooing so hard it hurt her neck and her sinuses clogged up with mucus and she couldn't even get up to get a handkerchief to blow her nose.

The front door banged and Alice swept into the house. From Faye's vantage point on the floor, Alice looked even taller than she really was. She wore her ankle-length mink—no one would dare spit on Alice!—and it billowed around her like a monarch's mantle as she strode across the kitchen floor.

"Good grief, honey, you look awful!" Alice knelt next to Faye. "Where does it hurt?"

"My ankle. And my neck."

"Your neck, huh? Can't take any chances with that. I'm going to call 911, get an ambulance here. Don't argue. And you're cold as ice."

In just seconds, Alice had the phone in one hand and a blanket in the other, multitasking, as usual.

Four hours later, at eight o'clock on Christmas Eve, Faye was released from Mount Auburn Hospital. She'd been examined, x-rayed, ultrasounded, fitted with a soft ankle cast, presented with crutches, and enclosed in a neck brace that squeezed the flab around her jaw-line up, so her head seemed to be resting on a ring of Silly Putty.

"I look like a walrus," Faye complained.

"And a very pretty one, too," Laura assured her.

Alice had stayed with Faye for the first three hours, until Laura could get her husband and child settled in her mother's house. Then Laura drove Faye's car to the hospital so Alice could return to her own Christmas Eve plans.

The good news was that no bones were broken. Faye's ankle was only sprained, but sprains could be the devil to heal, the physician assured her. She had to stay off her feet.

Christmas, and she had to stay off her feet!

The bad news was that the tests had revealed Faye's neck showed signs of osteoarthritis, caused by aging. Faye moaned when the physician told her *that*. Now, when everyone asked her what had happened, she'd have to confess that she was *aging*. As if it weren't already apparent. None of her vertebrae were cracked, but she was supposed to wear her neck brace for the next few days, to support her neck and her weakened, arthritic old neck bones.

"It couldn't have happened at a better time," Laura assured Faye as they drove through the dark evening. "Lars and I are here, we can take care of you. You can lounge about in bed or on the sofa and we'll wait on you hand and foot."

"But it's Christmas!" Faye protested. She'd forced herself to be cheerful in the hospital, but now here came the tears again. She'd had the pain medication prescription filled but refused to take one of the pills until bedtime. She didn't want to be dizzy and drugged on Christmas Eve. She *had* taken two aspirin, which helped, but they didn't completely alleviate the pain. The whole time it was as if someone were pressing an iron set to "linen" up against her neck.

Laura reached over to pat her mother's hand. "Hey, remember. If Fate gives you lemons, make lemonade!"

"Oh, no!" Faye groaned. How many times during Laura's childhood had Faye given her exactly that advice? "Did that irritate you as much as it irritates me?"

Laura tossed her a grin. "What do you think?"

Faye smiled, sniffing back her tears. It was, after all, *lovely* to be in her daughter's company again. And if Laura had become, well, *assertive,* that was a good thing, a sign she'd really grown up. Faye closed her eyes, resting. She'd have some Champagne when they got home. Certainly there'd be plenty of it. The new *über*-competent Laura had used her cell phone to call everyone who was invited to the Christmas Eve party to explain Faye's fall and regretfully cancel. What a disappointment for Laura and Lars, to miss seeing their friends! And all that food going to waste!

Aubrey had been wonderful, though. He'd wanted to come to the hospital, but Faye had asked him not to—she hadn't known how long she'd be there, not to mention (and she did *not* mention) how very much she did not want him to see her in such a vulnerable and unattractive state, carted around in a hospital gown like a suet pudding.

When Faye got the news that she was going home, she'd phoned Aubrey again, and he agreed to drive to her house so he could meet Laura and her family. So, they would manage to have, if not a *perfect* Christmas Eve, at least a pleasant one. The blow to Faye's vanity from Aubrey seeing her in a neck brace and on crutches would be balanced out by the windfall of his very presence in her life. She was so glad to have her daughter know she could attract such an elegant, charming man. She was even a little proud about it.

"Your new house is adorable," Laura said, as they pulled into Faye's drive. "Gosh, is that a Jag?"

Faye's spirits rose as they parked behind her beau's elegant vehicle. "Yes, it's Aubrey's."

"*Nice.*"

"He's nice, too." Faye smiled like a satisfied cat. It was all going to be all right. The lights on the Christmas tree twinkled gaily in the living room window. The wreath swathed in candy-stripe ribbons brightened the front door. Soon she'd be settled on the sofa with a glass of Champagne and her granddaughter on her lap and her loving family gathered all around, getting to know her delightful gentleman friend.

Laura rushed around to open the car door and assist Faye in the cumbersome task of hopping out and onto the crutches without hurting her neck or ankle. Slowly, Faye toddled up the walk, swinging the crutches clumsily, not yet used to the rhythm, feeling rather like a piece of unassembled furniture.

Laura opened the door. Faye bumbled inside. Too eager to wait to take off her coat, she clumped into the living room, leaning on her crutches, her head wobbling on its brace like a bobble-head doll.

Aubrey was standing by the fireplace, a glass of scotch in his hand. Lars was kneeling by the Christmas tree, Megan next to him, looking at all the packages.

Sweet, darling little Megan! She wore the red sweater with the white snowman that Faye had knitted for her. And a pair of jeans, and a pair of those dreadful Doc Martens boots the young seemed so obsessed with. Why would Laura buy those for her little girl? Still, it was *Megan*.

"Megan!" Faye cried with delight. She swung one of her crutches forward, hurrying toward her grand-daughter.

Megan's eyes grew wide with alarm as she watched Faye lurch toward her like a creature from a sci-fi film. With a shriek, she threw herself into her father's arms.

"Honey, honey," Lars soothed. "It's Nanny. You remember Nanny. You talk to her every day on the computer phone. She gave you your pink princess doll."

Megan stared. Her lower lip quivered.

"It's the crutches." Faye hurried to make excuses for her grandchild, even though her feelings were crushed. "And the neck brace." She backed away, not wanting to traumatize Megan any more than she already had, and as she did, a fierce hot flash exploded through her. Sweat popped out on her forehead. Her underarms were ovens. Her entire body itched with heat and irritation. In front of everyone she loved, she was turning into a walking prickly pear cactus.

Dropping her crutches, she hobbled around on one foot, clawing at her coat, desperate to get out of it.

Megan gawked and tightened her grasp around her father's neck.

Laura hurried over. "Here, Mommy, let me help you."

"I'll support her while you take her coat off," Aubrey suggested.

Together, Aubrey and Laura got Faye out of her coat and onto the sofa, with her bad ankle elevated. Aubrey put a flute of cold Champagne in her hand.

"Thank you," Faye said. "Just what the doctor ordered." She tossed back a hearty slurp, then held the cool glass to her forehead.

Megan clung to her father, peering in Faye's direction from the safety of his shoulder.

"She's gotten shy recently," Laura confessed, easily curling up on the floor next to Faye. "It's not just you. I'm sure she'll come around."

"Did she see her bedroom?" Faye asked.

"Oh, yes, Mommy, it's *amazing*. Although Megan's going to sleep with us while we're here. The shy business again. I know she'll get over it, but until she does, we're allowing her to sleep with us whenever we're away from home."

"Oh," Faye said in a very small voice. "I see."

"I think Megan's hungry," Lars announced. "I wouldn't mind eating, either."

"The refrigerator—" Faye began, automatically struggling to get off the sofa and into the kitchen.

"Don't move, Mommy," Laura ordered. "I've seen the tons of food you've prepared. I'll organize a dinner for us all, here in the living room. We'll put everything on the coffee table. Lars and Megan and I can sit on the floor. It will be fun, like an indoor picnic!"

"Let's go help Mommy." Lars carried his clinging daughter out of the room.

Faye looked mournfully over at Aubrey. "I feel like a beached whale."

"You need more of Dr. Sperry's Miracle Tonic." Aubrey poured more Champagne for them both, then gently lifted her legs so that he could sit on the other end of the sofa with her feet in his lap. "Merry Christmas, Faye," he said, raising his glass in a toast.

"Merry Christmas, Aubrey," Faye echoed. She sipped the cold elixir. "Oh, Aubrey, I'm so glad you're here! But with this neck brace on, I look like—*Burl Ives*!"

Aubrey laughed. "That's all right, Faye," he assured her, patting her ankle. "I can't see very well."

Their mutual laughter made Faye relax, surrendering into the comfort of the cushions. The Christmas tree twinkled merrily, and from the kitchen floated the aromas of food being warmed. It wasn't the Christmas Eve she'd dreamed of, but it would certainly be one Faye would always remember.

3

Polly steered her car into the garage and clicked the door closed. She staggered into the kitchen, her arms full of last-minute holiday groceries. She'd probably bought too much, but better too much than too little, that was her opinion.

The light on her answering machine was blinking. She listened to the message as she took off her cap, gloves, and muffler.

Faye, asking for help!

"Oh, Faye!" Polly cried. Hurriedly, she dialed her number.

A male voice answered.

"Hello, this is Polly Lodge, I'm a friend of Faye's, she phoned—"

"Hi, Polly, this is Lars, Faye's son-in-law. Faye's gone off to the hospital with Alice. Laura's on her way there now. I'm here with Megan."

"Is Faye all right?"

"I think she will be. She fell down the stairs. Sprained or broke her ankle, did something to her neck."

"Oh, dear, and at Christmas!"

"I'll have her call you when she gets back, okay?"

"That would be great. Thanks, Lars."

Polly hung up the phone and just stood in the middle

of her kitchen, miserable. *Darn it!* She had missed a rare opportunity.

As the newest member of the Hot Flash Club, she often felt like the baby sister scrambling to catch up with the big kids. Faye, Alice, Marilyn, and Shirley had met a year before Polly met them, and during that year they'd gotten up to all sorts of adventures and formed a tight bond of sisterhood. Polly was thrilled to be admitted to this casual club, but she wanted more. She wanted to be closer to all of them, or at least to one of them.

Looking down, she saw her ancient basset hound, Roy Orbison, sitting patiently at her feet, staring up at her.

"Oh, Roy!" She knelt to pet and hug him. "You're right. I can't stand here daydreaming! We've got a lot to do."

Her son, his wife, and their toddler, little Jehoshaphat, were coming to her house for Christmas Eve. Polly felt like she was preparing for a delegation from another planet.

David dwelt with his vegetarian wife Amy and their darling baby Jehoshaphat on a farm outside Boston. Amy's parents lived there, too, just up the driveway, and together they all grew vegetables and ran a precious little country store full of sour homemade jellies and scratchy hand-knitted apparel affordable only to the wealthiest and purest of souls.

Polly often wondered at the currents of fate driving her family line. Her grandparents had struggled to survive on a potato farm in Ireland. Her parents had lived as penny-pinching but respectable citizens in South Boston. Polly had gone to college, where she met and married a handsome, adventurous, unreliable travel writer and explorer. Scott got Polly pregnant, then roamed away, eventually dying in a scuba-diving accident. Polly had raised their son David alone, until she met the love of her life, Tucker Lodge, a banker. Their marriage had been a happy one. David had adored his stepfather and, after college, had gone to work in Tucker's bank. Then Tucker died of a heart attack. And David married Amy. And now Polly's son was a farmer planting potatoes on Amy's parents' farm. Was there a potato-planting gene in her blood?

Well, Polly thought as she unpacked the groceries, wouldn't it be nice if that was the explanation? Wouldn't it be helpful if, in future years, scientists isolated genes responsible for certain life choices, such as marrying someone diametrically different from one's parents? *She* had certainly done that, shell-shocking her timid, safety-loving parents when she married her first husband.

Since her son's marriage to Amy, Polly had spent hours examining her early life choices. Really, she didn't think the desire to shock, hurt, or impress her parents had played any part in her marriage to Scott. She'd been infatuated, completely *dazzled* by the man. He'd seemed so glamorous to her, and the life she'd lived with him, traveling to Peru and Mexico and the wild Newfoundland coast, had been exciting beyond her wildest dreams.

Life after the divorce had been difficult, though. She'd made her living as a seamstress, and dedicated herself to providing a happy and safe home for her little boy. When David was twelve, Polly had married Tucker Lodge. Tucker was a reliable man, a wonderful provider, and a loving stepfather. His death three years ago had devastated Polly, and she knew David mourned him deeply, too.

Was it possible that Amy and her family, so entrenched in their farm, with their smug rural virtues, were as dazzling and fascinating to David as Scott had been to Polly? Certainly David was thriving, if you could call changing from a wiry, energetic banker who liked theater and opera into a lumbering, overweight, red-faced, tractor-driving, potato-planting country bumpkin *thriving*!

Oh, Polly wouldn't care what David wore or did, if only Amy would allow her to see more of her grandson! Vegetarian Amy and her family acted as if they were civilized human beings while meat-eating Polly was some kind of Cro-Magnon creature, hooting and picking fleas off her fur. When Polly helped her mother-in-law, the year she was dying of cancer, Amy had not allowed her to see little Jehoshaphat, claiming that Polly might transmit dangerous germs. For a year, Polly had felt like some kind of leper.

The silver lining had been that she'd taken a membership at The Haven, hoping to work off some of the stress. There, she'd met three younger women who became her friends, and later, the members of the Hot Flash Club, with whom she could laugh about the gritty realities of aging. Thanks to all her new friends, she'd developed the courage to persist in her attempts to forge some kind of relationship with her grandson and his mother's tightly knit, terribly superior family.

And tonight, on Christmas Eve, Amy had agreed to come to Polly's house! This was a magnificent milestone. Jehoshaphat was fifteen months old, and he'd never visited his grandmother before.

Polly began arranging her evening's culinary offerings as artistically as possible on plain white ironstone platters.

"Let's see, I've got cheese made from the milk of goats fed by the Dalai Lama and crackers made from flour ground by French nuns during a full moon," she joked to Roy Orbison, who waddled hopefully at her feet, waiting for something to drop. "I have several kinds of fruit. I have plain nuts and salted nuts. Carrots and celery. Everything from the health food store." Because it was, after all, Christmas, she'd also used her grandmother's recipes to make the gingerbread cookies and sugar cookies David had always loved.

She carried the platters into the living room, setting them on tables out of the dog's reach.

Back in the kitchen, she surveyed the drink possibilities. From a health food store: mango juice, carrot juice, papaya juice, apple juice. Also beer, which David used to drink, and Champagne, just in case. And eggnog, whole and skim milk, sparkling and plain spring water, and a staggering assortment of herbal teas.

She glanced at her watch: five thirty. They would be here in an hour. She rushed to the living room to double-check everything. The tree's lights—the only non-organic decoration—were glowing. Gingerbread characters grinned from the boughs, among angels, elves, and animals that Polly, who was a talented seamstress, had made from scraps of fabric. Presents for everyone lay under the tree, wrapped in paper Polly had recycled from brown paper grocery bags and tied with yarn. She was especially proud of this touch of environmental support; Amy *had* to approve of that! From the mantel hung stockings Polly had made herself for Amy, Jehoshaphat, and Polly's boyfriend, Hugh. David's stocking she'd made years ago, when he was a toddler. She'd considered giving it to Amy when they married, but quickly realized Amy would want to hang stockings of her own choosing.

She nodded admiringly at her mantel, decorated with laurel and candles. "I bought the greens myself, at Odell's farm, which is totally organic," she told her hound. "The candles are beeswax, also organic. I bought the wooden candleholders at a farm fair this fall. Can't wait for Amy to notice *them*!"

Roy snorted.

"I know, you think I'm going overboard, trying to please Amy, but come on, Roy, David's my only child. And Amy's the mother of my only grandchild!"

Her grandfather clock chimed. "Eeek!" she cried. It was time to shower and dress.

She'd laid a fire of natural woods—was there any other kind? Now she knelt to light it, so it would be blazing heartily when David and his family arrived. She clicked on the CD player, and Christmas carols rolled their golden notes out into the room. Everything was clean, dusted, polished, shining. She lit the candles on the mantelpiece. Their little flames danced, giving a lively, festive touch to the room.

"I don't think Amy can complain about a single thing," Polly assured herself.

She hurried up to her bedroom, stripped off her clothes, and turned on the bath water. As the tub filled, she stared in the mirror at her naked, sexagenarian body. She looked grandmotherly. That was appropriate. After all, she *was* a grandmother.

But she was also, to her surprise, at her advanced age, newly in love, or at least in serious like.

After Polly's mother-in-law died last year, her physician, Hugh Monroe, had asked Polly out on a date, at which point Polly, who liked to consider the glass half-full, decided Fate was getting around to balancing things out. Polly had taken good care of Claudia in her final months. She considered Hugh a kind of karmic reward. In her most sentimental moments, she even imagined that Claudia had engineered this somehow.

Hugh was so wonderful! Polly sank into her bubble bath and closed her eyes, surrendering for just a moment to the heat, the peace, and her dreams. Fragrant bubbles surged over the mounds of her round thighs, belly, and breasts.

Hugh didn't seem to mind how much Polly weighed. A jovial, energetic, portly man, Hugh liked to eat, cook, and drink. Polly hadn't discussed the philosophy of this with him, but she guessed that he alleviated the stresses of his work as an oncologist with as many vigorous sensual pleasures as he could conjure up on any given day.

She had such a good time with Hugh on their dates! He took her to elegant restaurants, but also to amusement parks where they rode roller coasters and merry-go-rounds and ate cotton candy. They'd spent a day on a small boat plunging around off Boston's coast on a whale watch—and they'd seen two whales. Polly would never forget how her heart leapt at the sight. On his next vacation, Hugh wanted to take her scuba-diving in the Caribbean, something Polly had never done, and he was trying to persuade her to take riding lessons with him. Polly wasn't so sure about that. She hadn't ridden since she was a teenager, and she had visions of swinging her hefty hind end into a saddle and the horse going "Oofh!" and fainting.

The good thing about Hugh was that she was able to confide such fears to him. When she'd confessed her equestrian vision, Hugh had replied, "Ah, Polly, any horse would be thrilled to bear your gorgeous derrière!" That night, he'd given her a full back massage that ended with kisses all up and down her spine and all over her round rear end. Until then, she hadn't realized her nerves had valiantly sneaked through the cellulite and were there waiting to receive the sweetness of his warm breath, his soft lips, like a hive when the bee buzzes back with its load of honey.

Polly smiled and hugged herself.

But enough daydreaming. She stepped dripping onto the bath mat, grabbed a towel, and began drying off. As she dressed, she could feel her courage fading beneath an onslaught of nerves.

David's wife, Amy, and her parents, Katrina and Buck, all lived and worked on the same farm. Their schedules were closely knit together, their conversation related to matters Polly didn't understand—fertilizer, insects, spinning wheels. The Andersons had lived on their land since the Revolutionary War, which indeed was something to be proud about, but the Andersons were more than proud. They were *smug*. They belonged to their own elite club with its private language and rituals, and Polly was not admitted. Last Christmas, she'd been invited for two hours only on Christmas night, to share eggnog with her son, grandson, and daughter-in-law while they exchanged presents that, Polly suspected, they never used.

Nothing Polly gave Amy and her family was ever good enough. When Polly mailed her grandson a funny card and present on Valentine's Day, she never heard whether it had even arrived. Very occasionally she was asked to baby-sit her grandson, but when she did, Amy was always just in the next room. What was *that* about?

Polly pulled on her wool slacks and the green cashmere sweater she'd knit herself. Cashmere and wool, *natural,* that ought to satisfy Amy. She sat on the edge of her bed to put on her socks and shoes. From the corner of her eye, she noticed the crystal bowl filled with Brach's Chocolate Mix that she'd brought upstairs, to keep away from Amy's critical eye.

For courage, Polly grabbed the bag, delved inside, and pulled out a chocolate-covered Brazil nut. It was especially satisfying to eat nuts, because she could crunch them. *Hard.*

The chocolate, sugar, and fat blasted into her system like a team of miniature superheroes, lifting her spirits high. She nibbled more as she brushed her red—well, *white* and red—hair and put on a bit of lipstick and eyeliner.

Any moment now, they'd be here. She'd get to hold her grandson, hand him a present, watch him as he opened it.

Where was the camera! She was standing here chewing away like a squirrel, and where was the camera?

In the kitchen? Probably.

The doorbell chimed. Polly raced down the stairs, Roy Orbison hurrying with her, his long, chubby body swaying, nearly tripping her as they went.

The air downstairs was smoky. Hadn't she pushed up the fireplace flue? She'd have to open the windows, let the smoke out. First, though, she hurried to the front door.

"David!" she cried. "Amy! And Jehoshaphat!"

Amy's brown braids were looped on the top of her head in a kind of Fräulein milkmaid look. Instead of a coat, she wore a hairy brown poncho. Jehoshaphat's chubby baby face stared over his mother's shoulder from her backpack.

They were really here! Polly was so thrilled, she nearly burst into a flamboyant flamenco. At her feet, Roy Orbison danced and barked his hoarse old dog bark. "Come in, come in."

David bent to pat the basset hound. He smelled faintly of manure and Lysol. "Mom, why is it so smoky in here?"

"Oh, darling, I lighted a fire, and I need to—" There were so many things to do at once, she couldn't finish her sentence. "Let me hold Jehoshaphat while you take off your things," she told Amy, reaching out for her grandson. Amy allowed her to lift the little boy from the backpack.

"Mom, something's wrong." David pushed past her, still in his coat.

"Darling, it's just—" Carrying Jehoshaphat, who was squirming around, looking in all directions at this new environment, Polly followed her son down the hall and into the living room.

"Jesus Christ!" David exclaimed. "Mom, call 911! The house is on fire!"

But Polly was paralyzed as she stood in the doorway to her living room. What she saw was so bizarre, her mind couldn't, for a moment, force it to make sense. Flames shot up from the mantel, where her organic greenery was crackling and popping as it burned, and her wooden candlesticks glowed orange.

"Oh my God!" Amy shrieked. Lunging forward, she snatched Jehoshaphat from Polly's arms. The little boy began to scream along with his mother as she flew back outside.

The dog, confused and frightened, stood in the middle of the hall, threw back his head, and bayed like a lost soul.

David had his cell phone out and was dialing 911.

"Hallelujah! Hallelujah! Hallelujah!" a choir sang from the CD player.

Fire, Polly thought. *Water.* Breaking out of her stupor, she ran into the kitchen, found her big lobster pot, set it in the sink, and turned on both faucets. The water ran and ran, and yet, as if she were caught in some kind of nightmare, the pot would not fill. Slowly, slowly, the level of the water rose, while black smoke drifted down the hall and into the kitchen.

Finally the pot was almost full. Polly hoisted it from the sink, turned, and started to run toward the living room. But with her first step, the water sloshed out of the pot, spilling onto her slacks and puddling onto the floor. Slipping, slithering, she almost went down.

Carefully, slowly, Polly regained her balance. She moved her legs as quickly as she could while keeping her upper torso and arms completely still, to prevent more water spilling. Arms stiff, she walked zombielike to the living room.

David was by the fireplace, poker in hand, knocking the burning greenery and blackened candleholders onto the tile hearth and into the fireplace.

"Oh, David," she cried, "be careful! Don't burn your-self!"

"It's all right now, Mom. I've got it under control. When the fire department gets here, they can check whether it got into the walls somehow, but I think we're okay."

Polly stood helplessly, holding her heavy pot of water. Above the mantel, the wall was streaked with black, and the beautiful oil painting she and Tucker had inherited from his family was scorched and curled into fragments of ruined canvas. Roy Orbison had stopped bellowing and sniffed nervously at her feet.

"Aaah, Mom, it's all right." David put the poker back in its stand. "I'll put the pot here on the hearth. In case we need it." He lifted the heavy vessel of water from Polly's hands. "Look," he said, trying to cheer her up. "The tree, the stockings, the presents—none of them burned."

Polly's lip quivered. "That's right. That's good."

"Come sit down here," David said gently. "You've had a shock."

Polly had forgotten how to move her legs.

"Mom." David put his arms around her and hugged her for a long time. "It's okay, Mom. It's really okay."

He ushered her to the sofa. Docilely, she sat. Her dog sat, too, leaning against her legs for comfort.

"I'm just going to check on Amy and Jehoshaphat." David left the room.

Because the front door was open to let the smoke escape, her son's conversation floated in with perfect clarity.

"It's okay now, Amy, come on in."

"I'm not going in there! I'm not taking my child into a burning house!"

"The fire's out."

"I'm not taking a chance. What if a spark got up in the ceiling? Everything could go at once!"

"Amy—"

"When the fire department says it's safe, I'll go in."

"Then take Jehoshaphat and sit in the car. You'll freeze out here."

Sirens sounded in the distance. Then, closer. The wails pierced the Christmas Eve air as they screeched to a stop at Polly's house. Moments later, Polly heard men speaking with her son and then two firemen stomped into the living room, garbed in rubber coats, boots, and gear.

Behind them came Amy, David, and the baby. Amy stood in the doorway, refusing to enter the room, which was just as well, because the room was crowded. Somehow the firemen were twice as big as normal persons. Roy Orbison waddled around, wagging his tail and sniffing the firemen's interesting ankles.

They checked the walls, ceiling, and hearth. They stomped upstairs and down again.

The older one, with grizzled hair, had kind eyes. "This happens more often than you'd think," he assured Polly. "Christmas candles, dry greenery, there you are."

The younger fireman said to Polly, "I notice you have smoke alarms upstairs and down. Didn't they go off?"

Polly cringed. "I took the batteries out this week. I was doing a lot of cooking, and they're so sensitive, they were going off all the time and driving me crazy."

Behind him, Amy's mouth crimped disapprovingly.

"Yeah, that happens a lot," the older fireman said. "You'd better connect them."

By the time the firemen left, all the smoke had dissipated. Polly longed to pour half a bottle of rum into a cup of eggnog and chug it down.

But instead she rallied. "Sit down, now, please. We can still have Christmas Eve," she told David and Amy.

"The presents and stockings are okay. And I've made some delicious—"

"I think we'd better go home," Amy said. "The smoke gave me a headache, and heaven knows what it did to little Jehoshaphat's lungs."

"But the smoke's gone!" Polly protested, waving her arms.

"Yes, and it's freezing in here," Amy pointed out.

"It will warm up soon," Polly promised. "I'll make you some tea. I've got so many different kinds—"

With a sigh, Amy acquiesced.

The next hour dragged by. With the patience of Mother Teresa tending to the ill, Amy accepted Polly's Christmas gifts and allowed her son to touch his. The entire time, Amy darted frightened little glances at her husband, making it clear she was terrified that the house was about to spontaneously combust. She did not allow Polly's grandson to taste any cookies—too much sugar— or to drink any of the juice Polly had bought. Instead, she pulled a juice bottle from her woven bag.

Amy and David's gift to Polly was a set of woven reed place mats that Polly had seen on the sale table of the Andersons' little store over the summer. But Amy did permit Jehoshaphat to touch the set of natural wood blocks Polly gave him, and for five blissful minutes, Polly was allowed to sit playing on the floor with her grandson.

In spite of the herbal tea Polly brewed, Amy complained that her headache was growing worse.

You need caffeine, honey, you need chocolate, Polly thought. *You need a personality transplant.*

She walked them to the door, waving until their pickup truck was out of sight. For a moment, she stood looking out at the black sky with its frosty stars. All the houses up and down the block glowed with Christmas lights.

Polly returned to her smoke-stained living room. Her artistically decorated brown wrapping paper and yarn ribbons lay discarded on the floor like yesterday's trash. The present from Amy and David, the woven place mats, looked like hair shirts for a clan of masochistic dwarves. Roy Orbison sniffed through the crumpled paper and found a bit of unsalted cashew. From the CD player, the little drummer boy drummed for the fifty-ninth time that evening. Polly turned off the music.

"Merry Christmas, humbug!" she told her dog, and collapsed on the sofa.

It was only a little after eight o'clock on Christmas Eve. If only Hugh had been here! He wouldn't have let the place catch fire. Or he would have assured everyone, with his gentle physician's authority, that everything was really all right. He would have lent authenticity and gravity to Polly's gifts and food.

But Hugh wasn't here, and he wouldn't be tonight.

Tonight Hugh was spending with his grown children, their spouses, and his ex-wife, Carol.

Carol was—Polly had seen pictures—a tiny size six, and if that wasn't irritating enough, she was also a dependent little princess. Hugh and Carol had been divorced for several years now, but Carol, who had kept the house in which she and Hugh had raised their three children, was forever phoning him when the downstairs bathroom's pipes froze, or a bat got into the attic, or one of their grandchildren lost a tooth. Carol desperately needed daily conversations with Hugh, and Hugh took it all in his stride, listening to her complaints and soothing her with the same kind manner with which he spoke to his patients when they phoned. Also, he was diligent about attending his grandchildren's plays, recitals, and soccer games as often as possible. Polly admired him for this at the same time she hated how it limited their time together.

When they'd discussed their holiday schedules, Polly had thought it made perfect sense for Hugh to be with his children—and their mother—on Christmas Eve, while Polly was with her son and his family. Tomorrow, when she got to see Hugh, she would be glad to have the Carol part of Christmas behind them.

But tonight she was irrationally lonely. For a while, she indulged in a morass of negativity, imagining everyone else she knew celebrating the season in the bosom of their families. Quickly she got bored with that scenario. She'd spent too many holidays in the home of her mother-in-law, Claudia, Queen of Disdain, to believe all other families in the world were happy.

Besides, it wasn't celebrating she missed—she did a lot of that, with Hugh and with her Hot Flash friends. It was a sense of being useful, of being part of the world, that made her feel so solitary now.

But then, how useful could someone be who set her house on fire on Christmas Eve?

4

MARILYN DIDN'T KNOW WHETHER HER MOTHER WAS truly an exceptionally pretty woman, or if it was just that Marilyn loved her so much.

Ruth came out of the guest bedroom, dressed for Christmas Eve dinner in a red wool dress and a strand of white pearls. Red lipstick brightened her pleated lips and cheerful rouge blushed her wrinkled cheeks. From her ears dangled shiny little Christmas ornaments, one red, one green. Her snowy white hair bobbed around in curls, and the bit of pink scalp showing through made Marilyn's heart ache. Her mother had had such thick hair when she was younger.

"You look great, Mom," Marilyn said.

Ruth's face lit up at the compliment. "Well, thank you, dear! I believe, no matter which God you believe in, it's important to keep rituals in your life. It helps you remember to be grateful. To reflect on the cycle of birth, life, and dirt."

Marilyn bit her lip. Ruth had been a brilliant biology professor. Now, at eighty-five, her discourse was peppered with little malapropisms. Marilyn had phoned her sister Sharon about it, and they'd agreed it was probably a result of Ruth's mini-strokes. They decided not to mention it to Ruth, who always seemed puzzled when they tried to correct her.

Ostensibly, Ruth was visiting her daughter for a few weeks, an unexceptional, ordinary thing for a mother to do. Tacitly, Marilyn was supposed to watch Ruth for signs of senility so she could share her observations with Sharon and help her decide whether or not their mother should be "persuaded" to go into an assisted care facility.

"I can't make this kind of decision by myself," Sharon had insisted during one of their many phone conversations this fall.

"I agree. You shouldn't have to," Marilyn had assured her. She already felt guilty because Sharon had remained in the same Ohio town where they'd grown up, while Marilyn had moved east for college and remained east all her life. Marilyn flew back at least once a year to visit her mother, and she sent Ruth cards and gifts and phoned her often, but that didn't compare with the time and care Sharon gave. But then Sharon, who was the older sister, and always bossy, liked to be in charge, while Marilyn, a paleobiologist and professor at MIT, craved huge quantities of solitude for her studies.

Marilyn's intellectual preoccupation was no doubt genetic, although nurture played its part as well, since both her parents, who had taught biology at a large state university, had spent much of Marilyn's childhood lying on their stomachs in the backyard, observing insects.

For a few halcyon years when Marilyn and Sharon were children, they'd been extraordinarily popular, because their parents loved to talk about nature and were full of amusing anecdotes, complete with illustrations. *The flatfish have both eyes on the same side of their heads, and the eyes can migrate from side to side! Some snakes have two heads! When the sea elephant becomes angry, his nose swells up like a balloon!*

During their adolescent years, however, their peers began to consider their parents dorky and even weird. Their father loved to tell jokes—*Two hydrogen atoms walk into a bar. One says, "I've lost my electron." The other asks, "Are you sure?" The first one says, "I'm positive."*—which made the teenagers groan and roll their eyes.

It didn't help that the professors, both of whom could describe in detail the colors of a deer botfly, dressed without any consideration of fashion. They wore clothes to keep from being cold or naked in public—the latter of which, they were always ready to discuss with the sisters' contemporaries, was practiced in other cultures.

Sharon had rebelled, becoming obsessed with clothing, hair, and current styles. She'd majored in economics and, after trying a number of jobs, had ended up as a corporate headhunter. Sharon was slick, stylish, and savvy. Marilyn had been the child who adopted her parents' ways. But Marilyn had moved away, while Sharon remained in Ohio.

So Sharon had been the one to help both parents, ten years ago, move out of their sprawling ranch house and into a small apartment in a comfortable retirement community. She had been the one to phone Marilyn when their father died, at seventy-eight, and when Marilyn flew back for the funeral, Sharon had been the one to suggest Marilyn help their mother sort through their father's possessions.

It had nearly broken Marilyn's heart to give away her father's beloved paraphernalia: the insect light traps and transparent insect-rearing cages, the beautiful ant house she'd built with him when she was a child, the Schmidt boxes filled with specimens caught and mounted with exquisite care.

"You *have* mineral hammers and rock cabinets," Sharon had argued when she caught Marilyn trying to

sneak her father's into her own luggage. "I've seen your
house and your lab. You don't need another bit of old
equipment!" Sharon was strong-willed and assertive.
They'd ended up giving anything useful to a children's
museum and taking much of the rest to the dump.

Finally they had the apartment sorted out, clutter-free
and airy. Ruth had been sad to see the scientific equipment go, but only because it reminded her of her husband. After retiring from teaching, she had turned her
attention to other things, small things, and lots of them,
including knitting, doing crossword puzzles, and com-
piling a recipe collection. During the past five years of
her widowhood, Ruth had accumulated a rather daunt-
ing mass of clutter of her own. Her increasing inability
to part with her new possessions was one of the reasons
Sharon thought she was no longer fit to live by herself.

Still, Ruth could shop for herself—she didn't drive,
but took the shuttle provided by the retirement community. She cooked for herself and kept her kitchen clean.
She bathed daily, and her clothing was fresh and spot-
less. True, she was developing a tendency toward keeping her food around longer than it should be . . . the
refrigerator was crammed with foil-covered packets. As
with her needlework, Ruth tended to lose interest in her
current meal, and being a child of the Depression, she
wrapped it up and saved it for the future rather than
throwing it out.

Ruth's health was good enough. She'd had a hysterec-
tomy years before, and suffered a few very minor strokes
that hadn't paralyzed her, only slowed her down. She
was active; she had friends she played cards with in the
lounge. Her sense of hearing was failing, she'd had
cataract operations, and she needed a cane to walk because of arthritis, but still she was self-sufficient, good-
humored, and happy.

And, perhaps, failing. She often forgot appointments,

names, where she put something, but then, Marilyn
thought, who didn't? Occasionally, Ruth's speech was
jumbled. Most worrisome: she'd fallen a month ago,
while stepping out of the bath. She hadn't told anyone,
hadn't wanted to make a fuss. But a week later, at her
annual physical checkup, the doctor had seen the bruises,
still purple and yellow, along the front of her torso, and
had told Ruth—and Sharon, who'd accompanied her to
the appointment—that she had most probably had a
transient ischemic attack, a momentary blockage of the
blood supply to the brain. He'd suggested follow-up
tests. Ruth had stalled. He'd suggested she use a walker.
These TIAs were transitory, but often recurring. They
were mini-strokes, the doctor warned her. They could
happen anytime. Ruth had delicately rejected the walker,
saying in her gentle way she would think about it, but
didn't feel she needed it *quite* yet.

"I really can't tell if I want to move Mom into assisted
living because it would make *her* feel better, or make *me*
worry less," Sharon had told Marilyn. "You have to help
me evaluate."

So Marilyn had invited her mother to visit for a couple of months, and Sharon had helped Ruth pack and
board a plane, and now, here she was.

After her divorce, Marilyn had moved out of the huge
Victorian where she and Theodore had raised Teddy—
what a mind-warping, backbreaking project that had
been! Much of her personal scientific paraphernalia and
most of her books were in a storage locker until she decided where to live permanently. For the time being,
Marilyn was renting a bland, furnished condo in Cambridge. She'd never been one to fuss about her surroundings or attempt coordinating curtains with carpets, and
she found the small, practical space worked well for her
life. Especially since she was thinking about taking a
sabbatical and doing some traveling.

Now they were preparing to leave for Christmas Eve dinner with Marilyn's son Teddy, his wife, and their family.

"I've got all my presents tucked away in these big shopping bags," Marilyn told Ruth, gesturing to the bags sitting by the front door. "Where are your presents?"

"Ooops! Left them in the bedroom."

"I'll get them," Marilyn offered.

"No, no, I'm not helpless." Ruth toddled away, returning in a few moments with a large book bag. "I've got all my fits in here."

"Um, well, good, Mom!" Marilyn leaned toward the mirror in the hall, checking her hair. She looked rather messy today. Her Hot Flash friends would want to fix her up somehow, cut her hair, give her a different lipstick, brighten her up with a colorful scarf. But having her mother with her was pretty much like having a toddler around. She didn't have much free time for herself, and what time she had was often interrupted.

"What time is Fraidy coming?" Ruth asked.

"His name is Faraday, Mom," Marilyn reminded her for the hundredth time. "He should be here any minute."

She knew she sounded cranky when she talked about Faraday. Faraday McAdam was a charming man, also a scientist, always fascinating and courtly and attentive. When Theodore left Marilyn for a younger woman, Faraday's flirtation had buoyed her up, convincing her as never before in her entire life that she was attractive.

The problem was that Faraday, who at his best, when they first met, had been only a one-minute wonder, was now completely impotent.

Whenever Marilyn tried to discuss this, *gently,* with Faraday, he changed the subject, turned on the TV, or left the room. Occasionally, Faraday hinted at their living together, traveling together, marriage . . . and Marilyn dreamed of Barton Baker, the cad who had betrayed her, but also had shown her just how amazing good sex could be. Marilyn didn't want to live the rest of her life alone. But did she want to live it without ever having delicious, skin-heating, heart-thumping, artery-flushing, serotonin-surging, passionate sex again?

"Are you having a hot flash, dear?" Ruth asked.

Marilyn jumped. "I am," she replied honestly, abashed. How could she *think* of sex with her mother in the room!

As Ruth adjusted a bow on one of her presents, she said, "Marilyn, did I tell you about Jean Benedict's daughter? She's about your age, you know. Well, she ran off with her gardener to the Dutch West Guineas! It was a shock to us all, because she had been a pillow of the community. But you see, you're never too old for romance . . ."

Marilyn gaped at her mother. Had she developed a talent for mind reading?

Her thoughts were interrupted by a knock on the door.

"Here he is!" Marilyn opened the door.

"Ruth! How nice to see you again!" Faraday, large, ruddy, and jolly, made a little bow to the older woman.

Ruth smiled sweetly. "Hello, Fruity. Good to see you, too."

"*Faraday,* Mother!" Marilyn quickly corrected.

"That's what I said, dear," Ruth placidly assured her.

"Hello, Marilyn." Unfazed, Faraday leaned forward to kiss Marilyn's cheek. "Merry Christmas."

"Merry Christmas, Faraday. You look festive."

"I try," Faraday admitted modestly. Today he wore his most replete and elegant apparel: a Clan McGregor kilt in a handsome red and green tartan, perfect for Christmas; his Prince Charlie jacket with the handsome buttons on the sleeves; a tartan tie; and a dress sporran. Between his high wool socks and the hem of his kilt, his legs, massive and covered with fine red hair, were bare.

Marilyn's mother threw her hands up in astonishment. "You look wonderful! I've never seen a real live man in Scottish garble!" Ruth bent forward, peering. "I've always wondered about the purpose of that little fur purse you've got hanging down. Is it to advertise the male's reproductive equipment? Like a stag's antlers or a peacock's tail feathers?"

"Mother!" Marilyn admonished.

"Well, dear, it *does* draw the eye," Ruth calmly pointed out.

Faraday seemed amused. "It's called a *sporran*, and it's exactly as you named it," he informed Ruth. "It's a little fur purse. The kilt doesn't have pockets, so this began as a leather pouch for carrying our necessary items. This sporran is for dress only. It's made from Greenland sealskin. Everyday sporrans are usually just leather."

"And what do you wear under the kilt?" Ruth asked.

"Mother, stop it," Marilyn intervened. "Come on, let's get your coat on."

"Why shouldn't I inquire?" Ruth argued. "You're never too old to learn."

"Allow me." Faraday helped Ruth into her coat. "Marilyn tells me you taught biology. Obviously you were asking in the spirit of scientific inquiry."

"Obviously," Ruth agreed, pleased.

"So I'll tell *you*." Faraday bent to whisper in Ruth's ear.

Ruth giggled.

Marilyn rolled her eyes but smiled. "I'll just get the presents."

She gathered up the bags full of gifts and followed her mother and Faraday out to his car. Faraday opened the trunk and set the gifts inside, next to his offering of several bottles of Champagne and wine.

"Now, then," he said, as he got behind the wheel. "Is

everybody comfortable? Marilyn, do you have enough room for your legs?"

"I'm fine, Faraday." Why did he irritate her so much today? He was behaving beautifully!

Faraday started the car and they were off, driving toward Marilyn's son's house.

"I know a joke about what's under a kilt," Ruth announced.

"Mother," Marilyn said quietly.

But Faraday encouraged her. "I love kilt jokes! Let's hear it!"

"Very well. A Scotsman spends an evening in a bar and has rather too much to drink. When he leaves the pub, he passes out on the street. Two young American women notice.

" 'My,' one says to the other. 'I've always wondered what's under a Scottish kilt.'

" 'Let's look!' says the other.

"So they look, and glory be, he's naked as the day he was born. The girls giggle. Then the first one mischievously takes a blue ribbon from her hair and ties it around the man's sexual reproductive member. They run off, laughing.

"A while later, the Scotsman wakes up. Feeling something odd, he lifts his kilt, looks down, and sees the blue ribbon tied around his hoo-ha.

" 'Well, lad,' he says. 'I don't know what you got up to while I was passed out, but I'm glad you won first prize.' "

They all laughed, and the shared laughter made Marilyn relax just a little. This was the first Christmas that Faraday had accompanied Marilyn to her son's family dinner. She wasn't quite sure what this implied about their relationship. She wasn't quite sure what she *wanted* it to imply.

"Now tell me again who will be there this evening," her mother asked from the front seat.

"Well, Teddy and Lila and your great-granddaughter Irene, of course, since it's at their house. And the three of us. And Eugenie, Lila's mother."

"But not Lila's father?"

"No. They separated last year. Lila's father's gone off with a younger woman. Lila and Teddy and the baby will spend Christmas Day with Lila's father. Eugenie got them for Thanksgiving this year, because I got them for Thanksgiving last year. Eugenie wanted them all for herself this Christmas, but now that she and her husband have separated, there aren't enough bits of time to go around."

"You need a computer to figure out how to divide the holidays up fairly," Ruth said.

"Or a psychiatrist," Marilyn said.

"Still," Ruth said, "there's no plague like home for the holidays."

Faraday looked in the rearview mirror and winked at Marilyn.

The evening blurred past in a flurry of kisses, gifts, Champagne, and laughter. Teddy and Lila served a veritable Christmas feast, Ruth and her great-granddaughter formed a mutual admiration society, and Faraday charmed everyone, as usual, with humorous anecdotes.

Only Eugenie, Lila's mother, cast a pall on the party. Always aloof, tonight she was especially remote, and no wonder. Poor Eugenie had had the face-lift from hell. She looked like a melted Madame Tussaud's mannequin. Marilyn could only imagine how horrible this must be for Eugenie, whose extraordinary feminine perfection had been a living advertisement for her ex-husband's plastic surgery business.

In the car on the way back to Marilyn's condo, Faraday said, "It was a grand party."

"My, yes," Ruth agreed. "Delicious food. And I got to have some time with my great-granddaughter."

Marilyn leaned forward, resting her arms on the back of the front seat. "What did you think of Lila's mother?"

Ruth took a moment to think. "Well, Eugenie's an unusual woman. She reminds me of the Portuguese man-of-war jellyfish. Beautiful, diaphanous, and poisonous."

"She was even more beautiful before she had that botched face-lift," Marilyn said.

Ruth yawned. "Well, beauty is only kin deep."

Back at Marilyn's condo, Faraday insisted on escorting the women inside, carrying their bags of presents for them.

"It was a lovely evening." Ruth turned to Faraday. "Thank you for everything."

"Yes, Faraday," Marilyn echoed, "thank you."

But Faraday showed no intention of leaving. "How about a little nightcap?"

Marilyn hesitated. She was yearning to crawl into bed with her new book on plate tectonics.

"You two youngsters can stay up, but I'm going to bed. Good night, Fairy." Ruth leaned over to kiss Marilyn on the cheek. "Good night, dear. Merry Christmas."

"Merry Christmas, Mother," Marilyn said.

Marilyn and Faraday watched Ruth toddle away down the hall.

Marilyn stifled a yawn. "I don't know if I'm up for a nightcap. I've had so much to drink tonight. All that Champagne. How about a cup of tea?"

"Actually, I don't want anything else to drink, either," Faraday told her. "I just wanted a little private time with you."

Marilyn's heart sank.

Faraday took her hand and led her to the sofa. Once they were comfortably seated side by side, he told her, "I have another present for you, Marilyn."

Reaching down, he unfastened the metal lid of his sporran.

And brought out a small black velvet box.

"Marilyn," Faraday said, his beautiful blue eyes shining. "Will you marry me?"

A hot flash that would have propelled a missile to the moon exploded inside Marilyn's body. She flushed from her belly straight up to the top of her head.

"Oh!" she cried, jumping up. "Hot flash, Faraday, excuse me!" She raced from the room.

In her bedroom, she ripped off her clothes. In her bra and panties, she went into the bathroom, ran the cold water tap, and stood over the sink, pressing cool water onto her face, letting it drizzle down her neck and shoulders. The intense sense of irritation that usually accompanied her hot flashes was multiplied by a power of ten right now. She felt wildly, almost *violently,* insane.

She gulped cold water from her hands. Soaked a washcloth with cold water and pressed it against the back of her neck. And cursed under her breath.

Damn Faraday! How could he *propose* to her! It made her feel so *cornered.* As her body temperature dropped back into the normal range, her emotions remained on Emergency Alert.

Why was she so panicked? Marilyn asked herself.

Because Faraday had pressed her into an existential corner. She cared for him. She enjoyed his company. She admired him. She shared common interests with him. But never in her life had she experienced that sweeping sense of falling in love so much praised by her Hot Flash friends. Not with Faraday, not with her husband Theodore, not even with that cad Barton, who had introduced her to the sensation of lust.

So late in her life, she *had* developed a sexual appetite. And Faraday, who was so good, so intelligent, so charming, could not satisfy that appetite. Didn't even worry about trying. Should she refuse his proposal for that reason? Or accept it, and be thankful any man wanted to marry her at all? She was no beauty, and more than that, she was fifty-four. This might be her last and only chance to have a companion with whom to share the rest of her life. Statistically, this was a miracle. Who was she, a scientist, to defy statistics?

A gentle knock sounded at the bathroom door. "Marilyn?" Faraday whispered. "Are you all right?"

Marilyn grabbed the bathrobe hanging on the hook, pulled it on, and opened the door. "Sorry, Faraday. That was a particularly hot hot flash."

"Come sit down," Faraday told her. "I made you some chamomile tea with the valerian Shirley gave you to calm your heart."

"Oh, Faraday, how kind!" Marilyn said.

"I poured it over ice," he continued, looking pleased with himself. "So it will cool you as you drink it."

"Oh, Faraday, how brilliant!" Marilyn told him.

She allowed him to take her hand and lead her back into the living room. She felt like someone being led to the edge of a diving board. *Damn, damn, damn!* What was she going to do?

5

ALICE HAD NEVER BEEN PARTICULARLY INTERESTED IN domestic matters. Oh, when her sons were young, she'd enjoyed the Christmas folderol, but now she was in her sixties, her sons were grown, and she didn't feel obligated to make a fuss. So this year, she'd just hung some mistletoe and holly over the doors and windows. After all, her handsome condo, in a restored warehouse on Boston Harbor, had a view like a Christmas tree itself, replete with twinkling lights from boats, cruisers, and planes going in and out of Logan Airport.

Now she slid open the glass door and stepped out onto her balcony. Her beau, Gideon, ensconced on the sofa with the remote in his hand, didn't ask why she wanted to stand out in the frosty night in her light silk caftan. He was well acquainted with her hot flashes by now.

Actually, she wasn't having a hot flash, as she leaned on the railing, breathing in huge gulps of cold, fresh air. More like a brain blip. No—more like an interior tantrum. It was as if she had a little Alice living inside her, a cranky miniature troll who was always complaining. Always wanting more.

An Id Alice.

An Id-iot Alice.

She imagined that everyone else in the whole world was probably content right now, sharing Christmas Eve rituals, anticipating tomorrow's festivities.

She wasn't.

Turning slightly, she looked through the glass door into her living room where Gideon was relaxing, zoning out as he watched television. Gideon was absolutely adorable, a great, big man who resembled the Red Sox hitter David Ortiz, or perhaps more accurately, Ortiz's father. His bald spot expanded daily, and although he tried to watch his diet because of diabetes, he still had a gut slung like a hammock holding a baby hippo. Even so, he was a gorgeous man.

And he loved Alice. Because of a prostate cancer operation, he couldn't really have sex, but Alice did her best not to mind. Marilyn's lover couldn't have sex, either. Faraday didn't have a prostate problem; he was just impotent. Alice grinned, thinking of Marilyn's complaints. God, laughter helped.

Feeling slightly less grumpy, she went back into the living room.

"Alice," Gideon said, "sit down and relax. You've been going all day."

Alice glanced around her dining area. Christmas Eve dinner was over. She and Gideon had finished clearing up. The dishwasher hummed in the kitchen. Nothing needed doing. It was nine o'clock at night.

Sighing, she collapsed onto the sofa. "I think Jennifer liked her presents, don't you?"

"Um-hum," Gideon agreed absently, his attention fixed on a taped rerun of Tiger Woods playing golf, the sport Gideon had taken up this past summer.

"And I think Alan and Jennifer were both pleased that *I* fixed Christmas Eve dinner for *them*," Alice mused aloud. Alan and his girlfriend, Jennifer, lived in the gatehouse of The Haven, a cozy cottage where they worked together, running their bakery and catering service. Because they were always slaving over an oven, Alice wanted to give them a real holiday. And she had. "I was as nice as pie to Jennifer, wasn't I?"

"Um-hum," Gideon said again.

Alice frowned. *I want him to praise me!* cried the demanding diminutive Alice, dancing up and down in frustration just inside Alice's left ear. *I want him to tell me I'm wonderful because I've gotten over my prejudice about Jennifer being white! I want him to tell me I'm a good-hearted, loving mother, not to mention a fabulous cook with the intelligence of S. Epatha Merkerson and the looks of Vanessa Williams!*

"I ate too much tonight," Alice moaned. "I look like the south end of a rhino going north."

"Drat!" Gideon exclaimed, completely ignoring his cue for a compliment.

Alice glanced at the television. Tiger Woods's ball had just missed the hole.

You've seen that exact same ball miss that exact same hole at least ten times already! Alice wanted to shout at Gideon. *You've watched every game Tiger Woods has ever played at least twenty times!*

But she kept quiet, musing on her own thoughts.

After a few moments, she said, "Did you see how much Jennifer ate? And she's still so tiny! This caftan's comfortable, but it makes me look like a camping tent with legs."

"Nonsense." Gideon's reply was absentmindedly dutiful. "You are a thing of beauty and a joy forever."

Well, that was a half-assed compliment if she ever heard one. Still, she was grateful for it. "Who said that, anyway?" she wondered aloud.

Rising, she went to her bookshelves. More and more these days, old phrases of songs and poetry popped into her thoughts. She didn't understand just why. Sometimes she thought it was because great, gaping vacancies had been left in her brain when she retired from Trans-Continent Insurance, and because nature abhorred a vacuum, her brain was substituting stuff she'd learned about years ago in high school and college. More likely, she was just getting senile. Whatever, she was glad people had gone to the trouble of making anthologies like her dictionary of quotations.

She sat down with the heavy tome on her lap and looked for the word "beauty" in the index. John Keats. Hm. English poet, if she remembered correctly. She turned to the quote and read aloud.

> "A thing of beauty is a joy for ever:
> Its loveliness increases; it will never
> Pass into nothingness; but still will keep
> A bower quiet for us, and a sleep
> Full of sweet dreams, and health, and quiet
>   breathing."

"Oh," Alice said. "Oh."

"All *right*!" Gideon said, as Tiger's ball flew seventy thousand feet into the air.

Alice burst into tears.

That got his attention. "Why, Alice, what's wrong?"

"Oh, Gideon," Alice sobbed. "I don't know!" But she did know. And because she knew Gideon truly loved her, she sputtered, "I guess it just makes me sad, that's all. I mean, sometimes I just plain *hate* getting old! *I* was lovely once! *My* loveliness sure as hell didn't increase! I'm sagging and bagging and bloating! I'm aching and I'm getting too tired too easily, and when I'm not tired, I'm cranky and bored! Plus, I *am* going to pass away into nothingness someday, and I'm so old, that day is just around the corner!"

Gideon struggled up out of the chair, came over to the

sofa, and held her for a while. When she caught her breath and dug a tissue out of her robe pocket, he said, in the kind, sensible tone of voice that had made him such an excellent high school math teacher, "Well, you know, Alice, the poem doesn't say 'A person of beauty is a joy forever.' I believe the word is a 'thing.' Like a vase."

She blew her nose. "That's a good point, Gideon."

"Plus," he added, stroking her back, "you *are* lovely, every sagging, bagging, cranky old pound of you. You're downright beautiful, Alice. And I'm changing, too. Look at me. I used to use Head & Shoulders. Now I use Mop & Glo."

She forced a laugh. How had she ever deserved such a wonderful man? And why in the hell wasn't she satisfied with her life, now that she had him in it? She gave him a long, affectionate kiss. He held her tightly for a few minutes, then returned to watching television, leaving Alice alone with her cranky thoughts.

The phone rang. She jumped for it.

"Hi, Hon," Shirley said. "How's your holiday going?"

Alice curled up in a chair, settling in for a good talk. "Pretty well, I think." She recounted the evening spent with Alan and Jennifer. Shirley wanted to know every last detail, what all the gifts were, what everyone ate. When she wound down, she asked, "How's your Christmas Eve?"

"Oh, fine." Shirley sounded oddly blue. "Justin's in his office, working on his novel. I slept a lot of the day, since nothing's going on at The Haven."

"Wise of you. You'll be glad you rested up tomorrow." Alice forced herself to sound sympathetic, and she *was*, toward Shirley. It was just that rat Justin she didn't trust. "What time do they all arrive?"

"About one o'clock. It means a hell of a lot of driving for Justin, not to mention it took the skills of a UN negotiator to organize a time when both his ex-wives would allow their children to be away from them on Christmas. Justin picks up Angel and Spring in Stoneham at eleven thirty. Then he'll drive to the Braintree mall to pick up Ben, who lives on the Cape. His mom agreed to bring him that far. Then, about forty-five minutes to drive back out here."

"And you're roasting a turkey?"

"I am! I'm even doing it a special way, so it will be nice and tender."

"Good for you." Alice knew that this was a sacrifice for Shirley's vegetarian heart.

"Well, I want them to like me, Alice. We see each other so seldom, and I know their mothers don't want me, the new woman, to be a part of their lives."

"No one could not like you, Shirley."

"Oh, I hope you're right, Alice. I'd like to think this was the first holiday for us as a blended family."

Alice squirmed. Shirley's romantic blindness made Alice as irritable as a cow with a bug in her ear.

Of all the Hot Flash friends, Alice loved Shirley the best. When they first met, Shirley had been a masseuse with a business sense as drifty as the smoke from one of her aromatic candles. With Alice as her mentor, Shirley had changed. She'd taken courses in management and finance. She'd stopped dreaming and actually made her dream of running a wellness spa come true. Alice felt proud of Shirley for all she'd accomplished, and protective of her, too.

Alice had been in charge of personnel for a major insurance company for most of her life, so she'd developed keen instincts for liars, schemers, and bullshitters. And Justin Quale was all of those. She just *knew* it. Alice hadn't criticized Shirley when she started dating Justin, thinking—hoping—the romance would die a natural death. After all, Shirley was twelve years older than Justin and thrilled that this man, who had a Ph.D. in literature and wanted to write novels, would choose Shirley, who had never even graduated from high school. When Shirley let Justin move into The Haven, Alice had expressed her displeasure in no uncertain terms, although when Shirley hired him to teach a writing course there, Alice hadn't made too much of a fuss.

But now, something fishy was going on. Alice could *smell* it, just as surely as she knew it when her boys were teenagers and tried to sneak past her with mint on their breath, too naïve to know she could smell the smoke on their clothes.

For all Shirley's chirpy optimism, in spite of how much she had learned about business and looked and acted like an intelligent, powerful woman, she was really quite vulnerable. In her heart, Shirley believed in fairy tales. Alice did too—as long as they were by the Brothers Grimm. Justin's princely façade covered the soul of a toad. Alice *knew* it. But what could she do?

"I can't wait for the kids to see the tree," Shirley rambled on moonily. "It's the first time I've ever decorated a tree for a family. It's on the small side, but you know my condo's cozy, a bigger tree wouldn't have worked. Besides, it's kind of cute, how all the presents sort of overwhelm the tree. I've spent *hours* wrapping each present."

"Better have a camera ready."

"Oh, I do! I've told Justin to hand the presents out one by one, so I can photograph each child opening it. I can't wait to see their faces!"

"I wonder what they'll give you."

"Oh, I don't care. Probably nothing. Christmas is all

about *giving*. Oh, Alice, this is going to be the best Christmas of my life!"

"I hope so," Alice said warmly, and she meant it, but as she hung up the phone, her face was creased with worry.

6

When Shirley awoke at six o'clock on Christmas morning, her heart jumped straight from slo-mo sleep mode into speed skating.

At sixty-two, Shirley knew a racing heart was not a good thing. And come on, why was her ridiculous heart flipping around like this? She shouldn't be nervous. When was she going to grow up? When was she going to stop being a coward? Hadn't she proven herself enough already?

Gazing upon the beautiful face of her beloved Justin, who snored lustily on the pillow next to her, she told herself, "I can *do* this!"

Pulling on the filmy peach robe that set off her tousled auburn hair, she went to the window and looked out upon her domain, the elegant grounds spreading around the magnificent stone building that once had been a private school and now was The Haven. Wasn't Shirley the director of The Haven, just as if she were an intelligent person with good business sense? The rule of thumb, she'd been told, was that new businesses didn't turn a profit until the third year. This was only the beginning of their second year, and already they were beginning to show one.

More than that, she'd provided a nurturing home base

for hundreds of women in the Boston area, including her best friends.

Not to mention that while doing all this, she'd continued to stay away from the seductive charms of alcohol. She'd been sober for years now. She was living proof that a person could change her bad habits.

She had all the evidence she needed that she was an intelligent, rational person, right? She should be able to trust her own judgment, right?

On the bed, Justin snorted and puffed volcanically. She'd let him sleep. He deserved it, after the way he'd made love to her last night. Shirley hugged herself. Looking at Justin made her as happy as, well, as a kid on Christmas. She *loved* Justin, and she knew that even though he was twelve years younger than she, he loved her, too, just as sincerely. Her Hot Flash friends just had to stop fretting. They didn't know all the sweet things he said to her, not to mention the sweet things he did to her!

Shirley padded into the living room and did a few minutes of sun salutations. Then she went through the dining area to the kitchen. She drank her orange juice, ate some fruit yogurt, and brewed green tea, all the time going over her plans for the day.

Because she was a vegetarian, she hadn't roasted meat for decades. But Justin's kids were coming for Christmas dinner, and that meant turkey. She'd researched ways to make it tender, juicy, and delicious. She'd bought tons of veggies. And she'd bought a pumpkin pie and a cherry pie from Alan and Jennifer's bakery, so she didn't have to worry about dessert.

She had to start the turkey now. She'd decided to put it in a brown paper bag to make it especially tender, so she turned on the oven, organized her roasting pan, and hoisted the heavy bird out of the refrigerator. It was a fresh free-range turkey from a farm. She rinsed it, then rubbed it all over with butter and olive oil. Getting it into the paper bag wasn't easy, but she managed it and slid it into the oven.

There. That much done!

She washed her hands and her few breakfast things with organic soap, setting them in the wooden rack to dry. She double-checked the living room. *Perfection.* The tree and its presents glittered. And Justin's present, her *real* present, was hidden in Shirley's purse. She'd give it to him tonight when they were alone together. Tears sprang to her eyes as she thought of how Justin would look when he saw it.

She puttered around in the dining area, spreading the holiday tablecloth she'd bought especially for the occasion, setting out the plates and silverware and napkins. For the center of the table, she'd bought a long, low arrangement of red and white carnations—not expensive, but festive.

Everything was ready for the best Christmas of her life.

At ten thirty, Shirley leaned over the bed, put her hand on Justin's gorgeous naked shoulder, and gently shook him. "Hon? It's ten thirty. You'd better get going."

"Mrrph." Justin opened his eyes. "Okay. Thanks."

As he showered and shaved, Shirley made the bed and tidied the bedroom. Another good thing she'd accomplished, she thought, was helping Justin get to see his kids more often. Both his ex-wives were angry with him, and Shirley didn't blame them, because over the years he really hadn't been very good about paying child support or showing up for scheduled visits. What they didn't understand, of course, was that Justin was an artist, a writer, a sensitive, poetic soul who just could not be bound by the rigid laws imposed on ordinary people.

Justin hurried out of the bedroom and began pulling

on his clothes, his silver hair in its ponytail still damp. Shirley perched on the end of the bed, watching him. God, he was beautiful! It was Fate, really, that had brought them together. They'd met in a management seminar. It was Justin's own brother, a Realtor, who showed Shirley the run-down old estate that was now the flourishing home of The Haven. No one could tell her that she and Justin weren't *meant to be*.

"Okay, Sweetface, gotta go." Justin bent over, kissed her, and went off.

Shirley headed into the bathroom for her own shower. The thing her Hot Flash friends just couldn't seem to get was that Justin was an *intellectual*. He had a bachelor's and a master's degree in English literature, and he'd taught at various colleges and universities, but he'd never been given tenure because the world was swamped with English professors. "Publish or perish" was the unwritten academic law, but as much as Justin had struggled, he hadn't been able to teach, grade a million papers, sit on endless committees, and still find the psychic energy to write. So when his contract at a junior college was not renewed, Justin had decided to try the business sector. He'd signed up for the management seminar, hoping to learn enough to land a decent day job. He went to work at a real estate office and tried to write at night.

It was a good plan, and Justin did work hard. No one could deny that. It wasn't his fault that the real estate deals he invested in fell through. His own brother had advised him, and his own brother had lost money, too. But his brother had a lot of money to play with; Justin didn't. While Justin had been riding his professional roller coaster on its downward plunge, Shirley, with the help of her Hot Flash friends and a few wealthy investors, had gotten The Haven off the ground. It was only natural for her to invite Justin to teach a few courses in creative writing at the spa. His classes were always filled to the max—again, a fact no one could argue with. For a while, Justin rented a condo at The Haven for a nominal amount, but that made Alice cranky, plus it was a slight—*very* slight—financial negative for The Haven, so Shirley had invited him to move in with her and they rented his condo to Star, the yoga teacher.

Finally, Justin had the emotional space and comfort for writing his novel. He'd slaved over it, Shirley knew. She'd carried endless cups of coffee to him as he sat typing away at his laptop on the dining room table. He'd written hundreds and hundreds of pages in a storm of creation. A few months ago, he'd declared the novel nearly finished. Shirley was sure the work was brilliant, although Justin was too shy to let her read the book.

Perhaps it was because he hadn't yet been able to get an agent. It wasn't Justin's fault. The publishing world was as corrupt and difficult as the academic world. Everyone knew that. He didn't have the right contacts. He was disappointed—close to despair.

Shirley studied her body in the mirror as she dressed for the day. So many wrinkles, so many lines! Her Hot Flash friends, Polly, Marilyn, Alice, and Faye, could console themselves that no matter how used up their bodies looked, it was all right. They'd given birth to children. Their bodies *had* been used. The same could be said for the sags and wrinkles on their faces—no one had gotten through the business of motherhood without some difficulties, disappointments, and sorrows. The love, worry, fear, and labor that made them good mothers marked their faces, and because of that, they would not change a thing.

But Shirley had never had children. She had wanted children. With all her heart, she had wanted children. But it had just never been in the cards, and now the marks on her face, the long, deep lines, seemed like the tracks of tears engraved in her skin.

Which was why Justin was so important to her. She could actually help make *his* dreams come true. That was a luxury she'd never experienced. Alice, Faye, Marilyn, and Polly could close their eyes and remember all the years when their kids went wide-eyed on Christmas morning, or when they gave their kids the puppy or the kitten or the new dress or the bike they'd been longing for. The greatest joy in life wasn't getting, it was giving. Just once in her life, Shirley was going to experience that.

She couldn't wait. It really made her *shiver*. It would be wonderful, seeing the kids open their presents. But it would be a once-in-a-lifetime event on the order of a miracle to give Justin his present tonight.

She knew what Justin was giving her, and it was very important that she give him his present first. She hadn't even been looking; she'd been dusting the condo. His briefcase had been sitting on the dining room table, next to his laptop and his stack of papers. It had been open, and Shirley had carelessly glanced inside. It was crammed with student essays and handouts for his creative writing course, but wedged down at the bottom was a small black velvet box.

The sight had electrified her as if she'd been struck by lightning.

"Oh my God!" she'd whispered, covering her mouth. Justin was just in the other room. They'd been talking about marriage recently, in a playful, daydreamy kind of way. She knew Justin loved her. She knew he liked to surprise her. She danced away from the dining room table, jubilant. His Christmas present to her was an engagement ring!

"Let's wait and exchange our Christmas presents on Christmas night," she'd suggested a week or so ago. "When we're alone and relaxed."

"Good idea," he'd agreed. Today was the first holiday

they were spending all together, as if they were a kind of family.

At one o'clock, her cell phone rang.

"Shirley," Justin said, "Ben's mom was late getting him here. We're just leaving Braintree."

"That's fine, Hon. Thanks for letting me know!" Shirley wondered what to do about the turkey. She didn't want it to dry out, so she covered it and left it in the oven.

At two fifteen, the door flew open and they all stomped in.

Angel and Spring wore low-cut jeans with cropped sweaters. Spring's hair was short, spiked, and blue. Angel's was long and curly. Both girls wore glittering gold eye shadow and thick, frosted lipstick. Shirley tried to take that as a kind of compliment, that they'd dressed up to come to her place. Ben, only ten, hulked behind his half-sisters, looking sullen.

Shirley chirped, "Merry Christmas, everyone!" Pushing a little switch, she turned on her necklace and earrings so they flashed.

Spring, the most sophisticated at fifteen, rolled her eyes. But thirteen-year-old Angel said, "Cute!"

Ben pulled off his down jacket, dropped it on the floor, and waded into the pile of presents. Grabbing one of the larger ones, he picked it up and shook it. "What's in here?"

"Well, let's all get settled and you'll find out! I thought your father could hand out—"

Ben read the tag. "Mine." With both hands, in one long, violent tear, he ripped the paper from the box. "Cool! A PlayStation 2!"

"You got PlayStation?" Spring asked excitedly. "Wow! What did we get?"

As if they operated with one brain, Spring and Angel,

in sync, threw themselves at the presents, scanning the tags, tossing ones without their names over their shoulders in Ben's general direction.

"Kids, kids!" Shirley cried. "Slow down! I want to get pictures of you opening your presents!"

But the three kids were like hounds digging for buried bones. They went at the presents in a frenzy, ripping the wrapping paper, shredding the beautiful bows without so much as a glance, tossing each present aside in their hurry to get to the next one.

"We got a DVD player!" Angel trumpeted, sticking out her tongue at Ben.

"*We* already have a DVD player, dummy," Ben sneered.

"We got the coats!" Spring screamed at Angel as she opened a large box. "I told you Shirley would get them for us."

Shirley perked up, waiting for them to thank her. When they didn't, she told herself to be glad the girls assumed she would do something nice for them. That was a start, wasn't it?

"A skateboard! Awesome." Ben jumped up. "I'm going to take this outside."

"Wait!" Shirley said. "Let's have Christmas dinner first."

"Aw, crap," Ben whined. "Dad! Come on!"

"Why don't you go try it out for just a few minutes," Justin told his son. "While we get dinner on the table."

"*I'm* not helping set the table if *he*'s not helping!" Spring snarled.

"No, kids, you don't have to help," Shirley hastily assured them. "Everything's done; I just have to put the food on the table."

"I'll just stay inside," Ben decided, grabbing up his new PlayStation.

"Well?" Spring demanded. "I thought you said dinner was ready. I'm starving."

Shirley was almost dizzy. The opening-presents event had been a free-for-all, over almost before it was begun. The girls were already ignoring their coats, DVDs, cosmetic kits, and other presents and sat on the sofa, fighting over the television remote control.

"MTV!"

"No, VH1!"

Ben leaned against the sofa, fingers flying over his electronic game, already lost in another world.

No one had brought her a present, Shirley realized, with a twinge of disappointment. But no one had given their father a present, either. That was just *mean*.

"I'll help you put the food on," Justin said.

She gave him the best smile she could conjure up. "Thanks."

In the kitchen, she heated the creamed broccoli, the cauliflower au gratin, the marshmallow-topped sweet potatoes, the carrots simmered in brown sugar and butter. Justin's kids all liked their veggies disguised by sauces, the sweeter the better. She dished them into serving bowls, and Justin carried them to the table.

"Okay!" Shirley said. "Now, Justin, if you'll just hold the big platter, I'll put the turkey on it."

She pulled oven mitts on and lifted out the heavy pan.

"Hey!" Drawn by the aroma, Ben stood in the doorway to the kitchen. "That smells good."

His half-sisters came to stand behind him, peering over his shoulder.

"Turkey. Cool," Angel said. "We have to eat *goose* tonight. Ugh."

"My mom's fixing leg of lamb," Ben said, making gagging noises.

"Ughghghgh!" both girls croaked.

Shirley's cheeks were hot with happiness—she'd done something *right*! She'd cooked a Christmas turkey!

Carefully she cut open the brown paper bag. The

turkey was gorgeous, golden brown, steaming with heat and flavor. Justin held the platter out.

Shirley put a long fork in each end of the turkey and lifted it away from the roasting pan toward the platter.

With a kind of mushy, squishing liquid sound, most of the meat fell away from the bones, splatting in greasy pieces on the floor.

"Oooh, gross!" Ben cried.

"I'm not eating that!" Spring exclaimed.

"Me, either!" Angel echoed.

Visions of a strong gin and tonic danced in Shirley's head.

Fueled by Shirley's optimistic energies, the day staggered on. Enough meat remained on the turkey to feed everyone. The kids even ate the vegetables. Justin went out to watch Ben on his skateboard while Shirley, on a whim, gave the girls a tour of The Haven. Then Justin drove the kids home, while Shirley gathered up the torn wrapping paper and bows and removed the various glasses, plates, and cups the kids had left around the place. She did the dishes and cleaned up the fallen turkey mess—what a literal pain in the back!

Now, *at last,* Christmas night was here. The condo was clean, the tree twinkled brightly, and Shirley had turned off all the other lights and set candles glowing around the room. Christmas music spilled softly from the CD player. Shirley redid her makeup and tousled her hair, wanting to look perfect for the coming perfect moment.

Justin came in, smelling of fresh air and snow. "Let me fix a drink, and we can open our presents."

"Lovely," Shirley said. "I've made myself a pot of tea."

Justin sank down on the sofa next to her. "Cheers, Shirley," he said, toasting her. "Thanks for making this such a wonderful day for all of us."

His praise touched her deeply. "I loved every minute of it."

He raised his eyebrows and grinned. "*Every* minute?"

She laughed. "The bit with the turkey was a little embarrassing."

"We'll all be laughing about it a few years from now," Justin assured her.

Hey! There was a long-range plan if she'd ever heard one. Shirley's heart swelled in her chest. She blinked back tears.

"I want to give you your present now." She bent to retrieve the little red box left under the tree. It looked like a cuff link box. She hoped he would think it was cuff links.

Justin set his drink on the table and put the present on his lap. Carefully, he undid the ribbon and lifted the lid off the box.

Inside was a check. From Shirley to Justin. For ten thousand dollars.

Frowning, Justin looked at Shirley. "What's this?"

Shirley was practically squirming all over, like a puppy who'd just dropped his bone at his master's lap. "It's money! So you can self-publish your novel! And pay for a graphic artist to give it a dynamite cover. And in a few more months, I'm going to give you another check, so you can hire someone to help you publicize your book."

Justin looked dumbfounded. He shook his head. "Shirley, I can't take this much money from you."

"But that's how much you need. You told me so, yourself."

"Yes, but—"

"Justin, take it, please. I want to help you make your dream come true."

He ran his hand over his head. "I don't know. I just don't know."

She waited, holding her breath.

When he looked at her, his eyes were shining. "Shirley, I've never had anyone love me this much. I don't know what to say." He stood up and paced the room, walking like a man in a dream.

Then he came back to the sofa, knelt in front of Shirley, and took her hands in his. "All right. I'll do it. I'll take your money and publish my novel. On one condition: every cent I make from it comes back to you, until I pay this debt off."

"It's not a debt, silly, it's a present," Shirley reminded him.

"I'm serious, Shirley. I'm going to put it in writing. Any profit from my novel goes to you."

God, she loved this man! He had such integrity! "All right," she agreed.

He pulled her down to him and kissed her passionately. "I love you, Shirley. I love you so much."

"I love you."

Rising, he said, "God, this is so exciting! I've already investigated several self-publishing presses, but now *I get to choose.* I've got to make a list, and actually, I'd better get some information off the Net. I'll want to go to their offices, meet these people, see what they propose to give me for my money."

Shirley pulled her knees up and hugged them against her, watching Justin in his excitement.

"Oh!" Justin said, stopping midpace. "I haven't given you your present yet."

Justin reached into his pocket and brought out the small black velvet box. Returning to the sofa, he sat next to Shirley and put the box in her hand.

"This is nothing compared to what you've given me," he told her somberly. "I'm sorry I couldn't afford something bigger. I'd like to give you a diamond as big as the Ritz."

"Silly," Shirley said, kissing him lightly on the lips. It

was, after all, the thought that counted. She didn't care if the diamond was the size of a grape seed; it was still an engagement ring.

She opened the box.

And gasped.

Inside, tucked into a slot in the black velvet, lay two tiny diamond ear studs.

She couldn't help it. Tears leapt into her eyes. Ear studs, and she'd thought it was an engagement ring! For a moment, a terrible bitterness filled her mouth like an acid. She felt like such a fool for assuming it was a ring!

"Don't cry, darling," Justin said. "You're worth it."

7

COOL, ELEGANT CAROLYN'S CHRISTMAS DECORATIONS
were all silver and white.

"It's rather like entering a spaceship," Hugh remarked,
as he and Polly went into the house.

"Polly, Hugh, lovely to see you! Merry Christmas!"
Carolyn, elegant in a red cashmere dress, air kissed them
both before pulling them into the living room, where a
bartender offered them flutes of Champagne.

The large, airy rooms were already crowded. Hank's
aristocratic and rather daffy mother, Daisy, was there,
carrying her pet Shih Tzu, Clock, everywhere in her
arms and talking to the dog more than to the human beings. One of Hank's sisters, Evelyn, was there, with her
husband and their three young children. Ingrid, Carolyn's new au pair, drifted through the room with baby
Elizabeth in her arms.

Faye was ensconced on the sofa, her legs stretched out
and one ankle elevated on a cushion. Her neck brace
made it difficult for her to turn her head easily, so anyone talking with her had to sit on the coffee table facing
her.

Polly made a beeline for Faye. "Merry Christmas, Faye!
How do you feel?"

Faye managed a smile. "Awful, to tell the truth. If I

don't use painkillers, I'm in agony, and if I do use them, I'm in the Twilight Zone."

Now that she was close to her, Polly could see how pale Faye was. Wanting to cheer her up, she said, "Well, you *look* gorgeous!"

A chiming noise vibrated the air.

Carolyn tapped a glass with a knife until she had everyone's attention. "Dinner's served!"

Aubrey leaned over the back of the sofa, placing an affectionate hand on Faye's shoulder. "I'll bring you a plate."

"Thanks, Aubrey." Faye made a little shooing gesture. "Go on, Polly, fix your own plate. I'll be fine."

Polly, Hugh, and Aubrey joined the line at the table. It was set buffet style, with the food served by a smiling young caterer. Suddenly, Carolyn materialized out of thin air.

"Here, Hugh." Carolyn handed him a plate heaped with food. "Take this to Faye, will you?" Deftly she turned to Aubrey. "Father, why don't you sit at the little table by the tree with Elizabeth? And Polly, could you hold Elizabeth for me? She knows you and Father, she won't fuss with you two." Before Polly could object, Carolyn lifted her baby out of Ingrid's arms and plunked her into Polly's.

So, smoothly Carolyn paired off her father with Polly. Of course, Polly loved holding the little girl. At eight months, Elizabeth was only seven months younger than Polly's grandson, still cuddly and full of bubbles and baby babble. Aubrey clearly adored his granddaughter, holding her while Polly ate. Then Polly returned the favor, and she couldn't help it; she enjoyed talking with Aubrey, no doubt about that. He was a handsome, charming man. She told him about setting her house on fire. He laughed heartily.

From time to time, Polly glanced over at Faye, reclining on the sofa, with Hugh close by. The two were talking and laughing quite happily, Polly thought. It's just a party, she reassured herself. We're supposed to talk to everyone at parties.

After dinner, everyone settled in the living room around the Christmas tree and the fire. Aubrey stationed himself next to Faye, sitting on the edge of the sofa, occasionally touching her lightly with his hand or leaning down to whisper something that made her smile.

Hugh returned to Polly's side, his jovial face flushed and bright. "What a feast! And such fascinating people."

So everything was all right, Polly thought, with relief.

Then Carolyn and Hank brought out the Perrier Jouët Champagne. Since Elizabeth's premature birth in April, Carolyn had lost her baby weight and regained her strong, healthy blond beauty. Her father had handed over control of the Sperry Paper Company to her, they'd moved into this new house, and Carolyn was thriving. She radiated confidence and well-being. Polly felt a moment of almost maternal pride as she watched the lovely young woman.

Carolyn's mother had died when she was young, and because of Carolyn's dedication to the company, handed down matrilineally through the generations, she hadn't had a chance to keep up old friendships or develop new ones. When Polly met her last year at The Haven, Carolyn was a very isolated woman. Polly, who was cold-shouldered by her own daughter-in-law, had loved the opportunity to talk about all the things women over the ages discussed: the eccentric physical problems of pregnancy, the doubts about being a good mother. Gradually, they'd become such close friends that when Carolyn went into premature labor while Hank was out of town, she had called Polly for help.

Polly alone had been privy to Carolyn's fears and struggles. She'd helped her uncover Aubrey's new wife's devious, money-grubbing scheme. Polly had been there when Elizabeth was born. She'd spent hours helping Carolyn adjust to the demands of motherhood. She'd become a kind of second mother to the young woman.

But that didn't mean Polly should pair off with Carolyn's father, even though that seemed to be what Carolyn wanted.

Now Carolyn raised her glass in a toast. "Merry Christmas, everyone!"

They all cheered and drank.

"I want to thank my mother-in-law and sister-in-law and brother-in-law for coming to spend this Christmas with us." Carolyn looked very beautiful as one of her great-grandmother's magnificent ruby-and-diamond necklaces sparkled around her throat. "This has been a year of many changes."

"You had a baby!" chirped her five-year-old niece, and everyone laughed.

"Indeed, I did." Carolyn looked at her daughter, nestled now in her husband's arms. Leaning forward, she kissed Elizabeth's nose. "And my father and I moved from the family home, which is being converted into a museum for the town. Hank and I have turned this new house into a comfortable home, we've hired Ingrid as our housekeeper/nanny, and the Sperry Paper Company has had the best year in a decade."

More cheers.

When the noise died down, Carolyn spoke again. "And I couldn't have done it all without you, Polly." She flushed as she spoke. Carolyn was always uneasy with emotion. "You were like the mother I never had. You've taught me so much, and you've helped me so much. I wish I could adopt you as my mother, but since I can't, Hank and I would like to ask you to be Elizabeth's godmother."

It should have been a poignant moment. Instead, Polly felt like an onion dropped into an emotional Cuisinart, sliced and diced by the various needs of the others in the room. Carolyn's request made Polly's heart swell with love and sympathy—she knew how hard it was for Carolyn to show affection. She knew how much Carolyn needed a mother. And baby Elizabeth was adorable.

But if Polly agreed to be Elizabeth's godmother, that would tie her in even closer to Carolyn's family. Would it drive a wedge between Polly and Faye?

Of all the Hot Flash Club, Faye was the one Polly liked the best. She was the one with whom Polly had the most in common. They were both widowed by men they had loved. They each had one child: Faye, a daughter; Polly, a son. They wanted to be grandmothers more than Marilyn, who was obsessed with her ancient fossils, or Shirley, who had never had children and was focused on running The Haven, or professional, no-nonsense Alice.

A volcanic blast of heat exploded through Polly. She couldn't think—she wanted to pour her Champagne right down the front of her dress, *anything* to cool off!

"Polly?"

Polly blinked.

Carolyn and all the others in the room were smiling at her, waiting for her reply. What could she say?

"I—I—Why, Carolyn, it's an *honor* to be asked to be Elizabeth's godmother."

Carolyn was never shy about closing a deal. "So you accept?"

What else could she say? "I accept!"

NEW YEAR'S DAY

8

New Year's Day dawned white and frigid and only got worse, as a howling wind blew tiny stinging bits of snow, like grains of sand, against buildings, trees, and cars, and into the eyes of anyone foolish enough to brave the elements.

The Haven was officially closed, most of its windows dark. But the lights were on in the locker room, and in the beautifully tiled Jacuzzi room, the hot tub bubbled and steamed. Five women in bathing suits were sinking into the healing heat of hot water and good gossip. Although they often phoned one another, the Hot Flash Club members tried to keep their juiciest news and latest crises for an occasion when they were all together, so they could all weigh in with opinions, argue, and brainstorm. But the holidays had thrown them off schedule. They had a lot to catch up on.

Marilyn held her mother's hand until Ruth was securely seated, her head resting against the back of the tub. Ruth wore one of Marilyn's bathing suits, and Marilyn couldn't help but think she was seeing the Ghost of Christmas Future in her mother's body. Like Marilyn, Ruth was slender, and for a woman in her eighties she was in good shape, but the top of the swimsuit hung loosely over her shriveled breasts while the tummy section bulged out in a little round pudding. Ruth's skin was freckled and wrinkled, creased like tissue paper, and beneath the fragile covering, her green veins wound around her bones like vines over a trellis.

Ruth's toenails were yellow, thick, and hard as ice cubes. Marilyn had cut them for her this morning, and painted them with the polish she had in the house only because her Hot Flash friends insisted she use it from time to time.

"I've always liked my toes," Ruth had confided. "I think of them as ten friendly little companions. Hello down there!" she called. Wiggling her toes, she responded in a squeaky voice, "Hello up there!"

Okay, she's senile, Marilyn thought.

Ruth continued, "You and Sharon liked your toes, too, when you were young, remember? You used to draw faces on your toes and make little caps for them out of bits of yarn or foil."

Marilyn slapped herself in the forehead. "You're right! We did!"

Memories flooded back: Long afternoons in the Ohio summer heat. She and Sharon had spent hours painstakingly drawing faces on and dressing each other's toes, tying bits of ribbon around them as neckties or tutus. Then they'd lie side by side on the grass in the shade of a tree, holding musical revues, making their toes dance while they sang songs they'd heard their grandmother sing. "Five foot two, eyes of blue," or "Hey, good lookin', whatcha got cookin'." Did anyone sing those songs anymore?

A door opened up in her mind. Marilyn felt she could step through it and reenter those summer days, which shimmered green-golden and fresh and sounded like little girls giggling. The innocence, the happiness, the *there*ness of it all swept through her. She remembered how she'd been especially fond of one of her birthmarks, the brown one on her left thigh. It had looked like a piece of a miniature jigsaw puzzle.

"Marilyn?" Her mother's voice interrupted her thoughts.

"All done!" Marilyn stuck the brush back inside the bottle and tightened it.

Later, as they drove to The Haven, Marilyn thought how her mother was a living repository of memories. When Ruth was gone, who would remember, who would care, about Marilyn's girlish toes?

Now, as Ruth bobbed in the Jacuzzi, she kept letting her feet float up so she could admire her painted nails. Marilyn noticed how Ruth smiled every time she saw the perky spots of pink peek up through the water. *Hello up there!* she thought.

"Did you have a nice Christmas, Ruth?" Alice asked.

Ruth's face lit up. "It was *lovely*. We spent Christmas Eve with Teddy and Lila and my adorable little great-granddaughter, Irene."

"Was Eugenie there?" Shirley asked.

"She was, indeed," Ruth answered. "We could hardly pry little Irene out of her clutch."

"And guess what!" Marilyn looked at her friends with a grin. "Eugenie had a *bad* face-lift. Very *Phantom of the Opera*." Seeing Polly's puzzled face, she hastened to explain, "I know it seems callous of me to be silly about another woman's bad face-lift, but Eugenie is so superficial and critical and such a terrible snob—"

Shirley was glad Marilyn was so chatty today. She loved her friends and, as always, loved being around them, but sooner or later she was going to *have* to tell them about her gift to Justin. She let herself sink deeper and deeper into the water, so that her mouth was submerged and only the top of her head from her nose up showed.

"You've got to tell Faye about this," Alice said. "After all, she 'worked' for Eugenie."

"I wish Faye were here now," Polly said.

"I do too." Shirley slid up out of the water so she could talk. "I told her we'd be glad to pick her up, or even go to her house so she wouldn't have to deal with traveling in a car. But she said she really needed to rest."

Marilyn frowned. "Still, it's not like Faye not to come out. I hope she's okay."

"I think she's depressed," Polly told them. "I saw her Christmas night for dinner at Carolyn's house. When we had a chance to talk alone for a while, she told me that her daughter's pregnant again."

"That's great!" Shirley looked puzzled. "That should thrill Faye."

"It does, but Faye also learned that Lars's parents are moving to San Francisco so they can be near their son and his family. Lars's mother plans to help Laura when she has the new baby, so they won't have to hire a nanny. Faye feels horribly left out. She almost started crying when she told me."

"Oh, dear, poor Faye!" Marilyn's face crinkled with worry.

Shirley tried to be optimistic. "Good thing she's got Aubrey to keep her occupied."

Polly considered holding her breath and sinking to the bottom of the tub. She wanted to share her discomfort about the whole Carolyn/Aubrey business with the Hot Flash group, but now, in the soothing intimacy of the hot tub, she decided to ignore her worries. "Yes, Aubrey seems quite smitten with Faye."

"How was your Christmas?" Shirley asked.

"Well, let's see." Polly was glad to change the subject. Playfully, she cocked her head, pretending to search her memory. "Well, I *did* set my house on fire just when my daughter-in-law arrived."

"You set your house on fire! Oh, Polly!" Marilyn's mother looked horrified.

Polly waved her hands in the air. "It's all right. No one was hurt." She didn't want poor Ruth to have a heart attack. "Some greenery on the mantel caught fire. It was quite spectacular for a few moments, but only one wall was ruined. Well, and the other walls and ceiling were smoke-damaged. Fortunately, my insurance covers it, so I'll have the living room repainted. The problem is, it gives Amy one more reason to stay away from me."

"What's the matter with that girl?" Alice shook her head impatiently. "She sounds loony."

"I know," Polly agreed. "I'll never understand why David married her."

Ruth piped up, "*I* never understood why Marilyn married Theodore. He was always such a pompous little rooster."

"We got Teddy out of the marriage, Mother," Marilyn reminded her.

Polly leaned forward. "Marilyn, what did Faraday give you for Christmas?"

Marilyn very busily adjusted the strap on her Speedo.

"Oh, boy," Alice chuckled. "This is going to be good."

"Oh, Alice!" Marilyn slapped the water in exasperation.

"Come on, out with it," Alice coaxed.

"Oh, no!" Marilyn was turning red all over. "I've got to get out for a minute." Pushing herself up, she left the steamy room.

"Those hot flashes make her miserable," Ruth told the others. "She's forever pulling off her clothes. I told her she should call herself Dixie Rose Lee."

The others looked confused.

"Gypsy!" Shirley cried. "You mean Gypsy Rose Lee."

"That's what I said."

Marilyn returned, slightly less flushed. "I'll just sit out here for a while." She folded herself Indian–style on the tiles.

"So," Alice prompted. "You were saying . . ."

Marilyn made a face. "Faraday asked me to marry him."

"Oh, my God!" In her excitement, Shirley popped up like a piece of toast. "That's so wonderful! Oh, Marilyn!"

Alice yanked Shirley back down into the water. "Calm down, Shirley. We don't know whether Marilyn accepted."

"Well, of course she did!" Shirley responded, indignant. Then she saw Marilyn's face. "Didn't you?"

"Well," Marilyn hedged. "I told him I needed some time to think about it."

"But why?" Shirley asked. "Faraday's so cute! And he's fun! And he likes all that scientific stuff you like."

"True. But—" Marilyn glanced sideways at her mother. "You know, he's got a little problem in the, um, romance department."

"Do you mean he doesn't satisfy you sexually?" Ruth asked, turning to look up at her daughter.

"Well, Mom!" Marilyn blushed again.

"I think you're right to take your time," Alice weighed in. "What's your hurry? It's not like we're young women who've got to worry about ticking biological clocks. You can't have any more children. You're not getting married to get away from home or satisfy your parents. You should only do it if you really want to."

"But if you don't accept," Polly added, worriedly, "he might be insulted or hurt. He might start seeing someone else!"

Ruth stirred in the water. "You know what they say. Marry in haste, repent in leisure wear."

"Well, look." Alice's voice took on its executive tone. "If the only thing holding you back is Faraday's sexual, um, incapacity, then be an adult and try to find a solution. There are some excellent medicines for that kind of thing."

"True. But every time I try to talk with him about this, he stonewalls me."

"Tell him it's a condition of getting engaged," Alice suggested.

Marilyn nodded slowly. "I could do that." Lifting an eyebrow, she subtly nodded in her mother's direction. "It's all so complicated."

Polly got the message and changed the subject. "So, Shirley, how was your Christmas?"

Shirley squirmed. It was now or never. Actually, it didn't *have* to be now. Actually, her financial affairs weren't really any of their business. Except, of course, they were, because her Hot Flash friends had invested, some more than others, in The Haven. It would all come out one way or the other, anyway. She just had to be brave and tell them. But she was already so filled with negative energy, so envious of Marilyn because Faraday had asked her to marry him! And envy was a destructive emotion.

"Boy, do you look guilty," Alice remarked.

Shirley considered simply sliding down into the hot water and staying there. Instead, she pushed her wet hair behind her ears. "Justin gave me diamond ear studs!"

Polly peered at the little gems. "Beautiful!"

Marilyn reentered the water. "Did his kids like their presents?"

Shirley brightened. "They did! But oh, my gosh, wait till you hear about my gourmet Christmas dinner!"

As Shirley laughingly told them about the disintegrating turkey, Alice settled back against the Jacuzzi, adjusting herself so one of the jets hit her right in a sore spot in her back. The heat mellowed her out, and she was just beginning to feel ashamed for thinking ill of Justin, when Shirley said:

". . . so I want to tell you about it. It was kind of my Christmas present to Justin, but more than that, really.

Remember when I said I thought this Christmas should be about dreams coming true? How we've talked about this time of our lives being about making dreams come true? Well, you know Justin's written a novel, but he hasn't been able to find a publisher." She held up a hand. "Just wait! It's hard to find a publisher. You all just don't have any idea."

"You're right," Marilyn agreed. "I've heard some of my MIT acquaintances talk about this. It's a real struggle to find a publisher for fiction. There are so many people writing excellent books these days."

Shirley threw a grateful smile Marilyn's way. "So my present to Justin was money. Enough money for him to get his book published, and to get a good cover designed for it. And later, I'm going to give him enough money to promote and publicize it."

For a moment, the only sound in the room was the burbling of the Jacuzzi jets.

Then Alice asked quietly, "How much money did you give him, Shirley?"

Shirley's shoulders drifted up toward her ears and her voice went little-girlish. "You have to understand. He's investigated this. He's checked around. It's not cheap . . ."

"How much?" Alice persisted.

"Ten thousand dollars," Shirley admitted meekly.

Alice exploded. "Ten thousand dollars! Girl, where did you get that much money?"

"It's *my* money, Alice!" Shirley shot back defiantly. "I saved some from my salary over the last two years, and I got the rest on credit card loans."

"Are you nuts?" Alice was volcanic.

"Justin's going to repay me as soon as his book starts selling."

Alice shook her head angrily. "And what if no one buys his book? What then?"

"I don't see why you have to be so pessimistic," Shirley argued.

"I can't do this." Alice hauled herself up out of the Jacuzzi. "Shirley, if you're going to think with your crotch, I'm not going to remain involved with The Haven. I've invested too much of my own time and money to see it jeopardized."

"You're crazy!" Shirley cried. "This doesn't jeopardize The Haven! It's *my* money—"

But Alice strode out of the room, leaving behind only wet footprints on the tile and four women sitting in stunned silence.

Ruth spoke first. "Oh, my."

Shirley was white. "Should I go after her?"

Polly and Marilyn looked at each other helplessly.

"I don't know," Marilyn said. "I wish Faye were here."

"I think you should let her have time to calm down," Ruth advised. "At the retirement community, some of us tend to fly off the hamper more than others, due, I believe, to hardening of the arteries, or feeling cranky because of some physical ailment."

"But Alice is only sixty-three," Shirley said softly.

"I understand," Ruth told her. "Yet anyone at any age can be bothered by something like, oh, constipation. That can affect your mood all day."

"Talk about having your head up your ass," Marilyn said with a grin.

"Indeed," Ruth agreed.

Shirley made little swirls in the water with her fingers. "I hate starting the new year off this way."

"It will work out," Polly assured her Pollyannaishly.

Ruth held up her hands. "My fingers and toes are turning into little white raisins. I think I'd better get out."

"Let's all get out," Shirley suggested. She was about to add that they could come up to her condo for hot chocolate, but she remembered that Justin was there, working on his book, and he wouldn't want to be disturbed. "We could all drive down to Leonardo's to have some dessert!"

"Not me," Polly said. "I'm so stuffed from holiday food, I don't even want chocolate."

Marilyn had her mother by the arm as they carefully made their way up the steps and out of the tub. "I think we'd better go home and have a little rest," she told Shirley, with a slight nod toward her mother, who was unsteady on her legs, leaning heavily on Marilyn.

The locker room was oddly quiet as the four women showered and dressed. Shirley said good night to Polly, Marilyn, and Ruth, then went through the building, checking to be sure all the doors were locked and turning out the lights.

The last thing she did was to unplug the twinkling Christmas tree in the lounge. Then that room was dark as well. Outside the snow fell swiftly, quickly obscuring the footprints and tire tracks of her departed guests. Justin was upstairs, but Shirley felt all alone.

9

THE SECOND RULE OF THE HOT FLASH CLUB WAS "IF you're depressed, get up, get dressed, and get out of the house."

But what if you can't?

On New Year's Day, while her Hot Flash friends communed in a hot tub, Faye lay on her living room sofa with her ankle resting on a pillow and her head wobbling in the neck brace like a soft-boiled egg in a cup. She was surrounded by new mysteries, boxes of chocolates, plates of delicious food brought to her by neighbors, the latest magazines, and a pile of DVDs.

She was very crabby.

She felt guilty for not enjoying this enforced laziness. She thought back to the years when the tasks of life had overwhelmed her, when on any given day she'd struggled to drive her little girl to school and ballet practice, organize an elegant dinner party for one of Jack's new clients, pick up the dry cleaning, help out at the church fair, and even try to grab some time in her studio for painting. Back then, she would have wept with joy at the thought of having a week to do nothing but lie around like this, eating and grazing through movies and books like a big, fat cow in a lush, green pasture.

She sort of wished she'd told the Hot Flash Club to

meet here at her house today. She'd thought about it. Shirley, Polly, Alice, and Marilyn had all phoned to say they'd drive her out, but Faye had refused, insisting she didn't feel well enough to leave the sofa.

But that was only partly true. While half of her wanted to be around her friends, the other half hunkered down in a gloomy wallow of misery, and Faye just couldn't be bothered to struggle up out of it.

The truth was, she felt worthless. She felt like a kicked dog who'd crawled under the house to nurse her wounds.

This Christmas had been so terrible! Faye grabbed a handful of tissues as the tears started again.

First of all, there was her foolish fall, incapacitating her and making everything difficult for everyone else. Not to mention making her feel old and helpless! And falling down her own stairs—why, it made her seem absolutely *senile*. If she'd had to fall, why couldn't she have fallen out on the ice, a *reasonable* place to fall. She kept flashing back to the moment her foot slipped. It had been so frightening! That sense of total vulnerability, lack of control, danger—and then the painful landing and her body's refusal to move without pain.

Then, to have her own beloved granddaughter shrink in terror from her! That had bruised Faye's heart, even though she understood the cause was her neck brace and crutches. Eventually, Megan got used to them and allowed Faye to hold her, but Faye knew the rich connection of their relationship had been weakened. And during the four nights of their visit, Megan hadn't once slept in or been even slightly captivated by the magical bedroom. Kind, sensitive *Laura* had made an enormous fuss over the darlingness of the room, the fairies, the colors, the attention to detail. Laura had insisted, the last afternoon of their stay, that Faye, Laura, and Megan all spend time in the room, playing Chutes and Ladders, and she'd taken lots of photos of Megan there. Faye knew she could expect a framed picture from Laura in the mail. Laura was thoughtful that way. But Megan would not carry the fantasy room in her dreams. Megan was enchanted with space cowgirls and superheroines. Faye felt oddly embarrassed, like a gawky suitor who'd brushed his pony and polished his wagon, only to find his loved one going off with a guy in a Corvette.

Christmas dinner at Carolyn's hadn't improved her self-esteem. Faye knew Carolyn adored Polly and wanted to pair up Polly with her father, but this hadn't seemed a real problem until the moment Faye found herself stranded on the sofa, unable to do more than observe.

Carolyn had sent Hugh to bring Faye her dinner, then organized Aubrey, Polly, and baby Elizabeth into a winsome trio. Faye pretended to listen as kindhearted Hugh chatted, but really she was watching Polly, who looked so happy, holding the baby. Polly's own daughter-in-law was such a strange little snake, wriggling between Polly and her son, keeping Polly from seeing her grandchild, that woozy from painkillers, Faye decided it seemed natural—it seemed *right*—for Polly to hook up with Aubrey. They could all be one big, happy family. They *should* be.

As she rode home from Carolyn's house on Christmas night, Faye's spirits had been lower than the road the tires rolled over, and just as flat and cold. She'd done her best to hide her depression from Aubrey, blaming her neck and ankle for her lack of witty repartee.

And then, Christmas night hit.

Shortly after Aubrey brought Faye home, establishing her comfortably on her own sofa before kissing her chastely and leaving, Lars, Laura, and Megan returned from Christmas dinner with Lars's parents. Laura put Megan to bed in the middle of the big bed in the guest room where she and Lars would join her later. Then she came downstairs for a nightcap with her mother and husband.

Lars poured a brandy for himself, a Godiva liqueur for Faye, and only a glass of water for Laura. This, coupled with Laura's weight gain, made Faye's senses flick on to Red Alert. She wasn't completely surprised when Lars said, "We have some news, Faye." Looking fondly at Laura, he announced, "We're going to have another baby. A little boy. In May."

"Oh, Laura!" Faye longed to give her daughter a big hug, but could only smile and raise her glass, struggling to move like a boar stuck in a snowdrift, every movement sending shocks of pain down her neck, into her back and shoulders. "How wonderful, darling!"

"I know, Mom." Laura had been glowing. "I'm so happy. I feel good this time, too. We haven't told Megan yet. I wanted to wait until I was five months along, just to be sure."

"Now let's see." Faye thought aloud, envisioning her daughter's house. "Will you put the baby in with Megan? You have a guest room, and there's that nice little storage room off the kitchen. Will you get a nanny?"

"We're considering that," Laura began, and suddenly she looked uncomfortable. "At first we won't need to—"

Lars cut in. "—because my parents told us today that they're moving to San Francisco! They want to be there to watch their grandchildren grow up, and they'll be able to baby-sit for us or help Laura with the baby, whatever!"

"Oh," Faye said weakly, digging her fingers into her palms, forcing herself not to burst into tears. "How wonderful for you."

Over the next two days, Faye had struggled to prevent Laura from guessing how jealous she felt, how left out. She'd laughed, joked, smiled, and chattered, and whenever Laura asked, "Are you all right, Mom? You look sad," Faye answered, "It's just the pain medication, darling. It makes me feel a bit drowsy."

But when the cab took them off to the airport, Faye sat on the sofa and sobbed.

Since Christmas, Faye had been sunk in emotional quicksand. Marilyn, Alice, Polly, and Shirley had called, offering to stop by with gossip and goodies, but she'd put them off, saying the doctor insisted she needed lots of sleep for healing. Aubrey phoned often, wanting to come by, but she gave him the same excuse.

The truth was, she'd spent the week after Christmas consoling herself and fending off complete despair by eating everything in the house. Boxes of chocolates. Tins of Scottish shortbread. Macaroni and cheese, potatoes and gravy, lasagna. Comfort food. She knew she was gaining weight, but she didn't have the energy to care.

Last night, when Aubrey insisted on coming for New Year's Eve, Faye had cautiously removed her various wrappings and braces and taken a long, hot shower. It hadn't hurt to stand on her ankle—well, maybe a twinge now and then. And her neck felt fine. For a moment, elation began to percolate in her system.

Then she stepped out of the shower and saw her body. A week of overeating, and she looked like Alfred Hitchcock. Worse, when she sorted through her clothes, she couldn't find anything that fit comfortably! She'd been wearing her caftans and loose robes for a week, and hadn't realized how her waist had thickened. Not long ago, she'd cheerfully named her stomach rolls Honey, Bunny, and It's Not Funny. Now the three rolls protruded in one giant blob like a beach ball. The zippers on her largest trousers and skirts wouldn't go all the way up. The buttons wouldn't meet the buttonholes. Her arms bulged inside the sleeves of her sweaters like puppies in a bag. Worst of all, she could see the fat accumulating on her face. Her eyes looked smaller. She was developing jowls.

She wanted to crawl under a rock. It would take a really big rock to hide her. Mount Rushmore.

She had put a caftan back on for Aubrey's visit, and wrapped her ankle to provide an excuse for not leaving the sofa. Aubrey had arrived with expensive Champagne and lobster dinners cooked at one of his favorite restaurants. They'd watched a Thin Man movie with Myrna Loy and William Powell, and at midnight, as they'd watched the ball descend in Times Square, Aubrey gallantly got down on his knees by the sofa so he could embrace Faye and kiss her soundly. She didn't wear her neck brace all evening, and when Aubrey kissed her, she felt, instead of a warm surge of sexual desire, an irritating twang of pain. Aubrey had offered to spend the night, to be there to cook her breakfast in the morning, but Faye sent him away, protesting that all she could really do these days was sleep.

Carolyn was having a New Year's Day buffet today. Aubrey was going, and he'd asked Faye to go with him, but she'd declined.

The bitter truth was that her ankle and neck were both almost completely healed, but her body and soul were shattered.

So here she was, on the first day of the year, back in her braces, useless, unloved, and fat.

Defiantly, she hobbled into the kitchen, microwaved the remains of a pumpkin pie, and covered it with Reddi wip. Then she went back to the sofa and stuffed the food into her mouth, fast, as if she were building a wall to hold back the tears.

VALENTINE'S DAY

10

On a gloomy February morning, Polly opened the door to her sewing room and looked in.

During the past year, Polly had let her alteration and dressmaking business slide into the background of her life. She'd been so busy helping her mother-in-law, Claudia, who was dying of cancer, that she hadn't had the time or energy to do more than finish the commissions she already had. So she'd told most of her customers she wasn't taking on any new projects for a while, and naturally, they found someone else to shorten their cuffs or fit a dress for a party.

But now Polly decided it was time to try to make a little money. Her husband had left her enough in his will so that she'd never be out on the streets, but any little luxuries in life she had to finance on her own. And that was fine. She enjoyed her work.

With a can of Pledge in one hand and a soft cloth in the other, Polly went around the room, dusting off her cutting table and sewing machine and the cupboard where she kept her fabric, threads, and other sewing supplies. Should she put an ad in the local give-away paper? Or even in the *Boston Globe*? Or perhaps simply phone all her customers, or send them a charming little note? That might be better.

In the far corner of the room, several cardboard boxes were stacked. Polly stopped to consider them. She hadn't really forgotten about them; she just hadn't had time to deal with them.

In November, her mother-in-law's lawyer had phoned to say they had finally finished assessing Claudia's belongings and were ready to make distributions. Claudia had willed several boxes of clothing to Polly; when could they bring them over?

Anytime, Polly had told them, shaking her head. How like Claudia, who had been a wealthy but puritanical old bat, to will her clothing to Polly, who was much too short and plump ever to fit into her lean, lanky mother-in-law's clothing! Not that Polly would ever wear them anyway—Claudia had liked plaid wool skirts and trousers, brisk little white blouses, and severe, shapeless black dresses. Her fashion style made L.L. Bean look like Versace.

Still, Polly thought, Claudia had always invested in good quality. And if Polly wasn't going to use the clothing, she should donate it to Goodwill or someplace else where it would be appreciated.

Taking up her scissors, she cut open the top box, which had been fiercely taped and marked with her name. Folding back the four leaves, Polly looked inside, expecting to see tartan trousers and ancient wool cardigans.

What she saw was so unexpected, it took her eyes a moment to adjust.

Lace. It looked like old lace. Polly dipped her hands in and lifted out an ivory lace evening wrap. Beneath it lay several pairs of lace gloves. Beneath those was a satin packet containing dozens of handkerchiefs trimmed with all kinds of lace. Then, lace nightgowns. Lace slips. Bits of lace, and more bits.

Polly lifted an ivory lawn nightgown out and held it

up to the light. It was delicate and beautiful, but ripped in several places. She took out a pale white blouse with lace cuffs and collar. The lace was lovely, but the body of the blouse was stained with dark spots.

She delved deeper into the box, coming up with a pile of lace jabots and dickeys—detachable blouse fronts popular in the early part of the twentieth century but hardly of use now. Lace fichus, scarves, veils, and tippets. How curious!

The second box was piled with lace antimacassars and doilies, lace-trimmed napkins and tablecloths. Beneath were lace pillowcases and lace-trimmed sheets—but not entire sets of sheets, and often not even the entire sheets. In most cases, the lace had been cut away, leaving only a bit of ivory linen or blue cotton attached.

The third box held more lace, and also what looked like hundreds of embroidered handkerchiefs, hand towels, pillowcases, and gloves. Again, every item was either ripped or stained beyond repair.

None of the items was particularly old. Claudia had been in her eighties when she died; perhaps the oldest item was the remnants of a christening gown that might have been hers. None of the lace was of museum quality, yet all of it was lovely. So many different patterns and kinds . . .

Trust Claudia, Polly thought with a laugh, to leave her all this stuff that was not valuable, but was too good to toss out. Probably Claudia's estimate of Polly herself.

She ran her hands over various bits of lace. Could she piece together a pretty blouse for herself? Probably not.

The phone rang, interrupting her thoughts.

"Hi, Polly!" Carolyn's voice was chipper but clipped. "What are you up to on this beautiful day?"

"I'm organizing my workroom," Polly told her. "I've decided to start up my little sewing business again."

"Oh, Polly, if you need money—"

Hurriedly, Polly interrupted Carolyn's offer. "Carolyn, I love my work as much as you love yours. And you are at work now, aren't you?"

"Yes, right. I wanted to call before I forgot. I've decided to give an intimate little dinner party at my house on February fourteenth. Can you come?"

Polly hesitated. "February fourteenth? Valentine's Day?" Carrying the portable phone with her, she walked back to her kitchen and the calendar hanging on the wall, even though she knew damned well she had nothing penciled in for that night.

As if Carolyn read her mind, she continued, "You don't have anything planned with Hugh, do you?"

Polly, who was a terrible liar, stuttered. "We—well, not formerly."

"What?"

"I mean, not *formally*. I mean, Hugh and I usually spend time together on the weekends, and the fourteenth is a Saturday this year. But I could bring Hugh—"

"Oh, Polly, I was hoping you could come alone. Hank's *other* sister, the one you haven't met yet, will be in town that weekend with her husband, and I wanted you two to get to know each other. I want to have just a little *family* affair."

Polly closed her eyes and leaned against the wall. What Carolyn meant was that she wanted her father to come, but without Faye, and she wanted Polly to come, but without Hugh.

"After all," Carolyn continued, "you're part of the family now. You're Elizabeth's godmother."

Carolyn was such a forceful personality, Polly thought. All right, perhaps she was a little spoiled, too, but didn't she deserve to be? She'd lost her mother when she was only seven. And perhaps she was a little bossy, but like many younger women, she had had to learn to be assertive. She ran a large business, after all. Polly didn't want to hurt Carolyn's feelings. She cared so much for her, and was so grateful to feel valuable in, and connected to, someone else's life. Certainly her own son and daughter-in-law were not inviting her for Valentine's Day dinner.

Still, it *was* Valentine's Day! A day to spend with your lover, not your family.

"Let me talk with Hugh," Polly said decisively. "I'm not sure what our plans are. Can I call you back?"

"Sure. If I don't catch the phone, leave a message on the machine."

They spoke a few more minutes. At ten months, Elizabeth was starting to crawl, which meant she also investigated minute bits of mud, fluff, or food accidentally dropped to the floor, bits so small Carolyn and Hank and the nanny couldn't see them from their vantage point. Since Elizabeth considered tasting part of her investigative skills, Carolyn spent much of her time on the floor with her, being sure she didn't pick up the wrong thing.

"Last night," Carolyn said, "Elizabeth found one of those cloth-covered rubber bands Ingrid holds her hair back with. She started gnawing on it before I could stop her, and when I took it away from her—she could choke on it so easily!—she threw such a tantrum, you wouldn't believe it!"

Actually, Polly thought, I *would* believe it. Carolyn's daughter was as strong-willed as her mother. But she kept quiet.

Carolyn said, "Oh, the other line's ringing. I've gotta go, Polly. Call me!"

"I will," Polly promised.

Polly spent the rest of the day working. She checked out prices of newspaper ads and reviewed her list of customers. Getting out her colored pencils, she played around, composing a clever little communiqué announc-

ing her return to business. It was fun, drawing in bob-
bins, skirts, a measuring tape, a pincushion, and finally
a wedding gown. She wrote the body of the missive on
her computer, changing fonts and sizes until she found
exactly what worked, then with scissors and tape, cut
and pasted her drawings in the margins of the letter. She
copied it on her machine and found that it came off
quite nicely. She ran off fifty copies, then sat down to the
less creative business of addressing the envelopes.

When she decided to stop for the day, she was surprised to find it was after five thirty. The sun was staying
out longer. Spring wasn't far away. No wonder she felt
cheerful!

She stretched to release the tension in her neck and
shoulders, then flicked off the computer and the lights in
her workroom and went through the house, turning on
lights for the approaching dusk.

Her old hound, Roy Orbison, lay on the sofa, snoring
like a powerboat. Usually by five thirty Roy was agitat-
ing for his dinner, but tonight he was still sound asleep.
Polly gazed down fondly at the dog.

"You're getting on in years, old boy," she said softly.
"And so am I."

In the kitchen, she prepared an enormous salad with
tons of vegetables and heated up a big mug of chicken
broth. As always, she was trying to diet, and tonight she
didn't feel especially hungry. Alerted by her noise, Roy
woke and joined her in the kitchen, eating his dog food
as if he'd just returned from a sixty-mile run. Lucky
Roy, who didn't even know the concept of dieting!

After dinner, Polly started a fire in the fireplace and
curled up on the sofa with a cup of herbal tea and a fat
new mystery. In January, she'd had the smoke-scorched
living room repainted in pale yellow while she sewed
new drapes and throw-pillow coverings from a gorgeous

blue silk printed with birds, boughs, and blossoms. All signs of the Christmas Eve fire had disappeared and the room, even at night, looked fresh and cheerful.

Sometime tonight, she knew, Hugh would phone. On most weeknights he didn't visit Polly, but collapsed in his own apartment, tired from his day at the hospital. He always phoned her, though, and they talked, sometimes for hours, as current dramas reminded them of past events. One of the nicer things about being older, Polly thought, was that they had so much to tell each other, so many memories to recount.

It was almost ten o'clock when Hugh phoned.

"Sorry to call so late," he said. "I fell asleep when I got home. Just woke up a while ago, had a shower and a late meal."

"Busy day at the hospital?" Polly asked as she settled back to listen. Hugh seldom discussed his patients, having more than enough to complain about or entertain Polly with by talking about his staff, the secretaries, his fellow physicians, the hospital administration.

Polly told Hugh what she'd done during the day. Then she took a deep breath, screwed up her courage, and said, as sexily as she could without humiliating herself, "So, Hugh, do we have any plans for Valentine's Day? I noticed on my calendar that it falls on Saturday this year." Hugh was clever and creative about their dates; perhaps he'd take her to some ski resort where they could spend the entire time in the room, drinking hot buttered rum and making love. It had been a marvelous surprise to Polly, what a good lover Hugh was.

"Oh, hell, Polly," Hugh answered. "My daughter's having a Valentine's Day dinner party, just for the family."

Disappointment surged through Polly. What *was* it about this generation of children that they thought

Valentine's Day was a family occasion? Polly didn't have to ask whether or not Hugh's ex-wife Carol would be there. Of course she would. It irked her that Carol would be with Hugh on Valentine's Day.

"You still there?" Hugh asked.

"Yes," Polly said, weakly.

"I'm sorry, Poll. I hate to think of you alone on—"

"Oh, I won't be alone," Polly hastened to assure him. She didn't want him ever to pity her. "Carolyn has asked me to dinner at her place that night, but frankly, I'd rather spend it with you."

"Let's have our Valentine's Day dinner Friday night, what do you say?"

"I think we've scheduled our Hot Flash Club meeting for that night, and I'd hate to miss it. We haven't been meeting regularly."

"Sunday night then?"

This was good of him, Polly knew, because Mondays Hugh worked, and Mondays were hard. "Why don't we meet here after our Saturday-night dinner parties?" she suggested. "I'll have lots of Champagne and chocolate, and all kinds of treats, so we can celebrate Valentine's Day Sunday morning. In bed."

Hugh laughed, and Polly's heart went all gooey. Hugh had a wonderful, deep, hearty laugh. She could just see him, his belly trembling, his perfect white teeth gleaming in his handsome face.

"That's a great idea, Polly. Let's make that a date."

After they said good-bye, Polly considered phoning Carolyn to tell her she could come to the dinner, but it was too late, especially since they had a baby in the house. She'd phone first thing in the morning. As Polly got ready for bed, she considered calling Faye tomorrow, to discuss this whole weird triangle they were caught up in, Polly–Carolyn–Faye. Or was it more a pentagon, because Aubrey and Elizabeth were both involved, too? Polly admired Faye so much, but she wasn't sure she could bring up the subject. It was awkward. It was terribly like high school. Oh, well, Polly thought, sliding into bed, at least that made her feel young.

11

It was February thirteenth, and Legal Seafoods was crowded on Friday night, but the five members of the Hot Flash Club were given their usual table tucked away in the far corner of the restaurant where they could chat without being overheard. They settled in, ordered drinks, glanced quickly at the menu—by now they all knew their favorite dishes—then leaned forward.

"Faye, you're here with no neck brace or crutches!" Alice observed. "How are you?"

Faye lifted a languid hand to rub the back of her neck. "I get twinges from time to time. And I think my chances for a speed-skating career are pretty much over."

"But you can always do yoga," Shirley reminded her cheerfully.

Faye flushed. "I *know* I've gained weight. Give me a break! I was hardly able to move for a month. I still have to be careful."

Shirley blinked, surprised at Faye's belligerence. "I didn't mean— Yoga's not about losing weight," she said softly.

Brightly, Marilyn asked, "So, Faye, have you been able to teach your art therapy classes this semester?"

Faye shook her head. "I had to skip the winter semester. I can hardly teach if I can't stand up or move my arms. And I hear the new art teacher is doing beautifully. I doubt if The Haven will need me again."

The other four women exchanged worried glances. Faye, being *negative*?

"Of course The Haven wants you to teach again," Shirley rushed to assure her. "Whenever you're ready."

Faye shrugged and said nothing.

Polly sagged in her chair, nearly ill with guilt. Obviously Faye was depressed. The whole Carolyn–Aubrey–Valentine's Day dinner arrangement had to be part of the cause. Could Polly bring this up now? *Should* she?

Alice turned to Marilyn. "How's your mother? Did she want to join us tonight?"

"She's fine. And there's an old movie on television she wanted to watch, thank heavens. I mean, I adore my mother, but it's nice to get away from her now and then."

"Are you managing to have any time alone with Faraday?" Shirley asked.

Marilyn folded her napkin in careful little pleats. "No, and I'm glad. I know I'm using my mother as an excuse to avoid talking with him about this marriage business, but I do have to decide about Ruth, that's the most important thing right now."

"You've had her with you for two months," Alice pointed out. "How's she doing?"

Marilyn frowned. "Well, you've seen her. She gets words confused now and then—"

"But so do I," Polly interjected.

"—and she forgets what she's doing sometimes—"

"So do I," Shirley said.

Marilyn nodded. "I know. I do, too. Sometimes I have to make a note on a piece of paper and carry it with me from one room to the other. Otherwise, I'll get distracted and forget what I came in for."

Alice laughed. "I hear you. The other day I was on a

tear, looking for my reading glasses, and all the time they were on top of my head. I said to Gideon, 'Good grief, Hon, how are you going to know when I'm senile?' "

"Exactly!" Marilyn agreed, then said in an irritated tone, "Oh, *damn*!" She unbuttoned her cardigan and tore it off.

"Hot flash," Polly said sympathetically.

Marilyn nodded and fanned herself with the menu. "What were we talking about?"

"Your mother," Alice reminded her.

Marilyn shook her head. "I really don't know what to do. I love her so much, and most of the time I enjoy her company. Plus, I feel obligated to Sharon. She's taken care of our mother most of our lives. It really is my turn now. And I don't think I can just dump her into an assisted living facility because she's forgetful and deaf."

Shirley chuckled. "Speaking of deaf, let me tell you what happened in Star's yoga class yesterday. Star had some new students, older people bused over from a retirement home, seven really cute little old ladies who want to stay limber. They'd never taken yoga before, so this was their trial class. So Star put them up front and went through the poses slowly, telling them not to strain themselves. You know the routine. So she had them all seated with their eyes closed, and she said slowly, 'Feel your breath.' And one little old lady yelled, 'Feel my breasts? What kind of class *is* this!' "

When their laughter died down, Alice pinned Marilyn with one of her no-nonsense glances. "But if you didn't have to think about your mother, would you marry Faraday?"

"Honestly? I just don't know."

"Did you talk to him about the sex thing?" Alice demanded.

Marilyn blushed. "I tried to. I mean, I sat him down

and told him how I felt, and suggested he get something like Viagra. He had that deer-in-the-headlights look. Trapped and tortured! Why is it so difficult to talk about this with men?"

"Because we don't want to hurt their feelings," Alice said. "Men's egos are so fragile. And their private parts are so private. Women are used to having their reproductive organs plumbed and scanned and inspected, not to mention expanded to give birth. We *have* to be more practical, less sensitive about it all."

"You know, Hugh's a doctor," Polly said. "And he's in his sixties, and has no hesitation about using an erectile dysfunction medication from time to time."

"Does it work?" Alice asked.

"Very well," Polly answered, blushing. "So, Marilyn, what did Faraday say after you suggested Viagra?"

Marilyn looked exasperated. "Nothing! He said absolutely nothing! Or, rather, he said there was a show on *Nova* right then that he wanted to watch. So we watched television, then he kissed me politely good night and left."

The waiter brought their food. For a few moments everyone was engrossed in tasting and exchanging bits with one another. Alice and Shirley, who were sitting the farthest from each other, didn't offer to give the other a taste of their dishes, which made Marilyn and Polly exchange nervous glances, while Faye continued to seem lost in her own private world.

"So, Faye." Marilyn turned to her friend. "How is Laura these days?"

Faye lifted her head and forced a smile. "She's well, thank you. She's very good about e-mailing me daily. Lars's parents are staying with them while they look for a house in San Francisco, so they take care of Megan every afternoon. That gives Laura a chance to nap. And Evelyn—Lars's mother—loves to cook, so she's been preparing dinner for everyone. Laura tells me she feels rather spoiled."

Alice tried to cheer Faye with her question. "So what are you and Aubrey doing—" She saw Polly shaking her head in rapid but slight little movements, as if she'd suddenly developed a Katharine Hepburn–like palsy, but didn't interpret the message in time. "—for Valentine's Day?"

Faye's lower lip quivered. "Aubrey's been invited to his daughter's house for dinner tomorrow night. Carolyn's sister and her family are visiting, and she wants them to have a family get-together."

"Well, that sucks for you," Alice said bluntly.

"And for me, too." The hell with it, Polly decided suddenly. The Hot Flash Club's first rule was, after all, "Don't let fear hold you back." Shoving her plate to one side, she rested her arms on the table. "I wish the rest of you could help me out here. You know I met Carolyn at The Haven. I got close to her during the time she was freaked about Aubrey's weird quickie marriage. And then I was with her when she had her baby. So she thinks of me as a kind of surrogate mother, and I have to admit I like that a lot, because my own idiot son and his demented little flying-nun wife won't let me see my own grandchild. But I have no designs on Aubrey! What am I supposed to do? Carolyn invited me to dinner there tomorrow night, to her freaking *family* dinner, and I said I'd go, even though—"

Marilyn cut in. "But what about Hugh? Don't you want to have dinner with him?"

"Of course I do!" Polly replied. "But Hugh's *kids* are having a family Valentine's Day dinner with him, all the grandchildren, and oh, yes, let's not forget, helpless little size-six Carol, Hugh's ex-wife. I don't understand these young mothers. Why can't they let us alone?" She leaned across the table and put her hand on Faye's.

"Faye, I'm not romantically interested in Aubrey. You've got to know that. And Aubrey adores you. You must know that, too. I would love to find a way to straighten this tangle out."

Faye gave Polly her best smile. "That's very nice of you."

"But how?" Polly asked helplessly.

"What about talking it over with her?" Shirley suggested. "Take her out to lunch and get it all out in the open."

Alice shook her head. "That won't work. Carolyn's a determined young woman. Strong personality. Used to getting her own way."

Marilyn looked thoughtful. "Stalactites."

"Oh, boy," Alice said. "Here we go."

Marilyn shook her head impatiently. "No, *really*. Think of caves, stalactites, stalagmites, some as much as several yards long, and all formed by the slow, patient, steady dripping of high-lime-content water." She brightened. "Or, think of tiny grains of sand, which the sea has—"

"We get your point," Alice interrupted. "You think Polly and Faye should just remain firm and relentless, reminding Carolyn that Polly is dating Hugh and Faye is dating Aubrey."

"Slow and steady wins the race," Polly mused, nodding.

Alice added, "Yeah. Polly, maybe you could invite Carolyn and her husband to dinner at your house, with Hugh there, so Carolyn could get to know him, and see how much you two like each other."

Polly nodded. "I guess you're right. I hate confrontations, anyway."

Marilyn grinned. "Did you know that in some caves they've discovered stalactites that drip sulfuric acid in a kind of mucusy glue? They've named them *snottites*."

Alice pushed her plate away. "Thanks for presenting us with that image during dinner."

"Good," Shirley said mischievously, "maybe you won't gain weight tonight."

Alice glared at Shirley and bit her tongue. She was doing her best not to be a total bitch about Shirley giving all that money to Justin. Shirley ought to reciprocate and get off her back about her weight.

Defiantly, Alice said, "Maybe I *will*. Because I'm going to order a big, fat chocolate dessert!"

APRIL FOOL'S DAY

12

MARILYN AND HER MOTHER SAT SIDE BY SIDE ON THE sofa, both in quilted robes, their feet cozy in quilted slippers. They were watching one of Marilyn's favorite movies, *I Know Where I'm Going*, made in 1940, starring Wendy Hiller as a saucy city woman trying to get to a private island off the Scottish Highlands. It was in black-and-white, slow-paced but infinitely charming, and when Marilyn curled up in bed at night, she often sent herself to sleep on fantasies of meeting the male lead, Roger Livesey. Actually, it wasn't the actor she wanted to meet but the slow-smiling naval officer he played, and since modern science posited that there were an infinite number of worlds, Marilyn allowed herself to believe, deep in her heart, that in one of those worlds she could meet just such a man, tall, gentle yet rugged, with laughter dancing in his eyes and a Scottish burr that would flutter a kilt.

"That was lovely, dear." Ruth folded up the scarf she was knitting—it was already about seven feet long, but Ruth didn't seem to notice, and Marilyn didn't want to deprive her of the familiar pleasure knitting brought. "I think I'll retire now. It's late, isn't it?"

"Almost ten o'clock," Marilyn told her. "Here, let me help you up."

Marilyn held out her arms. Ruth fastened her bony hands on her daughter's wrists, and Marilyn lifted. Ruth grunted with the effort of getting her body up on her spindly legs.

"There!" she said triumphantly. "Let me catch my breath, and then I can make it on my own."

Marilyn handed Ruth her cane, and after a few moments, Ruth tottered off down the hall to the bathroom. Marilyn watched nervously, glad that the rented condo was so small, Ruth didn't have far to walk from room to room. Marilyn put their cups in the dishwasher—they'd been drinking Postum, a drink Marilyn had forgotten existed until her mother's arrival. She wiped the kitchen counter one more time and plumped up the sofa pillows. Her briefcase was in her bedroom on her computer table, which was squeezed up against her bureau. She scarcely had room in her bedroom to turn around, but she wanted to keep the dining area free for meals with her mother, and she couldn't concentrate on her work with her mother in the room, anyway.

"All right, dear," Ruth called from her bedroom door. "I'll say good night now."

Marilyn went to her mother and bent to give her a kiss and a hug. "Good night, sleep tight, don't let the bedbugs bite."

Ruth patted Marilyn's cheek. "You're a good daughter." She went into her bedroom, shut the door, then opened it again and stuck her head out. "A jumper cable walks into a bar. What does the bartender say?"

Marilyn grinned. " 'I'll serve you, but don't start anything.' "

Ruth laughed, blew a kiss, and closed the door.

Marilyn got ready for bed herself, wondering when Mother Nature would finally blow winter away and let spring arrive. She turned on her electric blanket and bedside lamp, then went around the apartment, double-checking that the kitchen and living room doors were locked and all lights were off. In the hall she paused, quietly opened her mother's bedroom door, and peeked in. Ruth lay tucked beneath her covers like a little doll, snoring gently. Ruth was never bothered by insomnia or hot flashes ruining her sleep, one good thing, Marilyn supposed, about old age.

In her own bed, Marilyn shoved her pillows into comfortable lumps for her back and neck, picked up her book, put on her reading glasses, and found her place on the page.

Then she heard pounding at the front door.

She frowned and took off her glasses, as if that would improve her hearing.

Her heart fluttered. Who would come around at this time on a weekday night? Dear God, she hoped it wasn't Teddy—had something happened to Lila or the baby?

Too alarmed to pull on her robe, she flew to the door and opened it.

Faraday stood there, handsome in his camel-hair coat, but red in the face and reeking of alcohol.

"Faraday!"

Faraday swept off his tartan cap and waved it as he bowed. "I have come to make love to you."

"Faraday, have you been drinking?" She stepped back, allowing him to enter.

He pulled her to him. "Yes, I have indulged in an aphrodisiacal libation, and more, my dear, much more."

"What do you mean?"

Faraday chuckled maniacally as he gripped her wrist and towed her toward her bedroom. "I mean, Marilyn, *mon amour,* I have finally committed the daring deed you have so often obliquely, and gently, propelled me toward." He removed his coat and gloves and dropped them on a chair.

"I don't understand."

Faraday took Marilyn in his arms and bent to kiss her. He had always been a wonderful kisser. But no matter how inventive, patient, or persistent Marilyn was when they tried to make love, "Little Johnny Jump-Up," as Faraday called his penis, had failed to rise to the occasion.

Marilyn let Faraday lead her to the bedroom and watched him pull his thick cable-knit sweater over his head. She knew from experience not to let her body get excited, because that always led to frustration. Still, she was fond of him, so she lifted off her nightgown and slipped between the covers.

As Faraday, naked now, slid in beside her, she said, "We should be quiet. I don't want to wake my mother."

"Ah, my darling," Faraday whispered, "I don't make promises I can't keep."

"You're speaking in riddles tonight." Marilyn snuggled next to him, enjoying the animal warmth of their touching bodies. His thighs and torso were warm, though his hands and face were still cold from the winter air.

"I mean," Faraday whispered, drawing his fingers lightly down Marilyn's body, "I did what you've been wanting me to do. I saw a doctor, who prescribed a helpful medication, and I took it just before I came over here. I'm good for four hours."

"Oh, my!" Marilyn reached up and stroked his bristly bearded jaw. "Faraday. How sweet of you!"

"Have to say," he continued, "I'm a little concerned about it. Just a *little*. I mean, there are side effects . . ." Turning his head away, he belched discreetly. "To build up my courage, I, um, imbibed most of the scotch you gave me for Christmas."

"What side effects?" Marilyn nuzzled his neck.

"Heart attack. Sudden death. Stroke. Irregular heartbeat. Increased blood pressure," Faraday recited glumly. Marilyn raised herself up on one elbow, looking down at him with concern. She put a calming hand on his hairy chest. "But, Faraday, surely those are very rare occurrences, or the FDA wouldn't allow the drug to be sold."

"I suppose—" A ferocious yawn swallowed the rest of the sentence. " 'Cuse me. Still, there's no guarantee something won't happen to me."

"I think you're very brave." Marilyn moved her hand down his belly.

He chuckled. "You wouldn't think that if you'd seen me guzzling down the scotch. Oh, yes, and I took a few Valium, too."

Alarmed, Marilyn drew back. "Oh, Faraday, that wasn't wise!" He would have to spend the night. She couldn't allow him to drive home with all those soporifics in his system. Her mother wouldn't be too shocked, seeing him there in the morning. "I feel so guilty," she told him.

"Now, now. That's not at all how I mean you to feel, my dear."

"But, Faraday—"

"Hush now." He silenced her with a long, amorous kiss.

Marilyn returned his kiss, hugging him tightly against her. She could feel his excitement rising, hard and long, against her abdomen, and her own heart began to pound in anticipation. The alcoholic fumes from his mouth were distracting, however; she was almost getting drunk herself, simply from inhaling his breath.

They arranged themselves together.

"Why, Faraday, I think it's working!" she whispered.

Faraday pushed himself up so that he could look down at her. "G-g-good." The word came out in a mumble. His face, always ruddy, was paler than usual, and his eyes weren't focusing correctly.

"Faraday?"

Suddenly, his mouth fell open. His eyes rolled up like a couple of struck billiard balls, disappearing beneath his eyelids. He let forth an enormous snort, shuddered all over, and collapsed on top of her.

"Faraday!"

Dear God, Marilyn thought, has he had a heart attack?

"Faraday?" She shook his shoulder.

Faraday sputtered, spraying her face, and began to snore loudly against her neck. His enormous torso sagged heavily against her as his breathing deepened. His beard and mustache scratched her chin and cheek.

"Faraday? I can't breathe." Marilyn tried to shift him, but he was a deadweight. "Faraday!" She panted, sucking in small gasps of air.

Faraday snored away, his lips smacking, his alcoholic breath streaming into the bedroom like a really bad air freshener.

Marilyn was five seven and weighed 120 pounds. Faraday was six three and weighed 230. She was strong enough, but he was so very large, and heavy, and limp.

Grunting, she pushed up with her legs and arms, straining to topple him off her, but he was as leaden as a fallen tree. She couldn't budge him.

She *really* was having trouble breathing.

What could she do?

She could call for her mother. But did she want her mother to see her like this, pinned beneath a large, hairy man like a chicken beneath a big, red bull? Absolutely not! Besides, Ruth wasn't strong enough to lift herself out of a chair, so how could *she* help get Faraday off Marilyn?

Sucking up every ounce of strength in her body, Marilyn bucked and heaved one more time. In vain. Faraday's breath sputtered against her hair. She was wheezing like an asthmatic as she strained to pull air into her lungs.

All right, Marilyn said to herself. Let's look at this sensibly. Faraday was bound to wake up sooner or later. Could she fall asleep until he did?

No, a little voice inside her screamed, *because you can't BREATHE!*

The truth was, she was getting scared. More than scared—she was on the verge of real panic, that horrible claustrophobic sense of desperate helplessness. Her left leg spasmed with cramp.

Twisting frantically, she tried to scoot out from beneath Faraday, but she was too weighted down. Frightened now, she began pounding on his shoulders and back. Faraday twitched, spluttered, and moaned, but slept on.

Tears welled in her eyes and rolled down toward her ears. Her sinuses filled with mucus and she couldn't even blow her nose, which was quickly becoming clogged. A feeling of suffocation overwhelmed her, increasing her sense of panic.

What on earth was she going to do?

Turning her head, she saw her phone on the bedside table. Stretching her arm out, she could just grasp it. She pulled it toward her.

911? Oh, Lord, how embarrassing, plus EMTs would make so much noise and wake her mother.

Who else? Who lived closest to her? Alice, who was strong! Fumbling, one-handed, she knocked the phone off its cradle. Straining uncomfortably, she punched in Alice's number, then brought the phone to her ear.

"Hello?"

"Alice, it's Marilyn."

"Are you okay? I can hardly hear you."

"I can hardly speak," Marilyn squeaked. "Listen, could you come over here right now? And tell Polly or Faye to meet you? I'm in a predicament. Faraday's passed out on top of me, and I'm trapped! I don't want my mother to find us like this. Besides, I can't breathe."

Alice sounded wary. "This isn't some kind of weird experiment, is it? Or a joke you're pulling on me?"

"Honest to God, Alice, I'm trapped and nearly smothered. Please come *now.*"

"I'm on my way. I'll phone Polly from the car."

"The key's on top of the lintel," Marilyn gasped. "Be quiet coming in, if you can. I don't want to wake Mother."

For the next twenty minutes, Marilyn labored to breathe. She developed a rhythm, putting both hands beneath Faraday's shoulders and heaving him up a few inches, using that release to inhale deeply. But her arms trembled with the effort, and soon she had to let him drop back down. She tapped his face. Lifted his eyelids. He snored on. She called his name. She pinched him, hard. Nothing worked.

At last, Marilyn heard noises at the front door. Alice and Polly burst into the room, accompanied by a surge of cold air. Alice's fur coat flew out behind her as she stormed in. Polly whisked off her wool cap and mittens and tucked them into her parka pocket.

When they saw Marilyn and Faraday, Polly's hands flew up to her face in alarm, but Alice smiled.

"*Nice,*" Alice said.

"Glad you're enjoying yourself," Marilyn wheezed. "In the meantime, I can't breathe!"

"You take that side, I'll take this," Alice directed Polly.

They stationed themselves on either side of the bed.

Alice grabbed Faraday's shoulder. "You shove while I pull," she directed Polly. "On the count of three. One—two—three."

Marilyn pushed upward with her hands. They shifted

Faraday a few inches, but his body was so limp, he landed back on Marilyn like a two-ton beanbag.

"Ooof!" Marilyn huffed as his body hit hers.

"Okay," Alice said. Quickly she removed her coat and rolled up her sleeves. Polly did the same. "On the count of three again, and this time, we're going to give it our all. Ready? One. Two. Three!"

Grunting with exertion, the three women shoved Faraday's warm, limp body. With a sucking noise, he came free of Marilyn and fell on his back, flopping down like a deflated plastic raft.

Marilyn scrambled off the bed, grabbed her robe, and yanked it over her naked body, taking huge, grateful gasps of air.

"He's a fine figure of a man, isn't he?" Alice remarked admiringly as she drew the covers up over Faraday.

"He's a whale," Marilyn puffed. "I've got to pee."

"I've got to laugh," Alice said. "I'll go in the living room and stuff a pillow in my mouth."

"Are you okay?" Alice asked when Marilyn entered the living room.

"Fine. Just embarrassed. And terribly grateful—I think I could have died!"

"I wonder if that's ever happened," Polly mused. "If any woman's ever suffocated beneath her lover."

Marilyn shuddered.

Alice grinned. "You'll see the humor of it in the morning. Will you be able to sleep?"

Marilyn nodded. "I'm sure I will. I'm exhausted. I'll have a bit of brandy and stretch out on the sofa." She hugged Polly and Alice. "How can I thank you? This was beyond the call of duty."

"Honey," Alice said, "I wouldn't have missed this for the world."

* * *

In the morning, Marilyn and Ruth had risen, dressed, and were sitting at the table, eating breakfast, when they heard the bedroom door open. A few minutes later, the toilet flushed. After a while, Faraday looked around the corner.

"Marilyn?" He was white and grim. "Could I speak with you?"

"Sure. Want some coffee?"

"No!" He disappeared. She heard the bedroom door slam.

She hurried into her bedroom. Faraday was dressed, but haphazardly, as if he'd just heard a fire alarm.

"Are you okay?" she asked.

"What happened last night?" He towered over her, swaying slightly.

She felt both accusatory and apologetic. "To be blunt, you passed out. You know you shouldn't mix alcohol and drugs."

"*When* did I pass out?"

"Um, when we were just beginning to make love." She put a reassuring hand on his arm. "It's okay, Faraday. These things happen. Mother doesn't know about it. I mean, she knows you slept over, but the rest she doesn't know. It was a little frightening, really. I couldn't breathe. I had to phone Alice and Polly, they came over to help move you off me—"

"You *what*?" Faraday looked like she'd slugged him in the stomach.

"Well, I couldn't lift you off me—"

"Your friends saw me naked and comatose?" His pale face flushed crimson. "What the *hell* were you thinking?"

She was stunned by his anger. "I was *thinking*, Faraday, that I didn't want to suffocate."

"This is unbelievable." Faraday rubbed his face with both big, hairy hands. "This is a nightmare."

"Oh, Faraday—"

He shook his head furiously. "I can't believe you did such a thing. I can't believe you'd embarrass me like that."

With a face like thunder, he strode from the room, grabbed his coat up from the back of a chair, and stomped out the door.

Ruth looked up from a crossword puzzle. "Was that Caraway?"

"Faraday, Mother. Yes."

"He seemed in a bad mood."

"He was just late for a class," Marilyn lied. She didn't know whether to laugh or cry. "I think I'm coming down with a cold. I'm going back to bed."

MOTHER'S DAY

13

Since New Year's Day, sensitive issues had flickered around the members of the Hot Flash Club like a kind of invisible miniature lightning. Alice was irritated with Shirley for her gullibility with Justin. Shirley was protective of Justin and annoyed with Alice. Polly was trying to be supportive of Carolyn without seeming to be flirting with Aubrey; Marilyn was preoccupied with Ruth; and Faye just seemed depressed.

Still, all five of them showed up for the May board meeting of The Haven, and all five remained in the conference room when the other directors left.

Alice stripped off her suit jacket, hung it over the back of her chair, and cranked open several of the casement windows, letting fresh air sweep into the room.

"That's better," Faye said, lifting her long, white hair off her neck.

Shirley opened a cupboard and brought out a plate of brownies.

Polly bent down to her book bag and lifted up a bottle of sparkling water and five paper cups. She poured the water and passed it around. "Shirley, are you okay?"

Shirley took her place at the head of the conference table, kicked off her dress shoes, and lifted her feet up to rest on the polished mahogany. "Thanks for the water. I'm fine. Why do you ask?"

"All through the meeting, you kept making faces at me and patting your chest, like you had indigestion."

Shirley laughed. "I was trying to instant message you that your jacket's buttoned wrong."

Polly looked down at the handsome tweed suit she'd made just for these board meetings. All the buttons were off by one. "Oh, no! I was in such a hurry—"

Her chagrin at a blunder any one of them could commit made them all feel sympathetic, and closer than they had for weeks.

"Don't worry about it," Faye comforted Polly. "If anyone noticed, they probably thought you were wearing some nouveau-chic asymmetrical style."

"Yeah, at my bridge group last week, I wore mismatched earrings," Alice confessed. "When someone pointed it out, I told them it was the newest fad. They believed me."

Polly unbuttoned her jacket and realigned it properly. "Good grief. When do we admit we're too old to appear in public?"

"Never!" Shirley hit her fist on the table for emphasis. "I was just reading about Stradivarius? The guy who made all the violins? He didn't start building them until after he was fifty, and he worked into his nineties."

"But let's be realistic." As she spoke, Faye removed her indigo silk jacket and fanned her face with the minutes of the board meeting. "We *are* older. We've *got* to make adjustments. We've got to accept changes."

"True," Alice agreed. "I nearly fall off the sofa laughing when I see a TV ad depicting a silver-haired couple waltzing on a cruise ship or backpacking up an Alpine path. Gideon and I are in good health and reasonably fit, but I can only be twirled on the dance floor if I take plenty of aspirin and remember to wear a panty liner."

Faye nodded. "You're right. When Aubrey tries to climb the stairs, never mind a mountain, his knees give out on him. Not to mention, I mean, excuse my bluntness, but *any* vigorous activity makes him fart like a popped balloon."

Polly laughed. "Tell me about it! The signature scent of senior romance definitely does not come from a perfume bottle."

"Still, we've got to keep dancing," Shirley reminded them.

"You are *so* 'The Little Engine That Could,' " Alice muttered.

"*So?*" Shirley shot back. "You want me to be 'The Little Engine That *Can't*'?"

Alice bit off her words. "Maybe 'The Little Engine with Headlights and Brakes.' "

Quickly, Marilyn derailed them. "So, Faye, how are things working out with Aubrey's daughter?"

Faye looked strained. "Well, I haven't felt like going out a lot. This winter's been so brutal, and my ankle hurts when it's bitterly cold."

"Welcome to my arthritic world," Alice murmured sympathetically.

Faye broke a chunk off a brownie, popped it into her mouth, and chewed while she talked. "Plus, I was down and out with the flu for almost three weeks. Also, Carolyn arranged a lot of 'family vacations.' They went skiing in March and to Costa Rica for two weeks in April."

Polly spoke up. "Carolyn invited me on both trips, but I refused. I said that I wanted to spend as much time with my *boyfriend* Hugh as I can."

Faye touched Polly's hand. "I'm not blaming you, Polly."

Shirley inquired softly, "Have you and Aubrey made love yet?"

"Not yet. But it's all right." Faye's expression denied

her words. "At our age, sex isn't as crucial or passionate as it was when we were younger."

"That's like saying it may not be Godiva, but it's still chocolate," Alice pointed out.

Shirley turned to Marilyn. "Have you heard from Faraday?"

Marilyn sighed. "Not since our Valentine's Day catastrophe. I've phoned him and e-mailed him, but he refuses to answer. I've tried catching him in his office at the university, but he gives me the cold shoulder every time."

Faye grimaced. "He must have been humiliated, passing out on you like that."

"I think what's worse for him is knowing that my friends saw him naked and comatose."

"I can sympathize with that," Alice said.

"I can, too," Polly said, "but at our age, we've got to have a sense of humor if we're going to enjoy sex."

"A sense of humor and total darkness," joked Alice.

"Even if it's entirely dark," Polly confided, "men can *feel* how different we are. I swear, my pubic hair is thinning out, but I'm growing whiskers on my chin!"

Alice chuckled. "Yeah, and my breasts used to feel like nice, hard pears. Now they hang down like a couple of eggplants."

"Come on, men don't love women only if they're young and beautiful," Shirley insisted. "I mean, look at Prince Charles. One of the most beautiful women in the world was his wife, and she was much younger. Still, he stayed in love with Camilla."

Alice snorted. "Camilla, that dried-up old twig."

Shirley pounced. "My point exactly."

"Is Camilla older than he is?" Polly asked.

"*Yes,*" Shirley stated defiantly. "At least a year or two."

Faye noticed Alice looking annoyed, as she always did when the subject of older women–younger men/Shirley–

Justin came up. So far Alice had remained on the board, but she didn't participate as much as she once had, and she seldom spoke directly to Shirley. Faye didn't feel very close to Shirley these days, either; she was always afraid Shirley would bring up the subject of health and weight.

Polly deftly switched conversational gears. "All right, everyone, let's compare notes on Mother's Day. Who got taken out to dinner?" When no one answered, she said, "Okay, who got flowers?"

Marilyn offered, "I brought Ruth flowers. And a pretty spring sweater."

"But what did *you* get?" Polly persisted.

Marilyn shrugged. "Teddy phoned to wish me a happy Mother's Day and to tell me he bought Lila a diamond tennis bracelet. That's perfectly fine with me. I've never cared much about Mother's Day."

"Nor I," Alice chimed in. "It was fun when the boys were little, but now that they're grown, I seldom think of it. Although Steven did send me a card."

"Laura sent me a card, too," Faye said. "With new pictures of Megan."

Polly pretended to pout. "That's more than I got. David didn't even send me a card."

"That's because Amy didn't remind him to send you something," Faye said. As the others raised their voices in objection, she continued, "I know it's not right, but it's true. Women are the ones who remember to buy birthday presents, Mother's Day cards, all that senti-mental stuff. I did it for Jack. I'd buy the card and put the pen in his hand and stand over him to make him sign it, as if he were six years old. Then I'd make him address the envelope. Then *I'd* mail it."

"You're right." Polly nodded, thoughtfully picking a chocolate crumb off her napkin. "Now that you men-tion it, I did the same sort of thing for Tucker. I'd order flowers delivered to Claudia, with a card signed, 'Love, Tucker.' "

"That doesn't seem fair," Shirley said. "*You* remembered, *you* went to the trouble of ordering flowers, and *he* gets the gratitude."

Polly snorted. "*I* could have sent Claudia a *tree* and she wouldn't have acknowledged it. But never mind." Polly's smile was slightly mischievous. "I was always glad to work behind the scenes. Because Claudia would phone Tucker and thank him for the flowers, and then Tucker would thank *me* for remembering for him." She waggled her eyebrows. "With something much nicer than flowers."

"Speaking of flowers . . ." Faye leaned forward. "I had the *best* idea the other day. I was thinking about Princess Di's death, and all those flowers people put at the gates in her honor. Remember? There were thousands of beautiful bouquets."

"It was so sad," Polly reflected somberly.

"Well," Faye continued, "what happened to those flowers? Did they all just get swept up and tossed out? Wouldn't it have been great if they'd gathered up all those flowers, dried them, put them in pretty little cloth bags, and sold them as Princess Di Memorial Potpourri?"

"That's a brilliant idea!" Shirley said. "I would have bought some!"

"Me, too," Polly said. "Gee, I wish we could do something like that. Has anyone wonderful died lately?"

Alice thought for a moment. "Rodney Dangerfield, but who would buy Rodney Dangerfield potpourri?"

Faye laughed. "Few people would have the same cachet as Princess Di."

"Or the same *sachet*," Marilyn quipped.

"True," Shirley said musingly. "The potpourri would

be a kind of constant memory, and how many people do we want to think of daily?"

"That reminds me," Polly said. "I'm still trying to decide what to do with the inheritance my evil old mother-in-law left me. Boxes of beautiful lace. I'd like to use it, even though it was Claudia's."

Shirley asked, "Can you separate the material from your memories?"

"I honestly don't know. Maybe that's why I can't think of anything . . . because the memory of her snotty old face gets in the way."

Alice turned to Marilyn. "Speaking of old people, how's your mom?"

"She's adorable." Marilyn played with her brownie, crumbling it into little pieces. "And I'm glad for her company, now that Faraday's no longer in my life."

"I sense a *however* in there," Alice said.

Marilyn looked around at her wonderful friends. She loved them so much. Yet she knew they all thought she was odd, and probably, she was. Certainly she couldn't speak to them about the matter closest to her heart.

Marilyn believed in the Loch Ness Monster. She was sure that Nessie was a descendant of the plesiosaurs, enormous, flippered marine reptiles that lived in the Mesozoic Era. Almost daily, science discovered new creatures in unexplored jungles and on the sea floor. It was possible, it really was, that the long, narrow, fresh-water lake, averaging four hundred fifty feet in depth and more than a thousand feet in some places, could hide a plesiosauroid.

To know Nessie existed had been Marilyn's lifelong dream. Too weird for her to share even with her Hot Flash friends, it was her own private mystery, as much a part of her as her scientific work or her maternal love or her sexual desires or her affection for her friends. It was the bedrock of her soul.

The more Marilyn learned about scientific matters, the more science unearthed facts about the universe, the more firmly she believed in God. She could not believe life was random. From the vastness of the starry cosmos to the nearly unfathomable worlds living inside one drop of water, an awesome order prevailed, and everywhere hints were hidden that sent man off on adventures his greatest imagination could not forsee. The universe was too beautiful, and too intricate, for man ever to come to the end of his searching.

The older she got, the more urgently she yearned to begin her own private quest.

"Earth to Marilyn," Alice prompted.

Marilyn's shoulders slumped. "I've taken a sabbatical. My courses end next month, then I'll be off for a year. I was hoping to go to Scotland for a couple of weeks, just by myself. But I don't think I can leave my mother alone. And I don't want to ship her back to my sister's just for two weeks."

"Hire someone to live in," Alice advised. "A practical nurse or someone like that."

Marilyn made a face. "I don't know. I'd feel awful, hiring a stranger to stay with her. She wouldn't say anything, but I know it would hurt Mother's feelings." She shrugged. "It's all right. I can go another year."

"Don't be silly!" Faye said. "Ruth can stay with me."

Marilyn looked at Faye. "Oh, I can't ask you—"

"But I'd love to have her," Faye insisted. "What do I have a guest room for, anyway? It's not like my own daughter is planning any visits. It would be good for me, Marilyn, really, it would."

"I'd help," Polly offered. "I mean, if Faye needs to go out of town, or has a date with Aubrey, or whatever, I can always take Ruth out to dinner or come sit with her. I think Ruth's a hoot."

Marilyn was dumbfounded. Had she had a minor

brain warp and told them how important this trip was to her? She was so shocked she was speechless.

"I'll bring her out here for some yoga," Shirley added. "We'll keep her busy."

"I've got season tickets to the symphony," Alice chimed in. "Gideon doesn't like to go to them all. I'll take her in his place."

Tears welled in Marilyn's eyes. "I can't believe you'd all really do this for me."

"Please," Alice chided. "You'd do the same for any of us."

Shirley took Marilyn's hand. "Isn't this your dream?"

Marilyn nodded. "It's the trip I've dreamed of for years." She frowned. "I should warn you. Ruth can be irritating. She says the same thing over and over again, and it takes her *forever* to move two feet. And she's practically deaf, and you have to repeat stuff a thousand times. And she—"

"Marilyn." Faye's voice was decisive. "We're doing it. We're taking care of Ruth. So make your plans. Two weeks, even more—we'll all do just fine."

Marilyn looked radiant. "You are all so wonderful! Oh, wow! I'm so excited!" She looked serious again. "But we're going to have to break this to Ruth gently. You should all come over to the apartment and visit, so she gets used to you."

"We can do that," Faye said. "It's going to be fun."

FOURTH OF JULY

14

THE SUN SHONE DOWN ON A PERFECT DAY: SUNNY, clear, and hot. Divine picnic weather.

Shirley bustled about on the large slate patio off The Haven's kitchen door, carefully setting, right in the center of each picnic table, a bowl of red, white, and purple-blue petunias with a cute little American flag in the middle. She felt festive in red cropped pants, a blue-and-white striped jersey, and red espadrilles. And her earrings were so clever—they looked like firecrackers!

All around The Haven, the grounds spread like green velvet. The gardener had mowed the grass two days ago, and now, at the far end, by the beginning of the walking path, Justin was stabbing croquet wickets into the ground. They'd already set up the badminton net.

Shirley paused for a moment to gloat.

A few years ago, she'd been lonely and just a hair above down-and-out. Now she was the director of this flourishing business, *plus* living with a literary genius who loved her enough to stop his important work and help her with the humble manual labor of preparing for this party.

It hurt that her friends didn't trust Justin, but their faith in *her* encouraged her to have faith in *him*. And he'd worked so hard over the past few months, and accomplished so much! He'd researched and assessed various self-publishing companies, finally choosing The Hemingway Group. Wasn't that the most elegant name! It gave Shirley shivers. The Hemingway Group was based in Boston, which was an asset, Justin informed her. This company not only knew how to package Justin's novel, but how to market it. They had contacts with the media. They were planning an extensive publicity campaign for the book's publication this fall. Justin went in about once a week to meet with Dee Sylvester, who had helped edit the book and was working with graphic artists to create the *perfect* cover. She'd promised Justin that this book would explode on the book-reading public, zoom to the top of the bestseller list, and bring editors from New York publishing houses pounding on his door.

Shirley couldn't wait until the fall! *Then* her friends would come crawling to her with apologies for not believing in Justin. Especially Alice!

Alan and Jennifer strolled up the long drive from their cottage, once the gatehouse for the property. Instead of paying rent, they helped out whenever The Haven had an open house or some event needing food. They'd helped Shirley prepare the food for today's party, but they were also guests, part of the Hot Flash Club's extended family. They greeted Shirley with a kiss on the cheek, then set to work.

Alan asked, "Shirley, is the bar good here?"

"That's fine." Shirley slid a rubber coaster under one of the tables to level it. "If you want to bring the ice out, I'll get the glasses."

They set up the bar, then wheeled out the state-of-the-art barbecue grill. Shirley was a vegetarian, but Alice and the others had protested that not having hamburgers and hot dogs on the Fourth of July was not only bizarre but practically un-American, so of course she gave in. She was also providing a full bar, even though she was a recovering alcoholic. Everyone else enjoyed a beer or wine, or a cool g-and-t; but she didn't crave the stuff at all these days, when simple air was like nectar.

"Hello!" Polly came around the corner of the building, her boyfriend Hugh following. "Oh, this is beautiful!"

Like Shirley, Polly had red hair, but Shirley kept hers dyed auburn, partly because Justin was so much younger than she, but also because it made her feel she looked less dated when she faced her board of directors. Shirley would never say this, but she was pretty sure she looked younger than Polly, who was letting the white grow in among the red and who also carried more weight than she. Shirley was naturally slender, and years of yoga kept her limber, while Polly was endowed with a more feminine kind of frame, with a substantial bosom and hips. Still, Polly looked lovely in her polka-dot sundress and the straw hat she wore to keep her freckled face from sunburn.

"Hello, Polly! Hello, Hugh!" she called, and the party officially began.

As the sun rolled high in the sky, the guests played croquet and badminton, strolled along the walking paths Shirley had created in the woods, and lounged about on the patio, nibbling appetizers and chatting.

Sometimes Shirley found her new work stultifying: running the spa, dealing with paperwork and administrative details. Just this week, she'd had to listen to Elroy Morris, the buildings and grounds manager, explain why they needed a new septic system—honestly, what could be more boring! And it was so expensive! She'd had to review the insurance with their rep; thank God Alice sat in for that, even if she had taken off right afterward, still too cranky about Justin to spend even a minute alone with Shirley. And then there were the endless problems with staff, illnesses, taxes—sometimes Shirley wanted to pull out her hair. She missed her massage clients, missed the immediate magic of feeling people relax beneath her hands, soothing away their knots and kinks, bringing balm to their souls.

Yet Shirley knew The Haven provided a sanctuary for many more women than she could handle alone. This was a little universe, where women could retreat from the real world, relax, heal, and renew.

Justin was playing badminton with Hugh, so Shirley joined her friends at a picnic table beneath the shade of a striped umbrella. Ruth had come with Faye, which was good for them both, because Carolyn had wanted her father with *her* for the Fourth of July, so Aubrey wasn't there. Polly sat next to Alice, and Gideon was on Alice's other side, so Shirley felt buffered from her critical friend.

Alice was talking with Ruth. "Have you heard from Marilyn?"

Ruth lit up. She looked very cute in her red, white, and blue sweater, with a little matching bow in her white curls. "I have! Just yesterday! She phoned to say she'd arrived in Edinburgh safely. She stayed there a couple of days to get over her jet sag. Then she rented a little car, and drove on the left side of the roads, all the way to Loch Ness! She said she misses you girls terribly." Ruth counted on her fingers. "She said Shirley would love all the Celtic magic potions and jewelry. Faye and Polly would love all the woolen shops. And Alice, you would have kept her from screaming every time she drove around the traffic circles they call 'roundabouts' over there."

"Sounds like she's having a wonderful time," Shirley said. "I'm so happy for her."

"Shirley?" Alan approached the table. "It's after five. Shall I start the hamburgers?"

"Not yet. Why don't you and Jennifer join us for a while?" Shirley looked around. "Where is Jennifer?"

"Oh, she's, um—" Alan looked nervous. "Putting final touches on a salad, I think. I'll check."

Poor Alan, Shirley thought. He loved Jennifer, and Jennifer loved him, and of course he loved his mother, and Alice adored him, but there were tensions between Alice and Jennifer. It was one of the frustrating things about Alice, who seemed perfectly content and comfortable being the only black woman in the Hot Flash Club yet worried that Jennifer, as a white woman, would somehow bring harm to Alice's son.

Alan went off, swinging his spatula. Alice leaned forward. "Faye, I love your outfit."

Faye smiled. "Thanks. I made it myself." She touched the lacy inset on her pale blue tank top. Over it, she wore a gauzy shirt of a darker blue that obscured her plump arms and draped smoothly over her rounded tummy and hips.

"You make most of your clothes, don't you, Faye?" Polly asked.

Faye nodded. "I do. I designed my own little outfits when I started having hot flashes. I got tired of pulling sweaters off over my head. I knew I needed layers. So I made up patterns for myself: tank top, shirt with short sleeves, jacket with longer sleeves. Of course in this hot weather, I leave off the shirt."

"And you make them in such wonderful colors," Shirley said. "And centering the first layer with bits of lace or embroidery like you do is so clever!"

"I wish you'd show me how to make them," Polly told Faye. "I think I told you, I have boxes of old lace my mother-in-law left me. I want to throw them out, because she was such an evil old queen, but I can't make myself do it. So they're just sitting in my sewing room, gathering dust."

Ruth set her wineglass on the table. Her white curls bobbed on her wobbling little head. "You should team up. Use Polly's lace and Faye's designs and make a whole lot of these pretty little outfits. I'll bet you could sell them and make money."

Shirley nearly jumped out of her chair. "Oh, my God! You could sell them here at The Haven! Hot Flash clothes!"

"Hot Flash *fashions,*" Alice amended.

Polly and Faye looked at each other wide-eyed.

Polly, whose sewing business was on idle, thought: *I could use the money! But Faye doesn't need money.* "Well . . ."

Faye thought: *This might be fun, and it would give me something creative to do, now that I can't paint.* "Maybe . . ."

Shirley said, "If you two did start a little business, Carolyn would *have* to see that you're not about to be driven apart by her machinations."

Alice looked excited. "I could do the bookkeeping for you. It would be fun for me."

Faye hesitated. "I don't know. I like to sew for myself, but I've never sewn for anyone else."

"But I have!" Polly reminded her. "That's what I *do!* And just think, wouldn't we be great models to set the patterns? We're both plump, and our weight has sunk down around our equatorial zone like that of a lot of women our age—except for you, Shirley—"

"And Marilyn," Shirley added.

Faye cocked her head, considering. "What if we make them and they don't sell?"

Polly laughed. "Then we wear them ourselves! We'll have a fabulous wardrobe!"

Polly's enthusiasm was contagious. Faye grinned. "All right! Let's do it!"

Shirley jumped up and hugged Marilyn's mother. "Ruth, you are a *genius!*"

Ruth beamed. "Well, girls, since it was my idea, I'll buy the first outfit!"

"Oh, no," Faye retorted. "Since it was your idea, you get the first one free."

"Nonsense," Ruth told her. "You'll never make any money if you give things away. Right, Alice?"

"As your business manager," Alice said, "I concur with Ruth."

From down the road, at a house inhabited by a family of five, came the pop of firecrackers, sounding like applause.

A little later, as the enticing aroma of barbecued burgers floated in the air, Alan announced that dinner was ready. Everyone helped themselves at the long table set with rice salad, potato salad, romaine and endive salad, chickpea salad, and piles of fresh sliced veggies. Alan remained at the grill, cooking more burgers, and Jennifer kept an eye on the food, whisking empty bowls into the kitchen and bringing back refills.

"Enough!" Shirley told Alan. "They've all had seconds and thirds. Sit down and eat with us. You two are guests today, not staff!"

"Oh, we're fine," Alan told her. "We'll sit down in a minute."

"Well, you'd better. Jennifer looks wiped out. Is she sick?"

A strange look of terror flashed over Alan's face. "She's fine," he muttered.

When dark fell, Alan and Jennifer finally pulled up chairs to join everyone else as they waited for the fireworks to begin. Last year, Shirley had noticed that the adjoining town held a fireworks display that bloomed so high in the sky it was easily visible from the grounds of The Haven.

"How perfect is this!" Shirley was so pleased with herself. Everyone was relaxed. They all had a drink in their hands, iced tea, or coffee, or sparkling water. "I think we should toast Alan and Jennifer, our fearless chefs!"

"Hear! Hear!" Gideon said, raising his cup.

"Hoorah and thank you!" cheered Faye.

There was just enough light for Shirley to notice how Alan glanced at Jennifer, who nodded her chin just half an inch.

"Um, this might be a good time," Alan said, his voice slightly shaky, "for us to make an announcement."

Shirley clutched her hair with both hands. "Oh, no! You two haven't gotten a better job somewhere else?" She loved having the two live in the gatehouse; it made The Haven seem more homey.

"Not at all," Alan assured her. Reaching over, he took Jennifer's hand in his. "Jennifer and I are going to have a baby in December." He took a deep breath. "So we got married last week."

Silence fell. Shirley could hear birds twittering in the trees. In the distance, a motorcycle roared.

Shirley could scarcely summon up the courage to look at Alice. When she did, she saw that Alice wore her implacable, executive, *mess-with-me-and-I'll-rip-your-guts-out* look.

"Alice?" Faye said softly.

"Alice." Gideon put a restraining hand on Alice's arm.

Alice felt paralyzed, but her thoughts were racing. Alan had gotten married without telling her. Without inviting her to attend. They were having a baby, even though they knew how hard life could be for mixed-blood children. And he was announcing this now, in front of everyone, instead of coming to her first? Alice felt betrayed and humiliated. She felt like everyone else thought she was some kind of monster. She was aware of her friends staring at her hard, as if they were using the force of the gaze to press her back in her chair. She wanted to go into a padded room, knock her head against a wall, and scream till her throat was sore.

"I didn't know about this," Shirley assured Alice.

"No one did," Jennifer said. "My parents are furious that I'm living with Alan. They'll probably disown me now."

Alice gasped. Jennifer's parents disapproved of her son? How *dare* they! Alan was a *wonderful* man, intelligent, hardworking, kindhearted—

Ruth touched Alice's arm. "Remember. *Carpe diem.* Squeeze the day."

"Mom?" Alan interrupted her thoughts. "Aren't you going to say anything?"

Alice swallowed. For some bizarre reason, perhaps because she'd spent her life working in a corporation, reading and writing and living by rules, a register appeared in her mind, clicking along like a David Letterman list. Oddly, these were not corporate rules, but the rules of the Hot Flash Club:

1. Don't let fear rule your life.
2. When you're depressed, get up, get dressed, and get out of the house.
3. Celebrate every chance you get.

Rule number three—that was the one she wanted now. It lay in front of her like a path.

She smiled. She tried to *beam.* "Congratulations!"

The surprised delight on her son's face was a blessing. Alice felt the air around her shift, as everyone released held breaths. "We should celebrate!" Alice hoped the others didn't hear the wobble in her voice. "Shirley, is there any Champagne around?"

"Yeah, there is, but it's not really *good* Champagne."

"Could we break it out?" Alice turned to Alan and Jennifer. Jennifer was crying quietly, smiling at the same time. Alan looked like he was going to faint. The sight nearly broke Alice's heart. "I hope you two will let us throw you a party."

"Could we invite our friends?" Alan asked.

They had friends? Alice's head spun. Of course they had friends! Alice had just never met them or heard about them, because she'd held Jennifer and Alan at arm's length.

Alice smiled. "Of course you could invite all your friends!"

Shirley said, "I'll get the Champagne."

Faye jumped up. "I'll get the glasses."

Jennifer said, "I—I—I have to go to the ladies'." Shyly, she confessed, "Since I've been pregnant, I have to pee all the time."

"Honey," Alice said, "I hear you."

She sank back in her lawn chair, exhausted, vaguely aware of all the others rushing in and out of The Haven's kitchen.

Gideon leaned over and whispered in her ear, "You did good, Alice."

"Thank you. My brain feels like a bath mat."

"Here's the Champagne!" Shirley called, her arms wrapped around bottles.

"And here are the glasses!" Faye followed, carrying a tray.

Everyone rose as Shirley and Justin and Faye opened the bottles, aiming out toward the garden. With a satisfying popping noise, the corks exploded. Champagne surged up in a froth of bubbles. They filled the glasses and passed them around.

Alice raised her glass in a toast. "To Jennifer and Alan!"

"To Jennifer and Alan!" everyone chimed.

With a noise like thunder, fireworks burst in the sky.

15

Wʜᴇɴ Mᴀʀɪʟʏɴ ᴡᴏᴋᴇ ᴏɴ ᴛʜᴇ Fᴏᴜʀᴛʜ ᴏғ Jᴜʟʏ, she lay still and smiling in her unfamiliar bed, allowing herself to savor the moment. She was here!

She was in Scotland, on the very shore of Loch Ness!

She'd found this little B&B on the Internet, made reservations, flown to Edinburgh, and driven here all by herself. She felt brave. She felt like a woman on a pilgrimage.

She jumped up and pulled on her khakis, sweatshirt, and hiking boots. She ran a brush through her sensible chin-length hair, which, she noticed, needed another touch-up. The white was showing through the auburn. She shrugged. Who cared? She'd worry about that sort of thing when she was back home. She fastened her money belt around her waist—a stylistic faux pas that would make her Hot Flash friends shriek with horror—grabbed her room key, and headed down the stairs for breakfast.

The dining room was small and oddly decorated, with a red-and-green tartan rug and orange-and-pink floral wallpaper. The delicious aroma of coffee curled from the urn on the sideboard.

A young, Nordic-looking couple glanced up from their table. "Good morning."

"Good morning," Marilyn replied.

She poured herself a mug of coffee and sat next to the window. Through the lace she could see the green hillside rising upward, and a steady rain pouring down.

That was all right. She'd brought a good oilcloth raincoat, knowing that it would rain at least half the days she was here, if not all of them. It was mild outside, nearly seventy, and once she started walking, she'd warm up quickly.

The vigorous, ruddy-cheeked owner of the B&B, garbed in a flowered, frilled apron, took Marilyn's order for a full breakfast, returning with a plate of scrambled eggs, sausage, fried mushrooms, a potato scone, white toast, and a mysterious blob of brown. Marilyn ate quickly, eager to start her day.

The Nordic couple went out. A man came in. He was around Marilyn's age, bald except for a rim of gray hair, spectacled, lanky, and lean. Like Marilyn and the young couple, he wore hiking clothes. He greeted Marilyn with a nod and a smile, then sat down at the remaining table, opened a folder, and took out a sheaf of papers. Marilyn strained to read them—it was an unbreakable habit of hers, spying on other people's work—but they were too far away.

She'd finished her breakfast, except for the odd brown substance. Now she decided to try it—why not? When in Rome, after all. She tasted a forkful—*hm*. Perhaps onions and pureed corned beef?

"Pardon me," the man asked from across the small room. "But do you know what that is?" He had a marvelous Scottish accent.

Marilyn hesitated. She didn't want to seem like an ignorant tourist. But actually, she *was* an ignorant tourist, so she confessed, "I have no idea."

"Blud pudding."

"Excuse me?"

"Blud pudding. Blood and suet and seasonings."

"Ah." Marilyn put her fork down. "Thank you for telling me."

"Some develop a taste for it." His eyes sparkled.

"Yes, well, perhaps not for breakfast." Washing down a big swallow of coffee, she rose. "Have a good day."

"Aye, you, too."

Back in her room, she checked her pack: bottles of water, some trail mix, a chocolate bar, maps, tissues, and sunglasses, in case the weather changed. She pulled on her rain jacket, skipped down the stairs, and went out into the Loch Ness day.

For twenty-three miles, Loch Ness cut like a narrow knife blade through the Great Glen dividing the north of Scotland from Inverness to Fort William. Geologists knew the loch lay in a fault line active since mid-Devonian times, 400 million years ago, but on this lovely summer day, Marilyn forgot all that, as her senses exulted in air softened by a gentle rain, the tantalizing azure sparkle of the water, and the emerald hills rising steeply on either side. She was here, now.

Leaving her car in the B&B lot, she strode downhill and along the road toward the Loch Ness Monster Exhibition Center. It was hardly a scientific headquarters, but she wanted to tour it nonetheless, and she was not disappointed. Ignoring the souvenir shop with its Nessie dolls and mugs, she focused on the sketches and detailed accounts by witnesses who'd testified to the creature's existence over the years. St. Columba saw the monster in A.D. 565. Would a saint lie? In 1987, a million-dollar sonar exploration called Operation Deepscan found evidence of a mysterious moving mass larger than a shark. And most recently, a member of the coast guard discovered with his own sonar an enormous underwater cavern, which he called "Nessie's Lair." A professor at

Harvard and MIT had also spent years searching for the creature.

Crowds shuffled past the exhibits and clogged the passageways. Most of them were families with children hugging soft stuffed toys of a friendly, smiling, slightly goofy Nessie. This wasn't a sweet cartoon character invented by Disney, Marilyn wanted to remind them.

Leaving the throngs, Marilyn returned to the fresh air. Just on the other side of A82 and down by the loch was Castle Urquhart, a stony ruin set on a small promontory. Marilyn wished its stones could talk.

The rain had stopped, and shafts of sun striped the landscape. Marilyn wanted to lean against the rocks and stare out at the blue waters, but a busload of senior tourists arrived, clucking like chickens as they fluttered down to the castle, so she dug out her map, planned a route, and set off walking.

Paths wound up- and downhill, through forests and bogs, past streams and rivulets. Marilyn wandered along, taking her time, never getting too far from a view of the lake. Occasionally, she thought of her Hot Flash friends, or wondered how Ruth was doing, and whether her granddaughter was over her cold. Sometimes she thought of Faraday, and wondered whether she'd ever be with a man she loved.

But mostly she let her mind drift through the ages. She thought about the geology of this land, the metamorphic schists underlying the hills, the altered limestones, the shattered granite. She imagined the last Ice Age, just a geological moment ago, when this great glen was occupied by an enormous glacier. Everything would have been white then, blindingly white beneath the sun. She thought about the moving on and holding of time, how it never stopped but often saved.

She loved the ache in her legs from all the climbing up and down the lumpy, uneven, tufty hills, so unlike the flat streets of the city where she worked. She felt she was breathing differently, seeing more, hearing more clearly. She felt her body sparkle as her lungs pulled in new air, skimming through her blood like transparent vitamins.

In her excitement, she forgot to eat. It was nearly four in the afternoon when she felt her physical system plummet. Shaky, tired, and weak, she collapsed on a rock on the edge of the loch while she munched her trail mix.

Today there was no wind, so the loch lay still, except for the occasional wake caused by a boat. Some enterprising soul motored by, his launch loaded with tourists fishing off the side or taking pictures or gazing through binoculars. Marilyn sat watching for over an hour, but not a ripple disturbed the surface.

When she'd regrouped, she rose and headed back to her B&B. She showered, then collapsed on the bed for a nap, waking two hours later with a rumbling stomach.

Outside it was still light—the sun stayed up past nine o'clock in the summer. She went down to the front hall to study the brochures and decide where to eat.

The Scotsman she'd met at breakfast this morning was there. He wore jeans and a flannel shirt and smelled of the same soap Marilyn had just used in her shower.

"Hello," he greeted Marilyn. "Did you have a good day?"

"It was *bliss,*" Marilyn told him.

"Are you a Nessie hunter?"

She hesitated. She didn't want him to think she was just some kind of superstitious cryptozoologic nut. "I'm a paleontologist, actually. I teach in Cambridge— the American Cambridge—and I study trilobites, which are—"

"Trilobites, you say! Indeed! I know what they are. I'm a paleoartist."

"Get out!" Marilyn exclaimed.

"But it's true." He held out his hand. "Ian Foster."

Marilyn looked at his hand as if it were made of diamonds. "*The* Ian Foster? You've done the restoration drawings of the plesiosauria?"

"That's right."

"Oh, my gosh!" Marilyn had to restrain herself from going into adolescent shrieks. "Oh, what a pleasure to meet you! What are you doing here?"

"The same thing as you, I imagine, taking a little holiday, going for walks, airing out my poor old brain." Folding his arms, he leaned against the wall. "I've just finished a critical analysis of existing and dependent phylogenies via cladistic methods."

"How fascinating!" Marilyn was too enthralled to be shy. "I'd love to hear about it."

The Nordic couple came through then, muttering to each other in guttural tones. They stopped to say hello, then passed on, out the door.

Ian looked at Marilyn. "Listen, would you like to join me for dinner? There are several fairly decent restaurants in Inverness, which is only about fifteen miles from here."

"I can't think of anything I'd rather do!" Marilyn told him, adding to herself, *Except wait on the banks of the loch, watching for Nessie.*

They sat together at a small table in a large pub, eating fresh trout, drinking Scots lager, and talking about paleontology like reunited old friends.

Thin and gawky, Ian was not a handsome fellow. His Adam's apple protruded sharply, bobbing up and down as he spoke, and pouches bagged beneath his dark eyes, slightly hidden by his heavy glasses. His forehead bulged out, and his bald head stuck up from his rim of hair like an ostrich egg from a nest. But his hands were beautiful, his fingers long, lean, and supple, and he had nice, even white teeth. Something about him was very attractive to

Marilyn. Perhaps she was high on simply being here, but the longer she spoke with Ian, the more she wanted to touch his elegant hands. She even found herself fantasizing about pressing her lips to his, and she didn't feel the slightest bit guilty, because Ian was widowed, with a grown son living in Australia.

After dinner, they ordered fresh berries for dessert. Wanting to linger, they asked for cheese and crackers, and after that, they had a brandy. Finally, they left the pub and drove back along the loch to the B&B. It was raining again, so for a while they sat in Ian's car, talking, until the windows misted over and Marilyn shivered— she assumed from the damp. They ran inside to find the lights were dim, the common rooms empty, the building hushed.

Ian looked at his watch. "It's almost midnight."

"Oh, dear. We should go to bed," Marilyn said reluctantly.

"How much longer are you here for?" Ian asked.

"Ten more days."

"Well." He hesitated. "Would you like to join me tomorrow? We could hire a boat to take us out on the loch. Have a little picnic."

"Oh, that would be wonderful!"

He smiled at her enthusiasm. "Good, then. I'll see you at breakfast." He held out his hand and shook hers. "I'm awfully glad I met you, Marilyn."

"Yes," she said, flushing. "Me, too."

In all her life, Marilyn had never experienced the kind of happiness she felt over the next few days. In her twenties, she'd married Theodore for three reasons. First: she knew she was a science nerd, too engrossed with her studies to be attractive to most men. Second, the time was right. Third, Theodore had been the one to ask her. But during the long years of her marriage, her own scientific interests had been overshadowed by her husband's brilliance, and by his lack of interest in anything that didn't further his own career or studies. Then he left her for a younger woman.

She'd shared common scientific interests with Faraday, but she'd never felt like she felt right now with Ian: as if they were two halves of a whole, two pieces of one jigsaw puzzle, best friends who'd been waiting all their lives to meet.

Ian made her laugh. She made him laugh. Often they said the same word at the same time. They walked at the same pace—they were so comfortable together.

Ian was from Edinburgh. He taught at the university there, and he was an ardent Scotsman. One day when the rains poured down, he drove her to visit Cawdor Castle, where Shakespeare set *Macbeth* and where, after a delicious lunch, Marilyn got to lean on a fence and gaze to her heart's delight at a herd of shaggy red-haired Highland cows. But mostly they hiked the hills around Loch Ness, sharing lunches from their backpacks, talking, or silently enjoying each other's company.

The night they met, Ian had shaken her hand when they parted. The next night, he pressed a gentle kiss on her forehead. The third night, he kissed her cheek. By the fourth night, Marilyn thought she'd hit him with a full-body tackle, wrap her legs around his hips, and clutch him like an octopus if he didn't get a little more passionate—and he either read her mind or sensed her urges, because that night he pulled her to him and kissed her heartily.

"Oh, my!" she sighed when he released her.

They were sitting in his little car, rain singing down all around them.

He pulled back, studying her face as well as he could. It was late. They could only barely see each other's face.

"Marilyn," he said softly. "What shall we do? I'd like

to take you to bed, but we're both practically strangers, and you're going back to the States in a few days."

Her mouth had gone dry. Her heart was thudding. "I think you should take me to bed."

Quietly, they crept into the B&B and up the stairs to Marilyn's room. They locked the door. Ian put his arms around her and they pressed against each other, all up and down. This kiss was different from the others, rougher, warmer, more urgent. Marilyn wanted him inside her so much she was afraid she'd explode.

They pulled the covers back and fell on the bed with all their clothes on. As they kissed each other's mouths and eyes and faces, Marilyn unzipped her denim skirt and wrenched it off while Ian unzipped his khakis. Ian rose up on his arms and Marilyn tilted her hips up. He slid inside her, fitting as perfectly as the loch outside fit into the glen. Marilyn felt her eyes go wide with surprise as her body adjusted to this delicious intrusion. Ian moved slightly, and they both groaned. He lowered his head and brought his mouth down to kiss her. She clutched him to her and kissed him back. They rocked together slowly, letting the tension build. Something loosened inside her. A landslide of sexual pleasure rode through her pelvis. Clutching him for dear life, Marilyn surrendered to a force she'd never known her body contained.

After a while, she opened her eyes to see Ian smiling down at her.

"Okay?" he whispered.

She nodded. He moved again, quickly now, and she felt his own release inside her. When he fell against her, drained, she hugged him to her while tears tracked down her face.

"Do you know," he whispered, stroking her hair away from her face, "we're both still wearing our shoes."

She laughed as she cried.

* * *

Over the next week, Marilyn made love more than she ever had in all her life. Even if she added together all the times she'd ever had sex with her husband or that cad Barton or Faraday, she thought the sheer quantity surpassed them—and the quality! My God! She'd never realized! They made love in her room and his, in his car and in hers, standing up in a forest, lying down in a valley, and every time she wept with joy. When they hiked, they held hands. When they drove to a restaurant, she kept her hand on his thigh. When they ate, they sat next to each other, or twined legs under the table. She was giddy with sensuality. She ate more than she'd ever eaten, she drank more wine, she sang when she showered, she laughed about nothing. She felt like a teenager—no, she felt like some kind of angel.

"Look," Ian told her on the eighth night, "I've got to go back to Edinburgh tomorrow. I've got several professional matters to attend to."

"I'm leaving for home in three days," Marilyn told him. "Tomorrow night will be my last night here."

"Do you fly out of Edinburgh?"

"Yes."

"Then spend the last night with me at my house. I'll take you to the plane."

Marilyn began to cry. "Oh, damn, Ian. I don't want to be away from you."

"Can you rearrange your schedule? Stay a little longer?"

"I wish I could. But I've left my mother with friends, and I can't impose on them any longer."

"I understand. Well, look. I'll come visit you, how's that?"

"Oh, will you? When?"

"I'll have to check my calendar. Perhaps sometime in early September."

"That's so far away!"

"We'll e-mail every day," he promised.

As Marilyn watched Ian drive away that sunny morning, she felt as if she were watching a lover go off to war or sail away to conquer new lands. She wanted to sob with grief. She felt as if her skin were being ripped from her body.

But the day was beautiful, and the hills surrounding the loch were filled with hikers who saluted her with good cheer as they stomped past. She couldn't allow herself to stand weeping like an escapee from an institution for the demented, so she blew her nose, packed her backpack, and went out for a long hike around the lake.

That night she had dinner at the B&B, too weary to care about eating a gourmet meal. She couldn't taste anything, anyway. She lay on her bed, staring at the ceiling, remembering every word Ian had said, every kiss he'd pressed against her. She cried some more.

Her mind was in turmoil. Was she in love? If she was, was Ian? Certainly he seemed to feel as strongly as she did.

Now she wished her Hot Flash friends were here. She longed to talk all this over with them. Since she couldn't, she tried to imagine what advice they'd give.

Faye and Polly and Shirley would all probably say, *Lovely, Marilyn, we're so happy for you!* But level-headed Alice would give her a look. *Girl,* Alice would say, *I'm glad you had fun, but don't try to make it into more than it is. Anyone who wants to base her future on sexual attraction is a fool.*

Thinking of her friends calmed Marilyn's nerves. She lay in the dark smiling, and her tears dried up and disappeared.

But her friends weren't through talking to her yet.

She couldn't tell which one it was—maybe it was all of them—but a voice in her head said quite clearly, *We thought you were on a pilgrimage, Marilyn. We thought this trip was about making your childhood dream come true, not about getting laid.*

Although, they continued, *getting laid is nothing to sneeze at!*

She was restless. Marilyn tied her sneakers, grabbed up her fanny pack and a sweater, and went back out into the Scottish night.

It had not rained all day, and it was not raining now. A moon, not quite full, rode high in the sky, the occasional cloud sailing slowly across its face. The air smelled fresh, of grass and wild garlic and clover, as Marilyn sauntered down the long bank toward the loch's edge. There was no breeze. The deep waters of the loch slumbered, dark beneath the sky, dark to their depths.

It was midnight, but cars still passed on both sides of the loch, their lights flashing off and on like signals as they wound over the curves.

She crossed the road, heading toward the loch, going slowly, for the land was boggy and uneven, perfect for turning ankles. As she walked away from her B&B and the road up the hill to other hotels, the civilized world retreated. Nature closed around her.

It felt good to walk. Concentrating on each step soothed her nerves. She came to a small, sheltered cove overhung with trees, dense with bushes, and settled into a gap just her size at the water's edge. She could almost dangle her feet in the water. Instead, she drew her knees up, wrapped her arms around them, and gazed out at the loch.

She thought: *Ian.*

She shivered, remembering his touch, his breath, his body, his laughter.

Even if she never saw him again, the time she'd shared with him was a revelation. Love *did* exist. *Love at first sight* did exist. Even for a woman in her fifties, miracles could happen.

She knew her Hot Flash friends would scoff. They'd tell her there are no such things as miracles. Life doesn't give you miracles, they'd remind her. You're a scientist, for heaven's sake, they'd adjure. Be rational. Be skeptical. Be logical.

Her sensible side took over: Don't dream of a future with this man, this Ian. He lives in Scotland, you live in the United States. The past week was lovely; be grateful for that much. Don't expect anything more. For heaven's sake, you know nothing about the man, really. For all you know, he has a wife tucked away back home, or a mistress or two.

Marilyn idly watched the sleeping dark water as her mind tempered the past week's sensual richness with the astringency of common sense. In a lecturing way, her mind presented the facts: She'd been fortunate all her life. She had a healthy son, and now a healthy granddaughter. She had wonderful friends and work that fulfilled her. She was middle-aged, too old for miracles.

Why was she suddenly so greedy? She'd never been greedy before. She'd settled for a lackluster marriage, believing it was the best she could do. She'd accepted her junior position at the university with gratitude, not dreaming of anything more. Perhaps it was the influence of her Hot Flash friends, who got her to change her hair and clothing (when she remembered to), assuring her she could be more than plain, she could be actually *pretty*. Pretty, even at her age. Yes, it was her Hot Flash friends who caused her to be greedy—why, it was Shirley who said these should be the days of Dreams-Come-True.

But of course, they couldn't really mean that. At their advanced years, they knew that life could disappoint as much as it could thrill, and they were lucky if life didn't bring hurt or even grief.

But *still*, a small voice in Marilyn insisted, still good things can happen. We can change ourselves for the better. We can meet men and fall in love, and they can fall in love with us. We can—

Something moved in the water.

Marilyn blinked.

Perhaps twenty yards out, in the middle of the loch, the water stirred, sending concentric ripples with a shushing sound to the shore.

Above, a cloud passed over the moon, dimming the night, and then it floated off, and the loch stretched away, exposed in the clear air.

A swelling bulged from the surface of the water.

Marilyn held her breath.

Gradually, in a stately, steady manner, the shape broke through the water to reveal itself as a heavy, almost equine, arrow-shaped head supported by a narrow neck. Up it rose, one foot, two feet, three, four—

"Oh!" Marilyn whispered, trembling with excitement.

—ten, twelve feet at least, the neck extended from the long humped body that breached the water's surface, sending waves rolling to the land. With infinite grace, the neck turned, dipping the head this way and that, as if the creature were scanning the area. For a moment, Marilyn saw the liquid gleam of an eye.

The creature tilted her head back, exposing her throat to the sky, bending slowly to the left and right like a sunbather soaking in the rays. A low hum emanated from her, a satisfied sound, almost a purr. Then, in one sudden movement, like a duck or a bird, she bent her head to brush intently at her side, as if she were any kind of normal beast scratching an itch.

Tears streamed down Marilyn's face.

The beast, at least forty feet long, slowly swam a few

feet, stopped, and turned its neck warily. Again it navigated down the middle of the loch, as if out for a stroll.

I should do something! Marilyn thought. I should take a picture or call someone!

But she couldn't take her eyes off the creature. She was paralyzed with awe.

Then, across the loch, the double lights of a moving car glittered, and with a smooth, fluid plunge, the creature dove, disappearing beneath the loch's surface.

The car passed, its red taillights flickering, then vanishing. Marilyn waited, but the water was smooth now, as if a hand had passed over it, leveling all wrinkles.

Marilyn was trembling all over, and after a few moments, she realized she was freezing cold. The night air was cool, and she was, she knew, in shock.

Still, she waited, watching.

She waited over an hour, hugging herself while her teeth chattered, but the creature did not return. Finally, reluctantly, she went back to the hotel.

In her room, her mirror reflected her face, flushed with excitement. Using the little in-room service, she brewed a cup of hot tea and drank it down without tasting it. The tea warmed her and brought her to her senses. She looked at her watch. It was almost four in the morning. She felt as exhausted as she had just after giving birth to her son. She fell on her bed, pulled the spread over her, and sank into a dreamless sleep.

LABOR DAY

16

On a steamy afternoon at the end of August, the Hot Flash Club, plus Marilyn's mother Ruth, gathered at Polly's house. Polly handed out glasses of iced tea sprigged with mint, then asked, "Is everyone ready?"

"Ready!" Marilyn, Ruth, Alice, and Shirley chorused.

"Behind door number one!" Polly waved her arms like Vanna White. "Our first design!"

The double doors between the living and dining rooms flew open. Faye stepped out. She posed, one hand on her hip, the other at the base of her neck. Her thigh-length russet jacket covered a pumpkin shirt over a tank top inset with leaves embroidered in emerald and garnet.

"Oh, my God! It's gorgeous!" Shirley cried.

Alice applauded. "Double wow."

Ruth held out her hand. "Let me feel that material. Is it Velveeta?"

"Washable velour." Faye walked around the room so everyone could feel the fabric.

Polly hurried into the dining room. She returned, pulling a rack of clothing.

The others jumped up and sorted through the selection.

"The colors are all autumnal because they'll go on

sale in September," Faye explained. "If they sell well, we'll start on Christmas and winter colors right away."

"How many sizes did you make?" Marilyn asked.

Polly answered. "We've got twenty finished, in all. Three each of size twenty down to size ten, and one each of size twenty-two and twenty-four."

"Hey," Shirley protested. "Then they're all too big for me!"

"You don't need to wear this style," Alice told her. "You don't have any bouncing blubber to cover up."

Faye and Polly signaled each other with their eyes. Faye whisked into the dining room.

"But you *should* wear one of these ensembles," Polly said, "because you're the director of The Haven, and it would be great advertising, so—"

"TA—DA!" Faye came out with her arms full. "We've made one for each of you."

Polly lifted two of the garments from Faye and helped distribute them to each woman.

"Oh!" Shirley clapped her hands in delight. "You made mine purple!"

"It's Panting Pansy, actually," Faye told her. "We're naming each color. With a Hot Flash Hyacinth shirt and a Melted Mallow tank top."

"Here, Ruth." Polly approached the older woman. "This is yours."

Ruth tottered to her feet, beaming. "You girls didn't have to make one for me. I'm past the hot flash stage, after all."

"But of course we had to make one for you! You're the one who came up with the idea!" Polly reminded her.

"Let's just try the jacket on for now." Marilyn helped Ruth slide her arms in.

"This is just *lovely.*" Ruth smoothed the sea green material over her hips. "This Friday I'm going to a lecher. I'll wear it then."

"*Lecture,*" Marilyn enunciated in a whisper over Ruth's head.

Alice slipped into her jacket. "Feels like butter. And the color's delicious."

"Mad Marigold jacket," Polly announced. "With Sizzling Scarlet shirt and Crazy Carrot tank."

Alice went out into the hall to check herself in the long mirror. "Good grief, Gertrude, this flows like water!"

"That's because we made a yoke across the shoulders and lots of little tucks." Faye ran her hands along the back stitching.

"I predict these will be a raging success!" Alice said.

Polly disappeared, returning with a chocolate cake. "*Now* we have to make a few business decisions. We thought we should have a little nourishment to help our brains."

"What a beautiful cake!" Ruth said. "Did you make it, Polly?"

"Oh, no. Haven't had time to bake, with all the sewing. I bought it at The Haven's bakery." Polly and Faye bustled around, bringing out teacups, coffee cups, spoons, and napkins.

Marilyn reached out for a plate. "Alice, your party for Jennifer and Alan was a great success."

Alice smiled. "Thanks. I enjoyed meeting their friends."

Faye spoke around a mouthful of cake. "And Alan and Jennifer look so happy!"

Polly turned to Shirley. "How's Justin's book coming?"

Shirley lit up. "It will be published in October. Speaking of parties, we're planning a *huge* event."

Alice cast a worried glance Shirley's way. "Have you read his manuscript yet?"

Shirley bristled. "Not a single word. Justin says he

wants it to be a surprise." Defiantly, she added, "The publishers swear it's going to be a bestseller."

"Lovely," Polly smoothly interposed. "*Now.*" She set her empty plate on the table and clapped once, briskly. "Time for business. We agree these outfits are fabulous, right? Show of hands? Okay, we want to have these outfits in The Haven's gift shop in September. First, we have to have a name for our business."

"So we can sew in the labels," Faye explained.

"What are the possibilities?" Alice asked.

Shirley waved an enthusiastic hand. "Havenly Yours! Heavenly, Havenly, get it?"

"I was thinking Wisely Woven," Polly suggested.

"But they aren't *woven*," Marilyn pointed out.

"Hot Flash Fashions?" offered Alice.

"Mmm . . ." Faye tilted her hand back and forth in a so-so response.

Marilyn had an inspiration. "What about Crones' Crafts?"

"No!" Polly objected immediately. "*Crone* has too much of a negative connotation."

"So does 'hag,' " Shirley reminded them. "And 'hag' comes from the early Greek phrase 'Haggia Sophia,' meaning goddess of spiritual wisdom."

"What does 'crone' come from?" Faye asked.

Ruth spoke up. "It's from the Scottish for 'withered old ewe.' "

"Eeeuuwe!" cried Polly.

"Ancient wisdom has divided the life cycle of a woman into three parts: Maiden, Mother, Crone. Crone's wise, and possesses knowledge of ancient secrets." Shirley stirred sugar into her tea as she spoke. "Crone is definitely associated with old age and death. The crone's colors are black. She's sometimes called 'The Dark Mother,' because she knows the secrets of passing over into death."

For a moment, everyone in the room was quiet.

Faye said, thoughtfully, "We're all going to be crones someday."

"With all the advances in technology and medicine," Marilyn added, "we'll probably live different lives from the older women before us."

"True," Alice said, "but still, if we're lucky, we're going to get really old."

"And not necessarily really wise," Shirley added, with a grin.

Faye turned to Ruth, clearly the oldest among them. "What do you think?"

Ruth deliberated. "I think 'Crones' Crafts' is cute." As she spoke, she turned the rings on her liver-spotted, wrinkled, bony old hands. "But technically, girls, you're none of you crones, not yet. *I'm* a crone." She held up her hand in a "stop" sign. "*Please*. I'm eighty-three! It's been a couple of decades since I've had hot flesh. I'm not sad, scared, or embarrassed, so please don't you be. I'm just saying, I vote for 'Hot Flash Fashions,' not 'Crones' Crafts.' "

"But I'd like to get the word 'crone' back into our vernacular. If we *use* it, it will become something people won't dread," Shirley protested. "I mean, look at you, Ruth. You're old, as you said, but you're not shriveled, toothless, and scary."

Ruth laughed. "You haven't seen me naked!"

Shirley continued, "I think part of the mission of The Haven is to present new ways of looking at all the ages of womanhood."

"Well put," Alice said. "I'm impressed by your argument, Shirley."

Shirley blinked, thrilled to have Alice compliment her.

"And," Alice continued, "I still think your suggestion, Havenly Yours, is the best. It's clever, and it advertises The Haven."

"Let's take a vote," Polly decided. "All in favor of Hot Flash Fashions, raise your hands."

Ruth raised her hand.

"Crones' Crafts?"

Shirley raised her hand.

"Havenly Yours?"

Marilyn, Polly, Faye, and Alice raised their hands, and then Ruth said, "Can I change my boat? I choose Havenly Yours, too."

"Then Havenly Yours it is," Polly told them.

17

"IT'S AMAZING," SHIRLEY SAID TO JUSTIN ON LABOR Day as she looked out the kitchen window at the green grounds of The Haven. "Sometimes I actually believe there's hope for humanity."

Justin plunged a corkscrew into a bottle of wine. "And that would be because . . ."

"Well, look." Shirley waved her hands toward the window. "Alice has made Jennifer sit on the recliner, while she and Gideon help Alan set up the tables. Not to mention that everyone decided to make this a potluck, so I wouldn't have so much work to do."

"Doesn't take much to thrill you, does it?" Justin smiled to take the edge off his words. He'd had his teeth whitened, and he was tan from playing tennis, so his smile was like a million watts.

Shirley was too happy to let the tone of his voice bring her down. As the publication day of his book drew near, Justin was becoming nervous, short-tempered, and cranky. She didn't blame him. He was, after all, an artist, naturally sensitive, and worried about the event of a lifetime.

"Here come Carolyn and Hank and their baby. I know Carolyn's father is bringing Faye! I just wish Carolyn would *get* it, that Faye and Aubrey are a couple.

Faye and Polly spent all summer sewing together. They're such good friends now. Polly—"

"*Your* name should be Polly," Justin growled. "Pollyanna." Carrying the wine bottle and his glass, he went through the door.

Poor Justin, Shirley thought. Then she brightened. "Oh, my gosh! Here's Marilyn with her Scottish lover!" She raced outside.

The summer heat lay heavily across the day, frizzing hair, driving everyone into the shade of the patio where the tables were set out. Shirley fluttered from person to person, kissing, hugging, loving them all.

She wondered, just a *little,* in her secret and critical mind, just what it was Marilyn saw in this Ian fellow who had come to visit her for a couple of weeks. He was bound to be brilliant, but gee, he was a funny-looking guy, all elbows and knees and Adam's apple. Shirley thought Faraday had been much handsomer, and sexier, too.

"I'm verra pleased to meet you," Ian told Shirley. "I apologize for not shaking your hand, but as you can see, both hands are full." With his chin, he motioned to the large bowl he carried.

"Mother made her famous hot potato salad." Marilyn was absolutely glowing with happiness. And she wore a darling frou-frou filmy yellow dress that made her look divinely feminine. "And I made curried chicken salad."

"I'll take your bowl," Shirley told Ian, "and you can help Ruth get settled."

Ruth chuckled. "I like the division of labor. You girls take the food, I'll take the man." She fluttered her eyelashes flirtatiously, looking adorable in a dress covered with hummingbirds, with a hummingbird hairclip in her white curls.

"Madam." Ian held out his arm. "May I?"

Ruth clutched it and winked at Shirley. "Little does he know, I'm as stable as a horse."

"Your mother looks good," Shirley whispered to Marilyn as they carried the food to the long table.

"She has good days and bad," Marilyn said. "Some days she's really foggy and forgetful. Today she's in great shape."

Polly and Hugh appeared with plates in their arms.

"Cold paella salad," Polly announced.

"Tuna tonnato," Hugh told Shirley, setting a brightly colored dish on the table. "We've got an apple pie in the car. I'll just fetch it."

Faye strolled up. "My gosh, look at all the food! No dieting today."

"It's a holiday," Shirley reminded her. "It's illegal to diet on holidays."

"Is that a Hot Flash Club rule?" Polly asked. "If not, I move that we vote it in!"

It was too hot to play badminton or even croquet, so everyone lolled around chatting until Shirley announced that all the food and guests were there. Alice told Alan to move the sun umbrella to the left, so it would more completely shade Jennifer, and Jennifer told Alice to put her feet up on the end of her recliner.

We're a lucky group, Alice thought now, surveying her friends over the rim of her gin and tonic. We're an unusual group—five women of a certain age, each with her own beau. Polly and Hugh. Faye and Aubrey. Alice and Gideon. Marilyn and Ian.

Shirley and Justin.

Justin was the youngest, and by far the handsomest. He had all his hair, and no belly sagged over his belt. Alice looked around the party for him and spotted him in fervent conversation with Carolyn. Carolyn's hus-

band Hank, who was pretty cute himself, was busy taking their daughter for a toddle on the grass, and Justin
had pulled his chair so close to Carolyn's that their
knees were just an inch away from touching. As Alice
watched, Carolyn smiled, blushed, and shook her hair
away from her face demurely, as if Justin had just paid
her a compliment. Which, no doubt, he had. Justin knew
Carolyn was wealthy. He was probably buttering her
up. But Carolyn was a businesswoman, not an easy
mark. Alice wasn't worried about Carolyn.

Alice looked around for Shirley. Dusk was just beginning to fall, softening the light and moderating the heat.
Shirley was with Marilyn and Ian.

"Let me show you the walking paths before it gets
dark," she said. Shirley escorted them toward the woods.

Alice watched the three stroll away. Gideon and Hugh
were engaged in a fierce discussion of the Red Sox.

Alice stood up. She was half-surprised by the direction
her thoughts were carrying her legs, but as she strolled
unnoticed into the kitchen of The Haven, she decided
that somewhere in her unconscious mind she'd been
plotting this all along.

Just waiting for the right opportunity.

Alice wanted a peek at Justin's novel. Shirley might be
shy about reading it, but Alice wasn't.

In the kitchen, Alice took a moment to let her eyes adjust to the different light. Then she hurried.

She knew the layout of The Haven well. She'd examined every inch when Shirley was considering buying it,
and during the past two years, Alice had made her way
countless times past the back corridor leading to all the
offices, into the great foyer, and up the handsome staircase to the second floor where the private condos were.
She'd been in Shirley's condo often, although not since
Justin had moved in.

Shirley's condo was at the end of the building. The

door was open. Not just unlocked, but wide open. Good.

Alice stepped inside. Quickly she scanned the place. It was so very *Shirley,* with lavender walls hung with paintings of nude goddesses. Batik cushions spilled across the sofa. Candles and incense holders sat on every table.

A short hallway led to the bathroom and two bedrooms. Alice peeked in. On the left, a violet paisley duvet covered a bed. A man's robe was tossed over a chair.

Alice went into the other bedroom. Aha! This was clearly Justin's study, where he was writing his purportedly brilliant novel.

Two walls were lined with shelves filled with books. A handsome desk sat in front of the window, a computer humming on top of it. Filing cabinets stood in front of the fourth wall.

Quickly, Alice surveyed Justin's desk. Well, well, he was a very tidy boy. She saw a calendar blotter, blank notepad, pens, tape dispenser, stapler, paperweight, Post-its, and telephone, but that was all. No sign of the precious novel.

She crossed the room, stuck her head around the corner into the hall, and listened carefully. No sounds on the stairs. Good.

Approaching the filing cabinets, she yanked open a drawer, swiftly flipping through the files, which had been carefully labeled in a firm hand: *Correspondence/ Agents. Correspondence/Publishers.* Those held only polite letters of rejection. Files of newspaper and magazine clippings and online essays about how to get published or how to survive the trials of refusals filled the rest of the drawer. Alice felt a twinge of sympathy for Justin.

It didn't last long.

She opened the next file drawer. It was crammed with lesson plans, sample tests, essays, and handouts from his days of teaching English. Another drawer held the boring paperwork of everyday life: a car insurance folder, passport information, receipts for tax purposes.

One more drawer. Alice pulled.

It wouldn't open.

Ha! This drawer, no doubt, held the priceless manuscript.

She tried gently enticing the drawer open. It didn't work. She yanked hard. It wouldn't open.

Her heart was pounding. How long had she been away from the party? She should have noticed the time when she came in. She hurried to the window and looked out—everyone was occupied, talking and laughing; no one was looking around for her. Justin was still smarming around Carolyn.

Okay. Alice forced herself to take a deep breath. Plunking down in Justin's office chair, she wiggled the mouse. The computer brightened and came to life.

She took a moment to study the icons on the screen, then opened the word-processing program. Clicking on the folder "C," she learned it contained correspondence. Appropriate.

Could the folder named "N" possibly contain the novel?

Only one way to find out.

With a trembling hand, Alice clicked. Dozens of files marched down the screen. She moved the cursor to "Title" and clicked again. Her heart drummed in her ears.

Spa Spy, a novel by Justin Quale.

The words leapt out at her so fast, Alice gasped. She'd found it! She'd found his novel! Her heart went pit-a-pat.

Hang on now! It was called *Spa Spy?* That didn't sound good.

She closed that file and opened the one labeled "Chapter One."

She read the first page. He wrote well. It read fast. But . . . Alice was literally on the edge of her seat as she scrolled hurriedly down to the middle of the chapter.

"Oh, no," she whispered. Stunned, she clicked and tugged the mouse, speeding the cursor through succeeding chapters.

Spa Spy seemed to be about a group of women who ran a wellness retreat for wealthy older women. Everything was rosy—until the second chapter, when it was revealed that spy holes had been placed in strategic spots in the walls of the locker room, Jacuzzi room, and massage therapy rooms. The managing group were using the spy holes to photograph and tape-record certain of their wealthiest clients, with blackmail plans in mind. The director's lover, a handsome man who bore a remarkable resemblance to Justin, was trying to foil their scheme.

"Oh, no!" Alice cried again.

Her heart contracted fiercely as the full horror of it hit her. Justin had appropriated details of The Haven. Anyone reading this trash would immediately withdraw their membership. Even if there was the standard disclaimer about this being a work of fiction bearing no relation to any living person, it would still kill The Haven's business. Shirley would be devastated.

And heartbroken. When Shirley realized what Justin had done, she would know the truth about the man she believed loved her . . . Alice's own heart cracked at the thought.

A searing pain shot from Alice's chest into her left arm. She clutched her arm, groaning.

What—?

What was happening?

She couldn't get her breath. An immense pressure weighed against her chest—dear God! She was having a heart attack!

She tried to reach for the telephone, but only managed

to knock the handset off before crumpling to the floor. She was aware of a suffocating pressure and a burning pain—and then it all went black.

"So that's the main walking path," Shirley told Ian as they came out of the shadowy forest onto the grassy lawn.

"It's wonderful," Ian said. "So many varieties of deciduous trees!"

Ian and Marilyn were holding hands and lingering in the shelter of the woods, as if the tree bark were amazingly interesting, which, Shirley thought, it just might be to this pair of scientific brains. Probably they wanted to press their noses up against the tree trunks, searching for bugs.

More likely, they wanted to remain hidden in the woods so they could kiss.

"I've got to run into the kitchen and get some candles," Shirley told them.

"Need help?" Marilyn called dutifully.

"No, thanks!" Shirley grinned as she fairly skipped across the lawn.

Everyone seemed to be having a good time. Gideon and Hugh were still deep in discussion, probably solving the Red Sox pitching problems. Jennifer, Alan, and Ruth were sitting with Carolyn and Hank, who bounced his daughter on his knee. No doubt they were talking about babies. Faye and Aubrey were at the far end of the grounds, playing croquet.

Where was Alice?

She spotted Justin slinking into the kitchen.

Something about the way he moved worried her. He looked so . . . *furtive.*

She hurried onto the patio. "Just getting some candles," she tossed over her shoulder.

The kitchen was dark, cool—and empty. Shirley went

through into the foyer just in time to see Justin's feet disappearing up the great front staircase.

She followed.

Where was he going? Why did she feel so nervous? Her palms were sweaty! Her heart was pounding! This was ridiculous! The poor man probably just wanted to take a pee.

But there were restrooms on the first floor, close to the kitchen.

Well, then, maybe he'd spilled something on his shirt and went to change it. Or something, *anything*—why was she so spooked?

She flew up the stairs after him.

At the end of the hall, the door to her condo was open, providing a direct shot into the foyer and down the little hall leading to the bedrooms.

Justin was standing in the hall. He was just standing there, staring. Staring into his own study. Not moving. Why would he do that? He looked oddly *satisfied*.

"Justin?" Shirley called.

He turned his head and saw her coming toward him. In a flash, he disappeared into his study.

"What's going on, Hon?" Shirley asked, hurrying into the condo and down the hall.

She turned into Justin's study. Justin was hurriedly moving the computer mouse—and Alice was collapsed on the floor!

"Alice?" Shirley ran into the room and threw herself down. "Oh, my God, Alice!"

18

ALICE LAY CURLED ON HER SIDE, UNCONSCIOUS.

"Justin! Call 911! Alice is—I think she's had a heart attack!" Shirley turned Alice on her back. Alice flopped like a doll. She wasn't breathing. "Oh, God, oh, Alice!"

Justin was speaking with 911. Shirley shoved the window up and screamed down at the backyard. "Hugh? HUGH! Come up here, please! Alice had a heart attack!"

Startled faces stared up at her from the patio. She dropped to the floor and began CPR on Alice. Shirley's hands were shaking—her entire body was trembling as if it were about to shatter—but she forced herself to concentrate.

Kneeling, she pinched Alice's nose tight, covered Alice's mouth with her own, and blew. Once. Twice. Three times? She couldn't remember how many times to breathe!

Alice didn't respond. Shirley put her hands between Alice's breasts and shoved down hard. Once, twice, three times—she knew she had to do it fifteen times at the rate of one hundred per second, or was it one hundred times at the rate of fifteen per second?

She blew again in Alice's mouth. Alice had a mole by her left eyebrow. She'd never noticed that before. She moved back to her chest and pumped. Beneath her tangerine chiffon poncho, Alice's chest remained still.

Suddenly Hugh was there, kneeling next to Shirley. "I'll pump. You breathe." He began to count aloud. Quickly they synchronized their efforts.

In a blurry kind of way, Shirley was aware of the others crowding into the room, asking how Alice was, what they could do to help. Justin bent down to unplug his computer, then lifted it off the desk and left the room with it in his arms.

"Mom?" Alan fell to the floor next to his mother. "Is she okay? What can I do?"

"Just give her room to breathe," Hugh told him. "We're doing what we can."

"The ambulance is here!" Faye called.

"She's got a pulse," Hugh said.

"Should we stop now?" Shirley asked.

Two EMTs ran into the room.

The closest hospital was Emerson in Concord. The ambulance tore down The Haven's driveway, siren blaring. The rest of the party followed in various cars. Since Justin had disappeared, Polly tucked Shirley into the back of Hugh's Range Rover and sat with her, keeping a comforting arm around her.

"Justin was just standing there," Shirley sobbed. "Just *standing* there, looking."

Hugh spoke up from the front seat. "Not everyone knows how to give CPR."

"Then he should have yelled out the window like I did. Phoned 911. Run back downstairs and grabbed you. *Something.*" Shirley couldn't stop shaking.

"Take some deep breaths," Polly told her.

Shirley tried, but her thoughts kept exploding. "And then, when I was giving her CPR, Justin was removing his computer from the room! As if he had something to hide!" She covered her face with her hands and wept.

At the hospital, the Hot Flash friends and their beaux clustered in a waiting room for what felt like an eternity. Shirley repeated her story over and over again, how she'd followed Justin, how sneaky he'd looked, and then how creepily he stood there staring into his study, looking alert and somehow *satisfied*. How Alice had lain unconscious, her face void of her formidable personality.

"If she doesn't recover, I won't be able to live with myself," Shirley whispered.

"She'll recover," Faye promised, because anything else was unthinkable.

Hugh returned to the room, a physician in a white coat at his side. Everyone knew at once that Alice hadn't died—both men were smiling.

"Alice is awake," the physician informed them. "She suffered a mild cardiac infarction. We have her on an anticoagulant, and we're going to run some tests on her to find out exactly what the problem is. She'll be in the hospital for a couple of days at least. Who's her next of kin?"

"I am!" Shirley cried eagerly, then added honestly, "Well, I feel like I am."

"I am," Alan insisted.

"I am," Gideon bellowed.

The physician smiled. Pointing to Alan, he said, "We need you to sign some forms." He looked at Shirley. "You must be Shirley. Come with me. She wants to see you. But only for a moment, you understand."

Enthroned on a high white hospital bed, an oxygen tube snaking into her nose, IVs dripping into her arms, Alice lay beneath white sheets, sleeping.

"Alice?"

Alice opened her eyes. Seeing Shirley, she turned her hand over, palm up. Shirley grabbed it with both hands.

"Oh, Alice!" Tears ran down Shirley's face, plopping on her shirt. "Oh, honey, I'm so glad you're okay."

Alice's face grew serious. "Shirley. Must tell you." Her voice was whispery, strained. "Justin's novel? It's called *Spa Spy*. It's—bad. You can't help him publish it."

A nurse entered the room. "Ladies? What are we doing to get the patient agitated?"

"Alice." Shirley bent close to her friend. "Don't worry. I promise you, Justin Quale and his novel are on their way out of my life."

"But—" Alice struggled to explain.

"Tell me the details later. I know all I need to know now."

"How—?" Alice's face creased anxiously.

Frantically, Shirley wondered how she could reassure her. "Justin gave The Hemingway Group ten thousand dollars this spring. I mailed them a check for ten thousand more last week. First thing in the morning, I'm calling the bank and canceling the check. Next thing, I'm throwing all his stuff out on the lawn."

Alice smiled and relaxed into the pillows. "Sorry, kiddo."

"I love you, Alice!" Shirley bent down and kissed her friend. "I'll spend the night here."

"Tell Alan and Gideon I'm okay." Alice closed her eyes. "Just really tired."

The other members of the Hot Flash Club volunteered to come with her, but Shirley insisted she needed to do this herself. So they arranged a schedule for sitting with Alice—Gideon and Alan would spend the night at the hospital; Polly and Faye would arrive early in the morning to take over; Marilyn would relieve them in the afternoon; and Shirley would join Marilyn whenever she was through with Justin.

Through with Justin.

When Shirley returned from the hospital, it was almost midnight. Someone had brought the food in from the patio, but empty plates and glasses were still scattered outside and the kitchen was in chaos. She checked her answering machine—perhaps Justin had phoned to ask how Alice was—but there were no messages.

Glad to have a use for her nervous energy, Shirley buzzed in and out the kitchen door, carrying trays of plates, utensils, and used paper napkins in from the patio. She sorted, tossed, rinsed, and stacked, until all that was left to do was turn on the dishwasher.

Its hum was comforting in the huge kitchen. It sounded kind, almost concerned.

"All right, now you're getting weird on me," Shirley said aloud, because that's what Alice would say.

She turned off the lights and set the alarms. She climbed the stairs to her condo—the door was still wide open. She looked in Justin's study. No Justin. No computer.

Still too restless to sleep, Shirley decided to pack Justin's clothes. It was a melancholy task, and as she folded his white terry-cloth robe, the tears began.

Perhaps she'd suspected just a *little bit* that he didn't love her. She could believe he'd pretended to because she provided free lodging and food, not to mention funds for the publication of his book.

But she'd never dreamed his novel was titled *Spa Spy*! It had to be based on The Haven. Oh, her poor clients would feel so invaded! Was she hopelessly naïve? She brought his robe to her face and sobbed into it, letting it absorb her tears.

The robe smelled so good. It smelled like Justin.

The worst thing, the very worst, was the memory of Justin standing there in the hall, alert, *waiting*. He'd been looking at Alice, collapsed on the floor, and had not done what any normal person would do. He had not run in to help her. He'd just stood there, watching, as if waiting for her to die.

She sobbed harder, in huge, heaving sobs that produced frightening noises, like some kind of jungle rampage. So what? No one was here to hear her.

That was all right. The pain of his betrayal hurt so much—but it was pain she had to bear alone. She'd never had a baby, but she'd heard other women talking about the agony of labor. Even though husbands, lovers, doctors, nurses, midwives, or coaches were with them, they all had to endure the pain in their bodies alone.

Shirley had to endure this pain alone. She could do it, she thought, if she could consider it a kind of labor, like giving birth to herself—a new and, *dear God, please,* less gullible self.

"Shirley?"

She woke. Sun streamed in through the windows. She was lying on her bed with Justin's robe in her arms. Her eyes were swollen and crusty. Her mouth was dry.

Justin leaned in the bedroom doorway, handsome in a crisp white button-down shirt with the sleeves rolled up over his tanned arms. He looked perfect. Shirley sat up, aware of her own disarray. Wrinkled clothing, hair no doubt sticking up in all directions, skin blotched from sleep.

"Is Alice all right?" Justin asked.

Shirley nodded, yawning. She needed a shower and a gallon of peppermint tea.

"Thank God." Justin sat down on the bed. "I was so worried." He tried to pull her into his arms.

"Don't, Justin." Wearily, Shirley put both hands on his chest and pushed him away. "Don't bother pretending. We both know it's over between us."

He looked shocked. "What are you talking about?"

"Oh, Justin." She gazed at his handsome, immoral face. "You didn't try to help Alice. She was dying, and you grabbed your computer and left."

"But you've got to understand!" Justin sputtered indignantly. "All those people—my work is private—"

"Your work is shit," Shirley told him. She dropped the robe on the floor and stood up. "We're through, Justin, and as far as I'm concerned, your work is no longer any concern of mine. I'm stopping the check to The Hemingway Group. And I want you to move out."

Justin jumped up, genuinely alarmed. "You can't do that! Shir', I'm so close to publication!"

"Yeah," Shirley spat, "publication of a novel called *Spa Spy*?"

"Shirley, it's a work of *fiction*."

"How dumb do you think I am?" Shirley demanded, immediately adding, "No, don't answer that. I don't want to know."

"Shirley. Please." He approached her, once again trying to take her in his arms. "Let's talk about this. Let's talk about *us*."

Shirley looked up at his handsome, smug face. Her hesitation sparked triumph in his eyes.

She stepped back. In a firm, level voice, Shirley said, "Justin. Leave. I mean it. Pack your clothes and leave. It's over."

He tried to grasp her hand. She wrenched away from him. She hurried into the bathroom and slammed the door.

Sometimes Justin had joined her when she showered,

soaping her back, pressing her against the tiles as he kissed her.

Today, she turned the lock on the door and took her shower alone. The sound of the water obscured any pleas he might have tried to make.

The warm water rinsed her clean.

COLUMBUS DAY

19

THE TANG OF FALL LANCED THE AIR ON THE FRIDAY
night beginning Columbus Day weekend. The five members of the Hot Flash Club hurried from the parking lot into Legal Seafoods, hugging themselves for warmth. The restaurant was crowded, but they were still seated at their favorite table.

"Alice," Marilyn said, "you look *amazing*. You, too, Faye. And you, too, Polly."

The three women glowed. When Faye and Polly had heard about the lifestyle changes Alice's heart attack was forcing her to make, they had decided to join her, partly for moral support, partly to prevent something similar from happening to them. So they'd all been on the same diet, and attended the same yoga and exercise programs.

"I've only lost eight pounds," Alice said as she unfolded her napkin. "Five in the hospital, three since."

"But it's only been six weeks," Polly reminded her. "We're supposed to lose it *gradually*."

"Do you feel better?" Shirley asked.

Alice nodded. "I hate to admit it, but I do. I think the exercise and yoga's helping my arthritis. I'm less stiff."

"Yes, well, *I'm* having trouble with—" Faye stopped talking because suddenly the waiter was there. When everyone had given her order and the waiter left, she continued. "*Gas,*" she whispered. "All these vegetables I'm eating have me as bloated as the Hindenburg. After dinner, you could hang Firestone ads on my side and float me over football stadiums."

"Me, too!" Polly chimed in. "I never used to have gas, and now I have it all the time! It's so embarrassing! Especially since the worst time is night, when Hugh and I make love. I'm so busy trying not to pass gas, I can't enjoy myself!"

Shirley looked thoughtful. "But *men* aren't timid about it. They love to let it rip."

"Men consider farting an art form," Alice agreed. "I swear, Gideon will walk through the condo to find me, as if he's presenting me with a gift or performing some kind of symphony."

Polly laughed. "I know. Hugh does that, too. But it wouldn't be the same if I did it. It just doesn't seem *feminine.*"

Marilyn nestled her chin in her hand, squinting as she thought. "Perhaps it was once some primitive form of communication. You know how male mammals fight for control of the females? They fight, and bellow, and snort. Well, perhaps the male who could produce the most powerful scent and the most terrifying sound announced his supremacy."

"In that case, Gideon would win, believe me," Alice chuckled.

"It's all natural." Shirley squeezed the lime slice into her sparkling water. "Your body at work."

"It's not just farting," Faye said. "It's acid indigestion, too."

"Hugh likes to speak his belches." Polly imitated him in a bullfrog rumble. "*Helllllllo. Goooood-bye.*"

"I get acid indigestion, too," Alice told Faye. "It kind

of scares me, actually, every time I get heartburn. I mean, I'm afraid I'm having another heart attack."

Shirley patted Alice's hand. "Hon, that's not going to happen. You're on Plavix. You're doing everything your doctor advised with lifestyle changes. When you get heartburn, just remind yourself that's a sign that you're eating all the great crucifers and fiber that are keeping you healthy and strong."

Alice shook her head. "It's hard to think that way when there's a Bunsen burner flaring up between my breasts."

"You should get a prescription antacid," Polly advised her.

"More *pills*!" Alice looked despairing.

"Alice, I take tons of pills." Faye counted on her fingers as she named them. "Blood pressure medication, which also helps heart arrhythmia. I've been on that forever. Cholesterol medication. Aspirin for mild arthritis. Pills for bladder control. Allergy medication during allergy season, which seems to be just about the entire year. Antacids. Vitamins and extra calcium."

"Is that all?" Shirley was surprised. "I thought you were taking those omega-3 fatty acid supplements I told you about. Really, you should all take them. Didn't I give you the literature?"

Polly nodded. "We all read it. But I'm like Faye. I hate to depend on so many pills. Doesn't seem natural."

"Well, that's just crazy," Shirley argued. "That's like saying you won't use the phone or drive a car. We're fortunate that so many researchers are finding supplements that keep us healthy and active."

Marilyn laughed. "I read there's a new medication to help stroke victims. It dissolves blood clots, and it comes from the saliva of vampire bats. Isn't nature amazing?"

Alice shuddered. "That's just too weird."

Polly said, "We probably don't *want* to know where most of our medicine comes from."

"If you want to take fewer medications for arthritis," Shirley advised, "talk to the nutritionist at The Haven. I know certain foods are great anti-inflammatories. Ginger, turmeric, celery. Debbie carries a range of supplements and natural medicines in the shop."

The waiter set their meals before them—everyone had fish and steamed broccoli.

Alice tasted her salmon. "How's the shop doing?"

"We've still got a limited inventory," Shirley told her. "We need to work up a complete business plan before we invest in a lot of stock."

"Speaking of business plans . . ." Faye's eyes sparkled with merriment.

"What?" Alice demanded. "I can tell by your face this is going to be good."

"Oh boy." Polly looked like she was going to crawl under the table.

Faye smirked. "Well, you know, Polly and I talked with several banks about getting a loan to start Havenly Yours. For industrial sewing machines, materials, salaries, et cetera."

"Go on," Shirley coaxed.

"So our first meeting was yesterday, with Third National in Lincoln . . ."

"Wait! Wait!" Polly interrupted. "Remember, I've never done a business meeting before! Tucker used to do all that kind of stuff."

Faye grinned. "So Polly and I made the appointment. I met Polly at the bank. She looked very efficient in a tidy little cream pantsuit. We were shown into the vice president's office. Evan Krause. Our age, *terribly* serious."

"Talks like his jaw's wired shut," Polly added. "All the charm of a robot."

"So we sit down in his terribly serious office and pull out our folders and go over the business plan with him.

And Evan doesn't see one of the figures—" Faye swallowed a snicker.

"—the health benefit package," Polly added. She was turning red.

"So Polly gets up, leans over his desk, and points to the line in our figures. And as Polly leans over, there's her rear end staring right at me." Laughter bubbled up around her words. "And it looks like five or six little brown *pellets* are dangling from her bum."

Marilyn, Shirley, and Alice gawked at Polly. Polly put her napkin over her head.

"I'm thinking what *are* those things?" Faye put her hands to her heart in mock shock. "They looked like little . . ." She glanced around to be sure no one was near. ". . . *turds!*" She snorted, trying to contain her laughter.

"I'm *so* dying of embarrassment," Polly mumbled behind the napkin.

"So Polly sits down again. But I can't concentrate. All I can think of are those little brown nuggets and how they could be on the *outside* of her clothing!" She rocked with suppressed laughter. "So she and Ichabod Banker are *staring* at me, which sends me into a hot flash, and then I *really* can't think. Oh, Jeez," Faye interrupted herself. "Just *thinking* of it is giving me a hot flash!" She grabbed her water glass and pressed it against her neck.

Polly removed the napkin from her head and carried on. "So to make a long and painful story short, we did not do a very professional job of presenting our business plan. I couldn't understand why Faye was so scattered. I had to do all the talking, while Faye sat there twitching like she was being inhabited by aliens. So the Robot Banker says he'll take it under advisement and let us know—"

"And we stand up and Polly leans over to shake his hand." Faye exploded with laughter. "And I look at her chair, and those five little brown pellets are lying there! Ahahahaha!" Tears streamed down her cheeks. "Like she'd laid five little brown eggs!"

Her laughter was contagious. They all howled. It was like junior high.

"What *were* they?" Marilyn choked out.

"Well, I was nervous, you have to understand!" Polly held out her hands, pleading. "While I was driving to the bank, I ate a bag of chocolate-covered peanuts. For the endorphins for courage and tranquillity. You know! I gobbled them down like mad. I guess some of them fell onto my seat and rolled down and got attached to my trousers."

"And when she scooted around during our presentation, they brushed off her clothes and got stuck on the fabric of the chair!" Faye finished.

Alice wiped tears from her eyes. "And I thought I had problems when the underwire in my bra broke free when I was in a business meeting."

Marilyn blew her nose. "So did you get the loan?"

Polly nodded her head eagerly. "We *did*!"

For some reason, this set them off again. They laughed so hard Alice stuffed her napkin in her mouth to stifle herself and Shirley's breath turned into little mouse squeals.

Finally, they settled down.

"My stomach hurts," Faye sighed.

"Why weren't you there, Alice?" Marilyn asked. "I thought you were doing the accounting for Havenly Yours."

"She is," Polly explained. "But her doctors want her to avoid stressful situations. They said she can work at home, or at The Haven, with us, but nowhere else."

"Which is a shame," Alice added, "because I could have *handled* that banker."

"But it's good for us," Polly told her, "to learn how to

do that sort of thing." She patted her own shoulder. "I mean, I did manage to stay calm, cool, and collected. I did manage to present the business plan as if I actually had a brain. I'm really proud of myself, Alice, for doing something that's as easy as breathing for you."

Marilyn asked, "Alice, are you still allowed to play competitive bridge?"

Alice made a face. "Nope. Too stressful. They want me to wait a few months."

Polly decided this was a good time to ask her question. She turned to Shirley. "What's happening with Justin?"

Shirley rolled her eyes. "I haven't heard from him since the day after the Labor Day picnic."

"And his book?" Faye asked.

"Not going to happen. When I withdrew the second check and they knew no more money was coming, The Hemingway Group pulled the plug on publication."

"But what about the first ten thousand dollars Justin gave them?" Polly asked.

"Gone. The Hemingway Group kept that. I knew they would; it was in the contract Justin signed with them."

"Do you miss him?" Faye asked gently.

"Of course I do!" Shirley's eyes went moist.

Polly leaned over to give Shirley a little hug. "You'll meet someone else."

"I doubt it." Shirley dug a tissue from her purse and blew her nose. "In fact, I don't even want to. I've decided I'm going to be chaste."

Alice snorted. "Yeah, right."

"Oh, *stop* that!" Shirley elbowed Alice.

Faye turned to Marilyn. "How's Ian?"

Marilyn's face went blissful. *"Wonderful."*

"It must be hard with him on the other side of the Atlantic," Polly said.

"It is. I miss him so much. But we e-mail each other

several times a day, and we call each other a lot. And actually, since you asked—" Marilyn bit her lip.

Faye read her mind. "You want us to take care of Ruth while you visit him?"

"Could you?"

Polly and Faye nodded eagerly. "Sure," said Faye. "Ruth's adorable."

"Oh, you two are so wonderful! I don't know how I'll ever be able to thank you!"

"We both want to be bridesmaids at your wedding," Polly said.

Marilyn's face fell. "I don't know if that can ever happen. I mean, his work is in Edinburgh, and mine's here. Plus, there's Ruth. She's doing all right, living with me, but I couldn't move her to another country; it would be too hard on her."

The waiter arrived to take their dessert orders. Virtuously, they all ordered fruit bowls.

"While we're all here," Faye said, in a more serious voice, "I'd like to discuss something with you all, before we meet with the entire board of directors of The Haven. Polly and Alice and I have been discussing the employee benefit package for Havenly Yours. We think we'll need to hire six women."

"After we get it set up, Faye doesn't want to be involved with the day-to-day business," Polly told the others.

"I enjoyed making the first round of outfits," Faye explained. "It was challenging, and it was fun working with Polly. But I really don't enjoy sewing that much. I couldn't do it all day. And I wouldn't be any good, supervising others sewing, but Polly's made her living as a seamstress. She'd know what to do."

"So we're thinking four women at the sewing machines," Polly continued. "One woman at the cutting table. One to sweep, clean, carry, et cetera. We've already talked with some women we'd like to hire." She looked at Alice, who took over.

"They're friends of the women who clean The Haven. They're all Hispanic immigrants, and they're all young and eager to work. And they all have children."

"And we thought," Polly went on, "that since The Haven is so large, it would make sense to have a day-care room for the children. That would mean paying another employee to work as a caregiver, but the salary would be minimum wage."

"I really believe in having day care on the site." Alice automatically reverted to corporate-speak. "I was the one who pushed through child care at TransContinent Insurance, and it made an enormous difference to the welfare and productivity of our employees."

"I think it's a great idea," Shirley said.

"I do, too," Marilyn agreed.

Alice looked satisfied. "Good. We'll add it to the business plan. It's a surprisingly small sum, and I think it will pay off in employee satisfaction."

Shirley scoffed. "What you mean is, you're a big ol' softie, and you like the idea of making life better for workingwomen."

Alice smiled. "If you want to put it that way. But the directors will like it better it we phrase it in more businesslike terms."

"I'm going to miss working with you, Faye," Polly said.

Faye squeezed her hand. "I'll miss working with you."

"What are you going to do?" Shirley asked. "Want to teach art at The Haven?"

Faye shook her head. "I don't think so. Maybe in the winter. I'm in a kind of restless mood these days."

"How are things with Aubrey?" Marilyn asked.

Faye played with her fork. "Oh, I'm still seeing Aubrey.

We have a date every weekend, and we have a great time. Symphony. Ballet. Theater."

"But Carolyn keeps her father on a pretty tight leash," Polly added. "I thought she'd realize, when Faye and I spent every day all summer sewing together, that we're good friends. I've hinted in every way possible that I really like Hugh and have no interest in Aubrey. I've invited Carolyn and Hank to dinner several times, at my house, with me and Hugh, just the four of us, and I do everything but sit on Hugh's lap to make it clear that we're a couple. But Carolyn keeps inviting me to her house for dinner, and *not* inviting Hugh, and inviting Aubrey, but not Faye. I've started turning her down. I don't know what else to do!"

"She's a very stubborn young woman," Faye pointed out.

"Well, I'm a very stubborn *older* woman!" Polly retorted.

Shirley asked, "Faye, have you invited Carolyn to your home?"

Faye shook her head. "Carolyn's so standoffish with me. I know she dislikes me, or at least wants her father to be with Polly instead of me. I guess I'm just being cowardly—but no," she changed her mind midsentence— "I'm not cowardly. I just don't have the energy to deal with her."

"Have you considered taking antidepressants?" Alice had been wanting to ask this question for some time now.

Faye closed her eyes. "I have. But I'm already taking so many pills." Seeing all the concerned faces, she said, "Don't look so glum! I'm not suicidal! I'm just— restless."

"Or *resting*," Shirley suggested. "It's only been three years since your husband died. Plus, you're grieving over the loss of your daughter and granddaughter. Even though they're alive and well, they're on the other side of the continent, and really not part of your life. You know how sometimes you get a cold because your body wants to make you stop racing around and spend a few days in bed? Maybe this is the mental equivalent."

"Maybe," Faye agreed. "I do feel kind of empty. Like a well, drained."

"Maybe *you* need to take art therapy," Marilyn suggested.

"Shirley's got a point," Alice weighed in. "You used to paint. I've seen your paintings in your house. They're amazing. I'd love to buy one of your still lifes."

"I stopped painting after Jack died." Faye's face fell. "I *tried* to paint, but everything just was stale, *blah*. I think I've lost it, you know? Whatever my gift or talent was, it's dried up and vanished with my hormones."

"Are you sure?" Marilyn pressed. "You won't know until you try."

Faye fiddled with a button on her jacket. "I'll think about it." Wanting to change the subject, she turned to Alice. "How's Jennifer?"

"She's getting big." Alice beamed. "She's been wonderful to me since the heart attack. She's made so many casseroles, I never have to cook. The food's healthy, too. She's got a little problem with edema, so we're both on low-salt diets. I call her every day to remind her to lie down, put her feet up, and rest."

Shirley reached across the table to take Alice's hand. "Did I ever tell you how much I admire you for the way you've handled Alan's marriage?"

"Thanks, Shirl'. I guess I'm so used to giving commands and manipulating things to fit some work directive, I had to learn how to relax and accept what life throws my way. And thank heavens I met all of you. I couldn't have done it without you." Worry flittered across her face. "The damned thing is, now that I've let myself be open to Jennifer, I really like her. More than that, I *care* for her. When Steven's wife had their kids, they were living in another state, and I was glad to be a grandmother, but they were distant, I was busy with work, and I didn't get as involved. Now that I see Jennifer several times a week, I'm actually getting excited about this coming baby, and nervous as hell every time she tells me her feet are swelling."

Polly nodded. "I often thought that expression, 'Love means never having to say you're sorry,' really should be, 'Love means never feeling safe.'"

"No, no!" Shirley objected. "Remember, we're not going to let fear rule our lives!" She turned to Alice. "I have a number of herbal remedies for edema. Ginger's really good and can be used in all kinds of recipes. I'll make up a list you can give her."

Marilyn looked at her watch. "It's late. I should get home to Ruth."

"Give her a kiss for me," Faye told her. "And make your reservations for Scotland. I'm looking forward to spending time with her again."

"Me, too," Polly said.

"But don't leave until after next Tuesday," Shirley reminded Marilyn. "We've got The Haven's board of directors' meeting."

"Right." Marilyn beamed euphorically. "I'll make my reservations for Wednesday morning! I can't wait to see that man again!"

HALLOWEEN

20

"THAT WAS A LOVELY EXCURSION!" RUTH LEANED heavily on her cane as she and Faye came in from the cold.

"Glad you enjoyed it. Let me take your coat, Ruth, and then I'll light the fire."

"Thank you, dear." As Faye hung their coats in the closet, Ruth slowly toddled into the living room. "I just love this house. It's like a little bit of heaven."

Faye smiled. "I'm not sure I'd go that far."

But Ruth's praise made her see the room with fresh eyes, appreciating the opulent colors, rich fabrics, and harmonious arrangement of furniture. As Faye moved around her home, lighting the fire, turning on the lamps, setting the kettle to boil, she realized she was more content than she had been for a while, perhaps for months. It was pleasant, having Ruth around. It was not simply that Faye was less lonely; it was more as if her pleasures were doubled, because she saw how Ruth enjoyed the simplest events and objects of everyday life.

Faye stuck her head into the living room. "Ruth, what kind of tea would you like? Earl Grey or apple cinnamon?"

"Apple cinnamon, please, dear." Ruth's voice was muffled. She had established herself at the far end of the

sofa, slipped off her shoes, and pointed her gnarled feet
out toward the fire. Her head was bent almost inside her
knitting bag as she burrowed around, retrieving her needles and yarn.

Faye hummed as she prepared the tea tray. She loved
it when Ruth called her "dear" or "sweetie." It made
her feel young again, and very little could do that these
days. She was reminded of her grandmothers, especially
her mother's mother, who had smelled like lilacs and
willed Faye some beautiful brooches and elegant gloves.
By herself, Faye drank from a mug, but Ruth was a
guest, so Faye brought out her grandmother's Limoges
teapot and cups, and Ruth was thrilled with the thin
china and its translucence. Setting the quilted tea cozy,
patterned like a plump cat, over the steaming teapot made
having tea more of an *event*. It made her stop rushing
through her day and relax. She experienced it all more
fully: The spicy aroma of the tea. The dollhouse charm
of the silver spoons, tea strainer, sugar tongs, cups and
saucers. The clarity of the peaceful moment.

"Well, isn't this just beautiful!" Ruth exclaimed as
Faye set the tea tray on the low coffee table. "It's like
being in one of Sargent's still lifes! Look at the way the
firelight gleams on the silver."

Faye served the tea the way Ruth preferred it, with
one lump of sugar, and handed it to her, then settled
back in her armchair to toast her own feet at the fire.
"Would you like me to put on some music?" This was
Ruth's second night at Faye's. Ruth had been thrilled to
see Faye's CD collection of classical symphonies, and
yesterday evening they'd listened to Sibelius's Fifth Symphony.

"Not just yet, dear," Ruth said. "I'm rather enjoying
hearing the wind howl. It makes me feel so smug, sitting
here, warm by the fire. Besides, don't we need to go over
the final arrangements for the party?"

"Oh, right." Faye pulled a pad and pen from her purse, tucked her fire-warmed feet up under her, and flipped the pad open.

At Ruth's instigation, Faye had decided to give a "Come as Your Favorite Person in History" dinner party on Halloween weekend. She'd drawn clever invitations and mailed them out, planned the menu—chili, jalapeño cornbread muffins, a green salad, and a Hot Flash cake—and was in the process of making decorations. Construction paper, scissors, and glue were spilled across the dining room table in various states of transformation into moons, black cats, witches, and ghosts.

Faye read over the list. "I've got everything for the dinner except the salad bits. I'll get those on Friday. Oh, and we have to decide on costumes for ourselves. Who are you going as, Ruth?"

"Madame Curie," Ruth announced decisively. "Not only did she discover radium, she worked with her husband, had two children, and won *two* Nobel Prizes. Oh, yes, and after she was widowed, she was involved in a scandalous love affair." Ruth smiled. "A real rain essence woman. Who will you be, Faye?"

Faye rearranged her legs beneath her. "I haven't decided."

"Why don't you come as one of the early women painters?" Ruth inquired. "Mary Cassatt? Rosa Bonheur?"

Faye looked deep into her teacup. "I don't paint anymore, Ruth."

"Yes, you've said." Ruth contemplated the large, gilt-framed, luminous still life above the fireplace, a bouquet of summer flowers. "You create such beauty, Faye. You have such talent. What a pity you've given up!"

Faye bit back a flash of anger. "It's not that I've 'given up.' It's more that *it* gave *me* up after my husband died."

Tears burned her eyes. "I did try. But nothing I did looked right. Everything was just bland. Lackluster."

"I understand."

The quaver in Ruth's voice made Faye look at her. "Are you all right, Ruth?"

"Oh, yes, dear, I'm fine." With a trembling hand, Ruth set her cup on her saucer. "It's just that I was trying to build up the courage to ask you a favor, but now . . ."

"What is it, Ruth?" Faye leaned forward, concerned.

"Oh, it's just silly." Ruth paid great attention to her knitting needles, her knobby fingers tangling the yarn.

"Maybe, maybe not," Faye said sensibly. "Tell me, and I'll decide."

Ruth peered shyly at Faye. "I was hoping you might paint my portrait."

"Oh." This was the last thing Faye could have imagined Ruth would ask.

Ruth blushed with embarrassment, her twisted hands fluttering in the air, as if she were trying to shoo her request away. "I know, it's ridiculous of me even to think of such a thing. I mean, no one paints portraits of old biddies like me. Well, unless they're someone *important,* like Queen Elizabeth or Elizabeth Trailer."

"It's not that—" Faye protested.

"It's just that all my life I've longed to have my portrait painted. Conceited of me, I know. I'm certainly not beautiful. I never was beautiful. But now that I have a great-granddaughter, I'd like to leave her something to remember me by, and a portrait gives a person so much more dignity than a photograph, don't you think? I mean, I'm not *someone* to the world, but I could be *someone* to my great-granddaughter. I'd like to give her—what do I mean? An illusion? Something to dream by." Ruth smoothed the loose flesh of her liver-spotted, bony hand. "Silly old woman," she muttered to herself.

Pity pierced Faye's heart. It felt much like a cupid's

arrow, stinging as it filled her, like an enormous invisible IV, with a kind of hopeless love and longing. Faye knew exactly what Ruth meant, because Faye thought the same kind of thing about her granddaughter Megan. She wanted to provide a kind of *message* to this child of her blood and love and history. Perhaps it was a desire bred in one's DNA, as tightly knit as the yarn in Ruth's endless scarf.

Faye swallowed a sip of tea, washing down the lump in her throat. "Well, Ruth, if you didn't mind that it's not a *good* portrait—"

Ruth looked up, her face childish with joy. "You'll do it?"

"Of course I will."

Faye didn't have a studio in her new home. When she'd bought the house, she was sure she'd never paint again. So the morning after Ruth's request, Faye walked through all the rooms with a judgmental eye, looking for the best natural light. Megan's bedroom won hands down, having the most windows and a northern exposure. With a mixture of sadness and satisfaction, Faye set about tacking plain white sheets up over the childish murals she'd painted. She rolled up the flowered rug and shoved it under the bed. She moved all the furniture into one corner, opening up a space large enough for her easel and the chair where Ruth would pose.

She wrestled the armchair in from her bedroom and placed it in the light, then asked Ruth to try it out for comfort.

"It's comfortable enough," the older woman said. "But I don't feel right, with my hands empty."

"Let's get your knitting!" Faye turned to go out the door.

"No," Ruth said firmly. "Knitting isn't right. And I don't want to be just sitting here, like a lump on a frog."

Faye blinked. "Well, then—I've got it!" Suddenly she was excited, as ideas swarmed into her mind. "We'll create a kind of scientific tableau. I'll have to borrow someone's microscope, and—and—"

Ruth understood at once. "Faye, that's a brilliant idea! We'll search Marilyn's storage locker. She's got her old microscope there, and all kinds of equipment. I think she's saved some of her early nature corrections, too."

The next day, Ruth accompanied Faye as she rushed around, lugging paraphernalia from Marilyn's locker, carrying a kitchen stool up to the bedroom, balancing a small end table on two encyclopedias to make it the right height. Finally she had the scene set: Ruth, wearing a shirt and glasses, bent over what could pass as a lab table, a microscope at her right hand, a pen, pad, ruler, scale, beakers, and collection jars at her left. Just behind her, on another table, lay several birds' nests, a mineral hammer, a specimen box, a pile of books, and a pair of binoculars. Before she began, Faye took a few Polaroid shots to show Ruth, who was delighted with the tableau.

"This is the real me!" she said. "Thank you, Faye."

Ruth was supposed to move to Polly's for the last five days of Marilyn's trip, but Faye asked Polly if she would mind if Ruth stayed at her house, because of the portrait, and Polly gladly agreed. She had her hands full, running Havenly Yours. Still, Polly insisted on providing dinner. Sometimes she arrived with carry-out food; sometimes she brought groceries and cooked in Faye's kitchen.

In the autumn evenings, the three women sat together, lingering over pork roast stuffed with apples and onions, or scallop bisque and pumpkin bread, indulging in a glass or two of wine, enjoying the light of the candles Polly set on the mantel and the table. Storms shook the windows as the play of shadows cast a dreamy mood. Polly and Faye asked Ruth about her life, and Ruth regaled them with bits of history, the years vanishing from her face as she talked.

"Oh, yes, I had fun as a young woman. I got to wear tipsy hats covered with glitter and beads to nightclubs. Black wool suits with huge splatters of rhinestones on the lapels. Bright red lipstick. Shoulder pads. I danced at The Stardust and The Blue Moon, and—don't tell Marilyn this, she might be upset—I promised five different men I'd marry them."

Polly and Faye were shocked.

"Well, dears, it was because of the war, don't you know. Those brave young men, going across the ocean to a foreign land to fight, not knowing whether they'd come back. I wanted to give them hope. I wrote them long letters and sent them parcels of food I'd cooked myself and gloves and socks I'd knit myself."

"Did you ever—" Polly hesitated, wondering how to ask this politely. "Were they ever, any of them, um—your lover?"

Ruth looked puzzled. "No, dear. I didn't have a brother. I did have a sister." Her face brightened. "Anyway, toward the end of the war, I met Marilyn's father. I knew at once he was the man for me. We married six weeks after we met."

Later, after Ruth had toddled off to bed, Faye whispered, "Perhaps Ruth needs a hearing aid."

"Perhaps," Polly agreed. "Or perhaps," she grinned, "she just didn't want to answer our question."

21

Wednesday evening, Alice lifted a gold circlet from its box.

She was dressing to go to the new, noncompetitive, pleasantly low-key bridge group she and Gideon had joined. Last week, for her birthday, her daughter-in-law Jennifer had surprised her with a dinner party and a gift Alice would never have expected: an ankle bracelet.

"I'm too old to wear an ankle bracelet!" Alice had protested, but secretly, she was pleased. She'd never worn an ankle bracelet before.

Now she bent to fasten it around her ankle. Its delicate links and tiny dangles gleamed playfully. She couldn't help smiling. No one could see it beneath her long trousers, but *she* knew it was there.

During the evening, she remembered it and felt oddly pleased. Her poor old aching feet might be bumpy with bunions and misshapen from years of wearing pointed high heels, they might be tucked away in comfortable, sensible sneakers, but her ankles were still trim and attractive. In fact, her legs were still good. She wanted to go shopping. She would buy some skirts and show off her legs! Distracted by such thoughts, Alice played bridge so badly she and Gideon lost most of the rubbers, but she didn't really mind.

Although Gideon kept his apartment, he spent most nights at Alice's, and when they returned from bridge they got ready for bed, even though it was not quite ten o'clock. Usually she enjoyed this comfortable routine, but now as she pulled on her warm flannel pajamas, the ankle bracelet sparkled at her. She felt oddly—*playful.*

Gideon was already in bed with a book, his pillows stuffed up behind him. Alice's book and glasses lay waiting on her bedside table. Alice lifted the covers and slipped in next to him.

"What do you think about Faye's Halloween party?" she asked.

"Sounds like fun," Gideon responded absentmindedly.

"I mean, who do you think you'll go as?"

Gideon lay his book on his lap. "I'm not sure. My favorite person in history? I don't know. I admire so many men. Frederick Douglass, I guess."

A hot flash hit Alice. Kicking off the covers, she pulled her legs up and wrapped her arms around her knees. The bracelet glinted around her ankle—a little beacon.

"You know who I'd really like to pretend to be?" Alice was surprised at how difficult it was to confess this to the man with whom she shared so many intimacies. "Cleopatra."

Gideon peered over the top of his glasses. "Cleopatra!"

"She's not the woman I admire most, but she would be so much *fun* to impersonate. I always thought she was so glamorous and mysterious. Not to mention brilliant and cunning. She ruled Egypt. She seduced Antony with her beauty." Suddenly Alice was completely mortified—to think she could masquerade as Cleopatra! "I've got to get some water."

In the bathroom she filled a glass, then held it to her

neck, cooling off. *Alice, you really are an idiot,* she scolded herself.

She couldn't even look at Gideon when she got back into bed. "Anyway," she began briskly, "I suppose—"

"You know, I'd love to go as Marc Antony," Gideon announced, to her complete surprise.

"You're kidding!"

"No, I'm not. As a kid, I used to fantasize about being a gladiator. I wouldn't want to be Caesar—he got assassinated. But I could really enjoy being Antony, especially if you were Cleopatra."

"Oh, Gideon!" Alice giggled. "This could be fun!"

Over the next week, they indulged in a kind of Egyptian-history orgy. On the DVD player, they watched the movie starring Elizabeth Taylor and Richard Burton. Inspired, intrigued, they spent a day at the Egyptian rooms at the Museum of Fine Arts. Getting into the spirit of things, they ate in several Middle Eastern restaurants. They visited costume shops, trying on different possibilities, unable to suppress their pleasure as the age-old, childish game of dress-up made them envision themselves anew. They brought home books and videos about Egyptian tombs and treasures. They discussed the possibility of traveling to Egypt to view the pyramids.

Because Gideon had been a schoolteacher before he retired, he suggested they read Shakespeare's *Antony and Cleopatra* aloud in the evenings. At first Alice felt awkward, even silly, but soon the power of the story, told in Shakespeare's intense, opulent language, drew her in. When they read of the extravagant barge with purple sails and silver oars bearing Cleopatra to Antony, Alice was captivated. She closed her eyes and allowed herself to be carried away when Gideon, in his deep, sonorous voice, read the famous lines: "Age cannot wither her, nor custom stale Her infinite variety; other women cloy

The appetites they feed, but she makes hungry Where
most she satisfies."

The night of Faye's Halloween party, Alice stood in
front of her bedroom mirror, scowling. She'd insisted on
sharing a bottle of wine with Gideon as they dressed. It
was one thing to try on costumes in privacy, quite another to appear in front of other people, especially her
friends, masquerading as one of history's most glamorous women. And at her age!

"Ready?" Gideon stepped out of the bathroom, adjusting his armor.

Alice wore a gold lamé tunic, cut low. A heavy half-
circle collar of faux gold and turquoise gleamed against
her chest. On her head was a wig of hundreds of beaded
tight black braids that made tantalizing clicks as she
moved. Set in the wig was a gold crown centered with an
asp. Snake bracelets wound up her bare arms. On her
feet she wore jeweled sandals, and just above, her ankle
bracelet. She'd painted her toenails gold.

Gideon wore a white tunic that ended just above his
knee. Leather straps of Roman sandals wrapped all the
way up his calves, exposing his sturdy, masculine legs.
Over his chest he wore a light, metallic shield. A red
cape hung from his shoulders. A gold laurel wreath circled his head.

"Alice, I swear, you make a dynamite Cleopatra."

"Thanks. You're a pretty snazzy Antony."

"I like your wig and the headpiece." As Gideon spoke,
he brushed his fingers against her neck. The beaded
braids whispered. "And the eye makeup, well, it suits
you, Alice."

She'd borrowed a book from the library and copied
the long, slanted black lines that exaggerated the size
and shape of her eyes. "Thanks, Gideon." She leaned
against him, studying their reflections in the mirror.

"But you know, I've learned something. I'm glad I live now, even as a humble wage-earner, rather than back then, even as queen."

Gideon grinned. "Because we've got movies, air-conditioning, and chocolate?"

"Well, yes, but also because we've got deodorant, soap, and antibiotics. Did you know, Gideon, in centuries past, people used to have wigs for their pubic hair? Called merkins. Because people had to shave off their hair because of lice, or lost it because of syphilis."

Gideon shuddered. "You know the strangest things."

"Marilyn told me." Alice accepted his embrace, her hair clicking, her tunic whispering as she moved. Wrapping her arms around him, she leaned her head against his chest. "And remember, Cleopatra lived only thirty-nine years." She hugged her sturdy, stocky friend and lover. "Plus, she never knew *you*."

Gideon tightened his arms around her and kissed the top of her head. "Alice. What a very nice thing to say!"

22

"THIS WAS A BRILLIANT IDEA!" QUEEN GUINEVERE told Zelda Fitzgerald as they stood side by side in Faye's living room, holding cups of mulled apple cider spiced with cinnamon and cloves and just a soupçon of rum.

"Thanks." Faye surveyed her party with pleasure. "Too bad Marilyn's not here."

"Oh, I don't know," Polly said. "I'm pretty sure Marilyn is quite happy to be in Scotland with Ian."

Lucille Ball swept up to them, a cup of alcohol-free cider in her hand. "Faye, this is so much fun! And thanks for inviting the board members of The Haven."

"I'm delighted to do it," Faye told Shirley. "I'd like to get to know some of them better. Like old Nora Salter. She's so cool, coming as Agatha Christie."

Polly leaned in to say, *sotto voce,* "Look at her over there on the sofa, head to head with Madame Curie. I'd love to know what they're talking about."

Faye grinned. "It's a good bet they're not discussing their bunions."

"I had a hard time deciding who I wanted to be," Shirley confessed. "If you want to know the pathetic truth, I wanted to come as Cinderella. I've always wanted to be Cinderella . . . in her ball gown, *not* in her

apron days! But since I'm Prince Charming–less, I settled on Lucille Ball."

"You won't be Prince Charming–less long," Faye pre-
dicted.

"I'm not so sure about that," Shirley told her, adding,
"Now that I'm single, I can really empathize with you,
Faye. You were so brave, dating all those men we forced
you to go out with last year. We *thought* we were doing
the right thing."

"You probably *were* doing the right thing," Faye admitted. "I needed to have a few starter boyfriends. It
helped me realize a bad date wasn't the end of the world,
and it certainly made me appreciate Aubrey!"

"I see that his daughter and her husband are here."
Shirley turned slightly, and kept her voice low. "That's
good, right?"

"Oh, absolutely. She's *got* to see how much of a *couple* Polly and Hugh are—"

"Queen Guinevere and King Arthur!" Polly, who had
overheard them, made a little curtsy. "And you and
Aubrey are F. Scott and Zelda Fitzgerald. So different!"

"The Fitzgeralds were Aubrey's idea," Faye informed
them. "He wanted to get his father's old tux out of the
closet. And Polly helped me pull together this flapper
costume. I must say I love the way it skims my waist,
and shows off my legs. And all the long ropes of pearls
camouflage my stomach."

"You look smashing," Polly told her.

"Well, I probably look more like Eleanor Roosevelt
than Zelda Fitzgerald, but it's still fun to dress up."

Shirley adjusted a button earring pinching her ear. "I
think you both have your hands full, trying to have your
way against Carolyn's wishes."

The three women nodded ruefully. Carolyn had come
as Superwoman, her husband as Superman.

"What are you three gossiping about?" Cleopatra swept up to them.

"Geez Louise!" Shirley exclaimed. "You look like a million dollars, Alice."

"It's true," Faye agreed. "You make a gorgeous Cleopatra."

"Yeah, and you're absolutely radiant!" Polly gushed.

Jennifer and Alan approached. Because Jennifer wasn't feeling terribly energetic these days, they hadn't given much thought to their Halloween personae but simply cut holes in white sheets, made halos of aluminum foil, and came as angels. Now Alan had a supporting arm around Jennifer's waist.

"This is a great party, but we're going to leave," Alan said.

Alice's eyes flew to Jennifer. "Are you all right?"

Jennifer looked embarrassed. "Oh, I'm fine, really. I just have a bit of a headache." Turning to Faye, she said, "Your party is wonderful, Faye. So clever. And the food's delicious."

"Thanks." Faye looked concerned. "I hope you're not coming down with a flu."

Alice put a gentle hand on Jennifer's forehead. "You don't feel like you have a temperature."

Jennifer's halo slipped down over one ear. "Oh, I'm fine, I'm sure. It's just this headache, and I'm having a little problem with swollen ankles."

"Have you mentioned this to your doctor?" Alice asked.

"Oh, sure. It's all right. I'll be better when I lie down." Jennifer waved her hand dismissively.

"Elevate your feet," Faye and Polly simultaneously advised.

"And Alan," Alice said to her son, "you wait on her hand and foot, okay?"

Alan made a comic bow. "Absolutely."

All four women walked Alan and Jennifer to the door. They stood on the porch, waving good-bye, so they were all together when an old truck pulled up and Polly's son David and his wife Amy stepped out.

"Amy! David!" Polly was over the moon. She didn't think they'd actually deign to come. "How wonderful to see you both!" She introduced her friends to her son and his wife.

Faye smiled invitingly. "Let me show you both to the drinks table. We've got spiked apple cider, and plain cider, too. And let me guess who you are—"

"Ma and Pa Kettle?" Alice's eyes glinted mischievously. "The Beverly Hillbillies?"

"No!" Amy's mouth pursed with displeasure. "We're Charles and Caroline Ingalls!"

Polly looked puzzled. "Um . . ."

"From *Little House on the Prairie*!" Amy looked offended.

"Of course!" Faye rushed to appease the stern younger woman. "That would have been my first guess! I'm so glad you came. How is little Jehoshaphat?"

Polly took a deep breath. Faye's question was perfect. Amy and David both lit up like lamps, chatting away as fast as they could, describing their son's latest prodigal achievements.

Finally their conversation ran down and they just stood there, holding glasses of alcohol-free cider, looking slightly puzzled and not particularly interested in their surroundings.

"Come meet Teddy and his wife, Lila," Alice invited, in a fit of inspiration. "They have a little girl about your son's age." Linking arms with Amy and David, she led them into the living room, making a funny face over her shoulder at Polly, Faye, and Shirley.

Beautiful Lila had come as the gorgeous seductress Delilah, with a slinky, revealing gown, bracelets high on her arms, and heavy makeup. Teddy wore a shield, white tunic, and leather thongs. He'd pulled a bare wig on over his own thinning hair in order to look like Samson after he was shorn, and the result was surprisingly attractive. Together, he and his wife looked exotic and sexy.

"Maybe introducing them isn't such a good idea," Polly murmured. "Amy is such a little prig, and Lila looks so sensual."

"Wait and see," Faye soothed Polly.

"And don't expect a great friendship to develop," added Shirley, who was feeling rather pessimistic these days. "They couldn't be more different."

Polly helped herself to another cup of spiked cider. "Amy is so damned *pure*. She'll think gorgeous Lila looks like a harlot, and probably drag poor David from the party."

"You're wrong!" Faye whispered to Polly. "Turn around! Look!"

Polly obeyed. The wholesome farm couple and the glamorous biblical lovers were retrieving photos from pockets and purses, passing them around, babbling and bonding as they shared pictures and anecdotes about their children.

Alice returned to fill her own glass of cider. "Well, Faye," she grinned, "I think we can safely say this party is officially a success." Her eyes dropped. "Although I am a little worried about Jennifer."

"She'll be fine," Faye assured her.

"I hope so," Alice said fervently.

THANKSGIVING

23

THE AFTERNOON SKY LOOMED LOW AND GRAY, THREAT-ening rain. As Alice and Gideon drove along the winding country road, a cold, intermittent wind flickered and gusted, making the fallen leaves heaped in the gutters suddenly skitter and jump like small, darting creatures. Tree boughs, bare and brittle, clattered and dipped toward the car like the animated trees in *The Wizard of Oz*.

It made Alice's nerves itch. She was cranky, when she knew she should be grateful. Damn it, she *was* grateful. She counted her blessings every night as she fell asleep, and reminded herself of them during the day, every day.

First, her sons were happy. Steven, down in Texas, communicated with her more than ever now that e-mail existed, and in January, Alice and Gideon both were going to visit Steven's family, which she hadn't done in years.

And Alan—well! Alan loved running the bakery and catering service—something Alice had never *dreamed* he would do, although given how much *she* loved food, why was she so surprised? And she had to admit, Alan was in love with his wife, and Jennifer obviously loved him deeply. They had only one more month to wait for the birth of their child—and here Alice's breath caught in her throat.

Jennifer had been diagnosed with preeclampsia and ordered to remain in bed for the rest of her pregnancy, which was why Alan was cooking the turkey but Gideon and Alice were bringing most of the Thanksgiving dinner out to the caretaker's cottage at The Haven. Alice had researched preeclampsia on the Internet, and what she'd learned had terrified her. It was a serious condition involving high blood pressure, protein in the urine, water retention, headaches, severe nausea, rapid heartbeat, and other uncomfortable and life-threatening problems. The child could die—or the mother.

Dear God, please let Jennifer and the baby be okay, Alice prayed. It was so frustrating for Alice not to be able to *do* something, to *fix* this problem, to take charge! That was what she'd done all her life both at home and professionally, but now she was utterly helpless. And it was driving her totally nuts!

She felt her heartbeat accelerate. Damn it! Deep breaths, she reminded herself. Deep, deep breaths. Shirley had said to breathe right down to her asshole. And think positive thoughts.

All right then. Well, she was healthy, more or less, as long as she took her medicine and exercised regularly and watched what she ate, although the thought of limiting caloric intake during Thanksgiving and Christmas seemed to her like some kind of sadistic joke. Go back to the Gratitude List, she told herself.

Well—*Gideon!* This burly, sweet man driving the car was a wonderful companion, friend, and lover. They had great fun together, playing bridge, attending movies and the symphony, or just lounging around the apartment, reading, listening to music, watching TV. And his health was good these days.

And her friends were amazing. She'd never had such close friends since her school days. She loved the sense of belonging to a group, especially this group, which made her laugh and kept her involved with the real world. She'd been afraid of retirement, fearing she'd feel useless, but with them she had more than enough work to do. She was on the board of The Haven, plus she'd helped get the business side of Havenly Yours set up, although she'd refused to take on the full-time job of bookkeeper.

Now she thought perhaps that had been a mistake. Because with all the richness in her life, Alice still felt a kind of gap, something not sharp enough to be called pain, something more like a sense of longing. She didn't feel *complete* yet. And she *had* felt complete for great hunks of her life, especially when she was working and raising her sons. But work and intellectual stimulation didn't fill that void these days; she'd given it her all, and still, even when immersed in calculations for some budget, she'd raise her head from her computer and gaze at the sun on the windowsill, and sit very still, almost *listening,* as if she'd just heard someone whisper her name.

"Alice?" Now Gideon actually did call her name, tugging her back into the present. "We're here." He undid his seat belt and peered at her. "Are you okay?"

"Oh, I'm fine. Just daydreaming." Impulsively, she leaned over and kissed his mouth. "I love you, Gideon."

"And I love you, Alice," Gideon replied with a smile, "but at the moment it's the aroma of the pumpkin pie that's making me drool."

"Fickle!" Alice scolded playfully. "Okay, let's go eat."

Alan came out of the house, hugged his mother, shook hands with Gideon, and helped them carry in the casseroles and pans.

Alice set the large, wooden salad bowl on the kitchen counter. Without taking off her coat, she hurried into the living room to see Jennifer, who reclined on the sofa in loose pants and one of the Havenly Yours jackets Alice had given her.

"Hello, honey." Alice bent down to kiss Jennifer's cheek. "You look beautiful!" But Jennifer's face was far too flushed, and she clearly was uncomfortable. "How do you feel?" She perched on the coffee table so she could take her daughter-in-law's hand. "Tell me true."

Jennifer smiled. "I'm glad to see you, Alice. Poor Alan's so worried, he's buzzing around me like a drunk mosquito. With you here, he'll calm down."

Alice cocked her head. "I'm sure he will. But you didn't answer my question. How are you?"

Jennifer's face grew serious. "I'm okay, I think. It's best if I just lie here, not moving, but that makes me feel like such a wimp. But if I try to do anything, the nausea and headaches start up again."

"How's your blood pressure?" Alice picked up the little home monitor lying on the table.

"We just took it. It's okay. Elevated, but not dangerous." Jennifer shifted impatiently on the sofa. "It's so boring, just talking about my health!"

"Hello!" Gideon came into the room, bending to kiss Jennifer's cheek. "You look like the bell curve, lying there."

"I feel more like a hot air balloon," Jennifer joked in reply.

"Take your coat off, Mom," Alan suggested. "The turkey's ready. I thought we'd all fix our plates and bring them in here, so Jenny won't have to move."

"Good idea." Alice squeezed Jennifer's hand.

In the kitchen, she tossed the salad while Gideon poured three glasses of wine and one of water. As Alan lifted the small turkey onto the platter and began slicing it, Alice watched him out of the corner of her eye. He was moving just a bit too quickly, just as he'd rushed them into eating now instead of enjoying a relaxing few moments of conversation. He was anxious, of course he was; he wanted to get this day over, and the next, and every day until his child was safely brought into the world. *Slow down,* Alice wanted to advise him, but she kept her mouth shut. The last thing he needed was a nagging mother.

Back in the living room, Alan adjusted Jennifer's pillows, lifting her into a sitting position so she could eat. He brought her a tray with a small plate of food, placed a pillow beneath her feet, then stood back to scrutinize her.

"Sit down, Alan." Jennifer flapped her hands at him. "Enjoy your turkey!"

The baby wasn't due until late December. Alice dutifully lifted her fork to her mouth, but worry dulled her senses. Jennifer wasn't going to last another month; that was obvious. Perhaps she and Gideon shouldn't have come; perhaps their mere presence was elevating Jennifer's blood pressure just that little bit more. Should they leave? God, what could she do?

"Did you know," Gideon said conversationally, "Faye's flown out to California to have Thanksgiving with her grandchildren?"

"Oh, I'm so glad," Jennifer said. "I know Faye misses her daughter a lot."

Thank God for Gideon. With the focus off Jennifer, Alice's own blood pressure dropped. She added, "Laura invited her out there for two weeks. Lars's parents, who've moved out there, are going on a cruise, so Faye will have Laura and Megan and the new little baby all to herself."

"Who's Aubrey spending Thanksgiving with?" Alan asked.

Alice snorted. "Who does Aubrey spend *every* holiday with? His daughter Carolyn. She's such a spoiled brat! She *insisted* that Polly come, too, because Polly's Elizabeth's godmother."

"Then where's Hugh having the holiday?" Jennifer inquired.

"With his kids, which means with his clingy little ex-wife Carol."

"I wonder," Gideon mused, sipping his wine, "which is worse, to be involved in family conflicts or to be without a family, like Shirley."

Alan took a bite of Alice's salad. "Good, Mom. Where's Shirley spending Thanksgiving?"

"With Marilyn and Ruth." Alice thought for a moment. "I'm not sure whether Marilyn and Ruth will be seeing Marilyn's granddaughter today or not. There's another difficult daughter-in-law."

"It's not Lila who's difficult," Gideon corrected her mildly. "It's Lila's mother, Eugenie."

Alan looked thoughtful. "Whatever happened to that guy Marilyn was dating—Faraday?"

Alice and Gideon exchanged glances. Alice had told Gideon about Faraday passing out on Marilyn, and they'd shared a good laugh, but it would be uncharitable to gossip about it. Although it was pretty funny.

Gideon said, "Faraday and Marilyn broke up. Too bad, because he was a good guy."

"Yeah," Alice added, "but Marilyn was never in love with him like she is with this Ian guy. With him, she's really found the love of her life, and she deserves some happiness. She was such a dutiful wife, I think she believed marriage was the same for everyone, sort of like plain bread, necessary but tasteless. With Ian, she's getting the bread PLUS a great big helping of strawberry jam."

"Trust you to use a food metaphor," Gideon teased Alice.

"Alan?" Jennifer's weak voice interrupted their lighthearted banter. "Alan—I'm going to—" Shuddering, she vomited all over her plate and her clothes.

In a flash, Alan was at her side. "Jenny, honey—"

Alice hurried into the kitchen, returning with a roll of paper towels and a wastebasket. Alan handed her Jennifer's plate and used a towel to wipe his wife's face.

"Alan." Jennifer's eyes were wide. "I feel . . . terrible. I'm so dizzy, and I've got a pain in my side, and my head . . ."

"Hospital," Alice said. "Now."

Alan supported Jennifer's head in gentle hands. "Is that what you want?"

Tears streamed down Jennifer's red face. "Yes. Please. Oh, Alan, I'm so frightened!"

"I'll call 911," Alice said.

"Maybe it would be faster if we drove her there," Alan said.

Alice bit her tongue just one millisecond to keep from yelling. In as calm a voice as she could muster, she said, "An EMT would know what to do right away. They'd be able to give her an IV. But whichever way you two want—"

"Ambulance," Jennifer said. "Please."

24

TOWARD EVENING, THE SKY FINALLY SPLIT APART, showering the New England area with thin, sharp raindrops that promised to change to sleet at any moment. Inside Marilyn's condo, it was warm and peaceful. Marilyn had roasted a turkey and set the table with a white cloth, china, and silver. Shirley had brought lots of vegetable dishes and a gorgeous centerpiece she'd made from autumn leaves and a few hardy roses and mums from the grounds of The Haven.

So much beauty, Shirley thought, such luxury! She refused to let herself mope simply because she wasn't with Justin. Because she wasn't with *any* man.

She'd wakened cranky, and grumbled through her lonely morning in her empty condo in The Haven's enormous edifice. Today the old stone building's elegance and solidity made her feel shabby and temporary. How had it happened, that of the five Hot Flash Club women, she, Shirley, the only one who couldn't have alcohol, was also the only one who didn't have a man? It wasn't fair! She was in the best shape of them all, with her limber, slender body. And she liked sex and loved men more than the others, too; she was sure of that. Plus, the other four all had children and grandchildren to love. Shirley didn't have any of that. She just felt so *rejected* by Fate!

Still, she'd forced herself to dress up and drag her unwanted, pathetic old body over to Marilyn's condo, and she was going to be a regular little ball of good cheer if it killed her.

And now that she was here, she was glad. She loved Marilyn, even if Marilyn had just returned from Scotland where she no doubt screwed her brains out with that man she adored, and Ruth was always a pleasure to be around. Shirley helped Marilyn carry in the food, and then took her place at the laden dinner table.

"Well, here we are!" Ruth wore a dark green sweater patterned with autumn leaves. She looked around the table, her wrinkled old face radiant with pleasure. She beamed at Shirley and Marilyn. "The three little figs!"

"Pigs." Marilyn sliced a tender strip of meat off the turkey breast and lay it, with its golden brown, salt-and-pepper–speckled skin, on her mother's plate.

"The three graces, I would say," Shirley amended.

Ruth glanced up from a bowl of sweet potatoes. "Just who *were* the three graces?"

"Goddesses from early Greek mythology," Shirley told her. "I can't remember their Greek names, but they stood for um, let me think: Brilliance or Splendor was one. Joy. And something like Optimism."

"Would you like sweet potatoes?" Ruth held out the bowl. "Were they young or old?"

"Young, I think."

Ruth spooned pecan-onion-apple stuffing onto her plate. "But with names like that, they could be any age, right?"

"Sure," Shirley agreed. "Why not?"

Ruth took a bit of creamed spinach. "Oh, Shirley, this is delicious." She nibbled on her roll, then observed, "Not many girls named Grace anymore."

"Fashions change." Shirley helped herself to the stuffing Marilyn had made especially for her, in a pan, with butter instead of turkey drippings. "Not many are named Shirley, either."

"Nor Ruth," Ruth said. "Nor Vagina."

"Regina," Marilyn quietly revised, using the British pronunciation.

Ruth cocked her head. "And they name girls such strange things these days. Like that beautiful actress with the big lips—Harlot Johnson."

"Scarlett Johansson," Shirley said quietly, flashing a smile at Marilyn.

Marilyn didn't respond to Shirley's smile, which made Shirley feel awful for just a moment. Did Marilyn think Shirley was making fun of Ruth? But now that Shirley paused to really look at Marilyn, she realized that Marilyn looked tired. Old. Absolutely *dragged down,* a look Shirley saw in the mirror all too often but had never before seen on Marilyn.

"Marilyn," Shirley said, "I haven't spoken with you since you went to Scotland. How was your trip?"

"Oh, it was fine." Marilyn didn't lift her eyes from her plate.

Shirley hesitated. "Oh. Well, how's Ian?"

Marilyn made a noise, an odd little moan. Still she would not meet Shirley's eyes. "He's fine. He's busy with his work." Her chin trembled. "I'll just get some more gravy." Lifting the gravy boat, she disappeared into the kitchen.

Bastard! Shirley thought, suddenly flaming with anger. Men were all alike everywhere; you couldn't trust any of them. Oh, Shirley knew all too well the signs of a woman betrayed.

Ruth patted Shirley's hand to get her attention. "Two termites walk into a bar. What do they say?"

"Um—" Shirley forced a smile. "I don't know. What do they say?"

"Is the bar tender here?" All the wrinkles on Ruth's face lifted up as she smiled.

"Very funny," Shirley chuckled.

"Oh, I've got lots more of those. Marilyn's father always had a slew of wonderful jokes. His students loved him."

Marilyn returned, her face composed, but guarded. Now that Shirley took a moment to study her friend, she realized that Marilyn, who had never been a clothes-horse, looked more—more downright *dowdy* than Shirley had ever seen her. Her gray sweater hung on her—why, Marilyn had lost weight! Shirley sent an urgent glance of concern toward her friend, who shook her head slightly and leaned over her mother. "More gravy, Mom?"

"Thank you, dear. I was just telling Cheryl about your father. He was so handsome, wasn't he? And as smart, I swear, as Allen Einstein. He could have gone on for a Ph.D., but he loved teaching high school–age students. So did I. We spent so much time concocting experiments!"

What could Shirley do to help Marilyn? God, Marilyn looked so tired! She looked *whipped*. Ruth was looking at Shirley expectantly. "Tell me about them," Shirley urged.

Ruth's face lit up. For the rest of the meal, she recounted the pleasures she'd shared with her husband, creating ant houses and aquarium tanks, sweeping nets and rearing cages for the butterflies, moths, caterpillars, turtles, reptiles, and lizards studied in the classroom. Equally fascinating to Ruth and her husband were water fleas, leeches, roaches, and bats. Well, Shirley thought, this explains a lot about Marilyn.

"Mother," Marilyn said, when she could get a word in, "would you like any more turkey? Or stuffing?"

"Oh, no, dear, thank you. I'm full." Suddenly Ruth's rosy face sagged. "In fact, I believe I'm just a little tired. All this chattering away I've been doing . . ." She looked at Marilyn, confused.

Marilyn took her mother's hand. "Would you like dessert now, Mother? Pumpkin pie?" When her mother didn't answer right away, she suggested, "Or perhaps a little nap? Wouldn't a little rest feel good?"

"Yes, dear. That's a good idea." Ruth's voice quavered, and when she tried to rise from her chair, her arms trembled.

Marilyn and Shirley jumped to assist her up.

"It's awful, getting old." Ruth shook her head. "I hate being dependent."

"You're not dependent, darling," Marilyn assured her. "For heaven's sake."

Together they accompanied the older woman into her bedroom. With a sigh, Ruth subsided gratefully onto her bed. Marilyn unfolded the light blanket at the foot and spread it over her mother. Then she and Shirley went out of the room, pulling the door almost closed.

"She'll sleep for about thirty minutes, then wake up all bright and bushy-tailed," Marilyn whispered.

"Fine with me. I'll help you with the dishes. I need to move around, after eating so much."

Shirley could tell that Marilyn was preoccupied, so they worked in companionable silence as they cleared the table, rinsed the dishes, and stacked them in the dishwasher.

"Coffee?" Marilyn asked.

"Not yet. I can wait till your mother wakes up. But tell me, Marilyn, what's wrong?"

Marilyn looked guilty. "Oh, dear. I didn't mean to spoil your Thanksgiving."

"Nonsense. This is a perfectly fine Thanksgiving. But I can tell something's not right. Is it Ian?"

Marilyn's face flushed bright red. Bringing her hands up, she covered her face, but Shirley could *feel* the misery emanating from Marilyn in a dark aura.

"Is it another woman?" Really, Shirley thought, that wouldn't be completely unreasonable. Marilyn and Ian lived an ocean apart.

But Marilyn shook her head. She grabbed for a paper towel. Her face was streaming with tears.

"Oh, honey." Shirley put her arms around Marilyn. "Oh, Marilyn."

"He a-a-asked me to marry him," Marilyn sobbed.

Shirley drew back. "And that's a bad thing?"

"No, of course not! But he wants me to live with him, in Edinburgh. And I can't, Shirley, I just can't. I can't leave my mother." Wrapping her arms around her stomach, she folded nearly in half as she wailed soundlessly. "Oh, Shirley, I love him so much!"

Sympathetic tears welled in Shirley's eyes. "Here, Hon, sit down." She grabbed a clean water glass and poured some wine into it. "Drink this. Come on. Take a sip."

Marilyn sank onto a kitchen chair, took the glass, and drank. She closed her eyes and sat very still. "God. I'm sorry. I didn't mean to be such a drama queen."

"You couldn't be a drama queen if you tried." Shirley pulled another chair up close, so she could hold Marilyn's hand. "Come on, Marilyn, let's think this through. There's got to be a solution."

"There's not. Really, there's not. I've thought about nothing else the past two weeks. Sharon's husband's ill. Cancer. It's serious." Marilyn shook her head. "And here I am, blubbering about myself."

"You deserve to blubber if you've met the love of your life and you don't think you can live with him."

"Well, *Sharon* can't take care of Mother. She's been the responsible one all her life. It's my turn now. And I can't put Mother into some kind of—of—*place*."

"Why not?" Shirley demanded.

"Oh, Shirley, come on. Ruth's not gaga. She's not incapable. She's just slightly . . . *frail*. Forgetful, sometimes, but usually she's great. I'd feel like a monster if I put her in an assisted living facility."

"But there are all kinds of facilities, Marilyn," Shirley argued. "Where Ruth could be safe, and have friends her own age, and medical or any kind of assistance at the touch of a bell."

"I couldn't do it, Shirley. She calls assisted living facilities 'finishing schools.' And she's so happy here. She was such a good mom to me and Sharon. If she were a little more incapacitated, or a lot more forgetful, then maybe . . ." Marilyn shook her head violently. "No. I need to keep her here with me."

"And lose the love of your life?" Shirley cried.

Marilyn closed her eyes and sagged against the chair. "What else can I do?"

Shirley glanced at the bottle of Burgundy. It seemed to be singing her name in dulcet tones, assuring her that if she'd just take a little sip, or maybe two, this terrible sympathetic pain in her heart would ease. She jumped up and paced the floor.

"There's got to be some solution. Damn it, where's the chocolate?"

This brought a wan smile to Marilyn's face. "The solution would be chocolate?"

Shirley hurriedly rifled through Marilyn's cupboards until she found a bar hidden in the back. Tearing off the wrapper, she broke it open, handed a piece to Marilyn, and bit into a piece. Her mouth was flooded with soothing, stimulating, glorious, dark sweetness.

"Did you know," Marilyn mumbled, licking her lips, "cacao trees can develop diseases called 'swollen shoot' and 'pod rot'?"

Shirley's laughter was laced with relief. If Marilyn

could joke at a time like this, she'd be okay. "I'm not surprised. I always thought there was something sexual about chocolate, and of course it would be masculine." She broke off another piece and handed it to Marilyn. "Now. Let's consider our possibilities. For one thing, you and Ian could continue seeing each other. Lots of people have transcontinental marriages, why not have a transoceanic one? I mean, for God's sake, Marilyn, you have gobs of money, why not spend it? You could hire a live-in caretaker, someone your mother would get to feel safe and comfortable with, and then you could visit Ian every other month, and he could come over and visit you every other month. Yeah!" Shirley nodded enthusiastically, pleased with her idea.

"It wouldn't be fair," Marilyn said. "Not to Ian, not to me. For one thing, we both have work to do, professional commitments, classes to teach. But actually, Shirley, we've discussed this kind of possibility, and we just can't feel good about it. Ian wants to be *married*. He wants to buy a home and share every day of his life with a wife. He wants domestic *permanence*, and I can understand that." Tears spilled down her face. "I want him to have that. I love him so much, and he's been so lonely, and he's such a lovely man. He wants to plant a garden with someone, and have dinner parties with friends, not pack up a suitcase every month and spend half his time with me suffering from jet lag. And I feel the same way."

"What if—"

Ruth toddled into the room, leaning on her cane. Her white curls were flattened on one side of her head from sleeping, and her pink scalp shone through. Her face was flushed and her lower lip trembled.

Marilyn sprang up. "Mom, are you okay?"

Ruth reached out and grabbed Marilyn's shoulder with one clawlike hand. "Oh, dear, I'm so embarrassed,

I feel so terrible." Looking completely mortified, she whispered, "I wet the bed."

Marilyn patted her mother's arm. "That's all right, Mom. I'll help you change clothes, and I'll change the sheets. It won't take a minute."

"*I'll* put on the coffee," Shirley chirped, "and warm up the pumpkin pie!"

Marilyn and her mother slowly left the room.

Ruth looked up at her daughter. "I think it's because I had so much to eat and didn't wee before I took my nap."

"I'm sure that's the reason," Marilyn agreed.

"I don't wet the bed often," Ruth insisted.

"No, Mom, of course you don't."

By the time the two women came into the living room, Shirley had set out a pot of decaf coffee, and cups and plates for the pie. She helped Marilyn lower Ruth into a chair and set up a little table next to her. Marilyn served the pie.

When she'd finished her helping, Ruth set her plate down. "Sherry," she said brightly, "did I ever tell you about my husband? He taught science in high school. He was as smart as Albert Feinstein, but he loved teaching more than research. We spent so many happy hours together, making peppermints for our students. We taught them to build sweeping nets, aquarium tanks, insect traps . . ."

Shirley smiled encouragingly as she listened to Ruth, but what she heard was the melody of Marilyn's sorrow.

25

Was she happy, or not, was life easy, or hard? *It's all relative,* Polly reminded herself on Thanksgiving Day, then laughed at her pun.

Hearing her laugh, Hank, seated on the sofa next to her, cast a puzzled glance her way. Everyone gathered here at Carolyn and Hank's for Thanksgiving dinner had been discussing world affairs, which were certainly nothing to laugh about.

Polly thought quickly. "Elizabeth," she mouthed to Hank, who looked over at his daughter. His face softened with adoration. The toddler, in pink padded corduroy rompers Polly had sewn for her, sat on the floor, concentrating very hard on putting a rectangular block of wood into a round hole.

They were having drinks before they went in to dinner. Polly tossed hers back like a private dick in a tough-guy novel. She wished she *were* a private dick in a tough-guy novel, or at least had some of his guts.

She had just come from an afternoon Thanksgiving feast with David, Amy, little Jehoshaphat, and Amy's parents, Buck and Katrina. Their wine was homemade and so sweet Polly felt little crystals of sugar clinging to her teeth like barnacles on oyster shells. The "turkey" was tofu, shaped, flavored, and baked into a curdled mass resembling, in texture and taste, a rubber rug pad. The conversation revolved around the farm, which was fine, but no one bothered to ask Polly one single question about her life. In fact, no one had particularly talked to Polly at all.

David was distracted. He'd kissed her when she arrived, then immediately run out to the barn. His favorite Border collie was having her pups today, so throughout the meal, David excused himself to check on her. Amy was also preoccupied; Jehoshaphat was coming down with a cold. He was irritable and fussy. Nothing Amy did could keep the little boy from whining, writhing, squirming, and now and then bursting forth in a full-scale tantrum. Amy looked frustrated and embarrassed by her son's behavior but allowed no one else to interact with him.

Polly left before dessert—pumpkin pie served with a homemade dessert wine, which Polly was sure would be even sweeter than the syrupy swill they'd had during dinner. It pleased her to tell them she had another dinner party to attend—proof that *someone* wanted her company!

But as she drove away from the farm, her body had sagged with disappointment and with fatigue from keeping a forced smile on her face for two hours. How different it would have been if Hugh had been with her just now! He would have lifted an eyebrow or twitched his mouth in silent humor or commiseration. As they drove away, he would have said, "Well, we've done our duty at the Bumpkin Banquet, now let's go to my house and treat ourselves to my best brandy!"

But Hugh was having Thanksgiving with his children and his ex-wife, and Polly was here at Carolyn's, where she was very much wanted, but where she didn't especially want to be.

Carolyn, sweeping around the room in a saffron cashmere dress that made her blond beauty glow, was beaming. Her little family was here—Hank and baby Elizabeth, Aubrey, and now Polly. Faye was safely on the other side of the continent. Carolyn didn't bother to ask about Hugh.

Am I getting to be a cantankerous old biddy, or am I allowing myself to be pushed around? Polly wondered. The Bible said to love one another. The Beatles said love is all you need. Stephen Stills said love the one you're with. She did love Carolyn and Elizabeth, but she loved her son more, and would certainly have loved her grandson if she'd had half the chance.

Perhaps the solution was tangled up in the definition of love. Perhaps, like sins, there were loves of commission and loves of omission. You did lots of committing when your child was a baby—nursing, rocking, feeding, bathing, sheltering, soothing. Later, attending recitals, driving to soccer practice, holding the line on disciplinary rules about curfew. But with a grown child, so much of love involved omission. Letting go. Shutting up. After all, if David had become an Air Force fighter pilot or, like his father, a wild adventurer who disappeared into foreign countries for years at a time, Polly would have gotten on with her own life and been grateful for an occasional sighting.

So, she admonished herself, she should just stop sniveling and enjoy the day. Here she was, in a gorgeous home, with people she cared for deeply. She hadn't been part of her grandson's birth, but she had been right there for Elizabeth's. The little girl's paternal grandmother, wealthy, batty Daisy, lived far away, and when she came to visit, she never put down her bug-eyed little dog long enough to hold Elizabeth—which was probably a good thing, because Daisy, adorable as she was, was also so scatterbrained she might forget whom she was holding. Maybe, Polly thought, when she was really old, she'd

look back to see that she'd been absolutely essential in
Elizabeth's life.

And maybe the fabulous Champagne Carolyn was
serving was blissing Polly out.

"Dinner's ready," Carolyn announced.

Polly went with the others into the dining room. Carolyn had set out place cards. Polly was not surprised to
find her place next to Elizabeth's. She helped Hank es-
tablish Elizabeth safely in her handsome wooden highchair.

"Yummy-yummies for our tummies," Polly babbled
to Elizabeth.

"Lolly yummy!" Elizabeth shrieked gleefully, and
threw her hands up over her head, waving her fat little
fists in the air. Elizabeth had a name for Polly—*Lolly,*
while Jehoshaphat, four months older, hadn't seen his
grandmother often enough to give her a name.

The table had gone quiet. Polly looked around. Everyone was smiling, waiting.

"What?" Polly said.

Carolyn inclined her head toward a gold foil packet
lying at the head of her place.

"Oh! A present? What fun! When can we open them?"

"No time like the present!" Carolyn punned, beaming.

Polly picked up the packet and untied the golden bow,
aware of Aubrey, across the table, performing the same
act.

Inside was a British Airways round-trip ticket to London and a printed itinerary. Ms. Polly Lodge had reservations at the Ritz in London, from December 20 to
December 31. Polly looked up, baffled. "I don't understand."

Carolyn clapped her hands with glee. In her highchair,
Elizabeth mimicked her mother.

"We're all going to spend Christmas in London!" Carolyn announced. "We've booked tickets for the best

plays, and we'll have Christmas dinner at the Ritz! I've made reservations—"

Polly couldn't hear the rest. From deep within her belly, a cyclone of sizzling intensity swirled, so furious and powerful, Polly couldn't tell whether it was a hot flash or her own pure indignation. She took a drink of water to calm herself, but her pulse flared in her neck and her heart pumped so hard she could feel it shake in her chest.

"—so divine!" Carolyn said. "If it snows, it will—"

"Carolyn." As if she'd been body-snatched, Polly looked down from the ceiling to observe herself rising from the table. "Forgive me, but I can't accept this. I *won't* accept this. I am dating Hugh Monroe, and *he* is the person with whom I want to spend my Christmas holiday." Interesting, how the words came from her boiling body with cold, clipped clarity. "My best friend, Faye, has been dating your father for over a year now, and if anyone should accompany your little family to London, it is she. Faye is a wonderful woman, as you would know, if you ever gave her a chance."

"Oh, Polly, silly," Carolyn trilled, laughing. "Sit down. Don't be so dramatic."

Polly met Carolyn's eyes. "It seems the only way I can get through to you about this, Carolyn, is by being dramatic. You should know by now, it's not in my nature. But you've ignored every kind of hint I've given about my relationship with your father." She turned to Aubrey. "Aubrey, you are a charming, handsome, wonderful man. I don't know, however, how intelligent you are, because you let Carolyn walk all over you. If you want Faye to be with you, you've got to be forceful with this beautiful daughter of yours." She looked back at Carolyn. "I'm going home now. And I hope the next time you invite me to your house, you'll tell me to bring Hugh."

"Oh, Polly!" Carolyn seemed more amused than upset.

Hank jumped up and followed Polly to the door. As he took her coat from the closet and slid it over her arms, he said, "Polly, you're trembling. Are you sure you want to drive right now?"

The conflagration had reached Polly's face; she knew she was crimson. "I'll be fine." She was verging on tears and needed to get out of the house.

Wanting to run to the car, Polly forced herself to walk, keeping her back straight, her head high. She settled into her little gray Volvo, grateful for its nestlike snugness. The amiable vehicle smoothly rolled out of the driveway and onto the road even though Polly's foot quaked on the pedal.

She looked in the rearview mirror. Carolyn's house grew smaller, then disappeared as other houses came into view.

"HA!" Polly expostulated triumphantly.

Then she burst into tears. Then she burst out laughing. As she stopped for a red light, she imagined people in the car next to her looking over to see a madwoman, laughing and crying at the same time. Oh, well, she thought, who would be surprised? It was Thanksgiving, after all, another family holiday!

Really, she was proud of herself. She had put her foot down firmly to Carolyn and it was about time. For if Carolyn really wanted Polly to be godmother to Elizabeth, she'd better welcome the *real* Polly; she'd better allow Polly to be herself.

"And now, Missy," Polly asked herself aloud, because if she was already laughing and crying, why not talk to herself as well? "What would the real Polly Lodge like to do right now?"

The answer came fast and certain.

She wanted to be with Hugh. She was proud, overwhelmed, excited. Her body was enormously *awake*.

She wanted to use this energy; she wanted to make love. She wanted to grab Hugh Monroe and kiss him like he'd never been kissed before.

So she headed toward his place. The daughter who was hosting the Thanksgiving meal had small children, so their plan was to eat early. Hugh might not be home when Polly arrived, but he might be, and if not, Polly had the key. She could slip in, *undress,* and surprise him when he arrived. Ah, what a delicious plan!

Since his divorce from Carol, Hugh had lived in an apartment on elegant Commonwealth Avenue, near the Boston Public Gardens. The magnificent building, staid and formal, was part of a block of row houses with marble stoops and neoclassical friezes and gargoyles above the doors. Parking was often a problem, but this evening the streets were empty and Polly easily found a spot.

No lights shone from Hugh's windows on the second floor; he wasn't home yet. Good. That would give her time to get ready.

Her key ring jingled as she opened the street-level outer door. She climbed the wide, curving stairs to the second floor and let herself into his apartment. It could have been a formal, stultifying place, with its acres of walnut paneling and its marble or parquet floors, but during his divorce, Hugh had given all his parents' antique furniture to his children or Carol. This new home he'd furnished with simple, expensive, modern pieces.

The front door opened into the enormous living room, dominated by a chocolate leather sofa facing a huge plasma television. Most of the walls held shelves of books, and one wall was almost entirely windows looking out onto the street.

Polly hung her coat in the closet. Humming, she crossed the expansive living room and closed the drapes. She didn't want the neighbors to see what she was about to do. Some logs were laid in the fireplace, so she knelt to

light them. As the flames caught hold and grew, they
threw out a romantic golden glow.

In the kitchen, she lingered at Hugh's wine rack. Did
she want wine, or Champagne? Champagne. She had a
lot to celebrate. Hugh always kept some cold in his refrigerator, and she opened it now, laughing when the
cork exploded across the room. She poured herself a
glass.

She emptied ice into a silver bucket and set it on the
living room coffee table, nesting the bottle in the ice to
keep it chilled. She brought in a flute for Hugh and a little bowl of nuts for herself, since she had eaten little at
her vegetarian son's, and nothing at Carolyn's.

Sipping Champagne, she went into the bathroom and
undressed. She was quite satisfied with her body, she decided, studying it in the mirror. The dieting she'd done in
comradeship with Alice had indented her waistline, and
with her full hips and heavy breasts, she had a luxurious
hourglass shape. Her bulging belly made it clear that
time and gravity had sifted most of the sand to the bottom, but because Hugh always made it clear that he
loved every ounce and inch, she tried to carry her ass
like an asset.

She brushed her teeth. Carefully, she redid her makeup.
She brushed her hair. She considered wrapping a towel
around her—she couldn't remember when she'd last, if
ever, walked naked around her house, let alone anyone
else's—but decided to go *au naturel*.

In the living room, the fire was crackling and gleaming, throwing out so much heat she was quite comfortable in her naked state. Sinking onto the sofa, she tried
several poses, imagining which would be the most seductive.

"Here I am," she will say. "Your dessert."

Plumping up a couple of throw pillows, she established them under her head, then reclined on her side as

if posing for a portrait. Her breasts hung low. So did her belly. When she heard the door open, she would rearrange all her bits. For now, she picked up the remote control and flicked on the television.

Polly waited an hour, fed two more logs to the fire, ate all the peanuts, drank half the Champagne, and peed twice.

Finally she heard Hugh's key scratch the lock. Quickly she ran her hands through her hair, mussing it. She positioned herself just so, head on hand, smiling at the door, one leg lying against the leather, the other bent at the knee, providing Hugh with a glimpse of what he privately called her "honey-well." The firelight danced. The room had grown hot, but that was fine. It made her nipples expand. Hugh liked that look.

"Here we are!" Hugh stepped into the room. By his side was a beautiful younger woman, her arm linked through his, her long blond hair falling against Hugh's shoulder.

"Oh!" said the woman.

"Oh," said Hugh.

"Oh!" cried Polly. Frantically she grabbed a throw pillow and held it over her naked torso. Of course, it was too small to cover *everything*.

Hugh began, "Polly—"

"No, no!" Polly babbled. Jumping up, she snatched the other pillow, and holding both pillows over her front, she ran past Hugh and the woman, shamefully aware of all her jiggling, lurching blubber. She scurried down the hall and into the bathroom, where she dropped the pillows and yanked on her clothes. She didn't bother to put on her pantyhose, but stabbed her bare feet into her shoes.

All she wanted in the world was to get out of there, now! Blood pounded through her body, making her completely deaf and nearly blind, but she moved as fast as she could, vaguely aware that she was sobbing. Throwing back the bathroom door, she raced down the small hall and spotted her purse where she'd left it on a table.

Hugh and the woman were in the living room. The woman had taken a chair. Hazily, Polly heard Hugh say to the woman, "Just wait here a moment—"

She didn't waste time taking her coat from the closet, but snatched up her purse, yanked open the door, and raced down the long, curving staircase so fast she slipped and nearly fell.

"Polly!" Above her, Hugh materialized, his ruddy face concerned. "Wait! Let me explain!"

But Polly flew out the door, down the street, and into her blessed Volvo. She was shaking so hard, it took her several tries to stab the key into the ignition. Finally, she connected, started the engine, and accelerated onto the street. Weeping, she drove home, so sick with humiliation and despair that she was halfway there before she thought to turn on the heater.

26

"M<small>RS.</small> D'A<small>NNUCIO?</small>" A<small>LICE</small> <small>GRIPPED THE PHONE SO</small> tightly she thought she'd leave permanent indentations in the plastic. She was on the hospital pay phone. Her cell phone only worked outside, and she didn't want to be too far away from the operating room.

Deep breaths, she reminded herself. "This is Alice Murray. I'm fine, thank you. I'm calling about Jennifer. No—she's—" For a few moments, Alice bit her tongue and tapped her foot, until the other woman stopped spitting out words.

"I'm calling because Jennifer is in the operating room right now, having a C-section. She—" Again, she listened to the other woman's shrill voice. "Yes, I know it's a month early, but you know she has preeclampsia—"

A barrage of sound hit Alice's ear. Alice inhaled so hard she was surprised she didn't suck the phone down her throat. No wonder Jennifer hadn't told her mother about her health problem. The woman didn't stop talking long enough for anyone to tell her anything.

"It's a medical condition involving high blood pressure and it's dangerous to the mother and the child—"

Alice held the phone away from her ear while Jennifer's mother screamed, "Oh, my God!" thirty or forty times.

The line was muffled. Alice heard rustling noises and arguing voices. Then a man's voice came over the phone.

"This is Jennifer's father. Where is she now?"

Alice spoke fast. "She's in Emerson Hospital in Concord. She's in the operating room. They're doing a C-section. Alan's with her. She was awake when they wheeled her in. I think they're planning to give a local anesthetic."

"We'll get in the car and come up at once. We're on the Cape, so it might take about two hours, depending on traffic."

"We'll be here." Alice doubted that he heard her, because his wife was in the background, screaming.

"Could you take our cell phone number and phone us if you know anything?" Mr. D'Annucio asked.

"Of course." Alice dug around in her shoulder bag, pulled out a pad and pen, and wrote down the information. She was surprised at how it helped, having *something* to do.

She returned to the waiting room. Gideon sat on a turquoise vinyl couch, thumbing through an old issue of *Newsweek*.

"Her parents are on their way up," Alice told him.

"That's good." Gideon patted the seat next to him. "Sit down, Alice."

"In a minute." She stayed on her feet, pacing the maternity-ward waiting room like a caged panther.

"Alice, come on and sit down," Gideon pleaded. "You're recovering from a heart attack, for God's sake. You know you're not supposed to get agitated."

Alice reached the end of the room, wheeled around, strode toward the opposite wall. "I'm supposed to get exercise, too," she reminded him. "So let's just call this exercise." She clenched her fists and opened them nervously. "I just wish I could *do* something."

"It's not going to help Jennifer if you have another heart attack," Gideon soberly reminded her.

"I'm not going to have another heart attack! I'm going to—oh!" Alice slapped herself in the middle of the forehead. "I know what I should do! I should call her best friend, Maya, remember, who came to the party we threw for Alan and Jennifer this summer? And what were the other girls' names? Two of them were married—Alisa and Morgan—but I think Maya was only engaged. Now, what were their last names?"

"Why don't you wait until Jennifer's out of surgery?" Gideon suggested. "You don't want everyone rushing down here."

"Well, if I were Jennifer, I'd want my friends to know!" Alice argued.

"But they're all having their Thanksgiving dinners," Gideon pointed out.

Alice stopped pacing, folded her arms, squinted into the distance, and debated Gideon's line of reasoning. "I understand where you're coming from," she told him. "I won't ask them to come down here, not unless they volunteer. But I want them to know what's going on."

"You want them to worry about something they can't do anything about?" Gideon asked.

"But they *can* do something," Alice insisted. "They can *worry.*"

Gideon exhaled noisily, like a principal with a recalcitrant child. "And their worry is going to help Jennifer?"

"Yes," Alice told him decisively. "Worry is a kind of prayer. It *helps*. Maybe it's a female thing, but it's what I feel is true, and it's what I'm going to act on. If *I* were Jennifer's friend, I would want to know."

She rushed to the nurses' station, borrowed a phone book, and made a list of phone numbers. The mental effort it took to remember Jennifer's friends' last names provided a moment's ease from her own anxiety. *God,* she thought, *I hope I'm not relieving my fear by passing it off onto these young women.* She stopped, searched her soul, then made the phone calls.

She was just hanging up for the last time when she saw her son striding down the hall toward the waiting room. For a moment, her legs went so weak, she nearly fell.

Then she saw his face.

"Alan?" The word came out in a croak.

"We have a daughter, Mom," Alan said. "Five pounds, one ounce."

That even one tiny ounce could be measured against the enormity of all their hopes and fears made Alice burst into tears. "How's Jennifer?"

"She's got a headache. She's going to have to stay in the hospital for a few days. She's not out of the woods yet, but she's going to be okay." Alan wrapped his mother in a tight bear hug. "It's okay, Mom."

"I'm so glad!" Alice dug a tissue from her pocket and blew her nose.

Gideon came out of the waiting room. Alan told him the good news while Alice pulled herself together.

"I phoned Jennifer's parents," Alice told her son. "And all her friends."

"And CNN and all the major networks," Gideon joked.

Alice made a face at him. "Her parents are on their way. I'd better phone them and Jennifer's friends again."

"Want to see your granddaughter first?" Alan asked.

Alice staggered backward, amazed. "Can I?"

"Sure. Come on." Alan wrapped a supporting arm around his mother and led her down the hall.

They passed through a swinging door into a room so bright it seemed like heaven. Jennifer lay on a high table, as white as the sheets covering her. Her eyes were closed.

But when Alan and Alice came to her side, she opened them.

"Look who's here." She adjusted herself slightly on her bed, turning so Alice could see the very small person bundled in her arms.

Alice bent over and gently pulled the blanket back from the baby's face. Her eyes were swollen nearly shut. Her tea-colored skin was blotchy, and her vulnerable scalp was covered with a few black curls.

"Oh, my," Alice breathed. "She's *beautiful*."

"We think so," Jennifer agreed. Reaching out, she took her husband's hand. "Her name is Alice."

CHRISTMAS

27

Shirley was in her office at The Haven on Monday afternoon when her phone rang.

"Shirley? This is Hugh Monroe."

"Oh, hi, Hugh, how are you?"

"I'm well, thank you, but I'm concerned about Polly. Have you spoken with her recently?"

Shirley thought for a moment. "Not since last Wednesday. Have you—"

"I've tried to phone her for three days now, and her line's always busy."

"How odd!" Polly frowned. "Have you called Carolyn? Polly spent Thanksgiving with her and the Sperrys."

Hugh made an ambiguous coughing noise. "Well, I saw Polly—briefly—Thanksgiving night, but that's a good suggestion. I'll call Carolyn right now."

"I'll check in with Alice and Marilyn, see if they've heard from her," Shirley told Hugh. "Faye's out in California with her daughter. Hugh—" She paused. "Is there any reason to worry? I mean, I don't want to pry, but did you two have a fight or something?"

Again, the ambiguous cough. "Not a fight, no. More of a . . . *something*."

"I see," Shirley said, although she didn't. "I'll call you back after I talk with Alice and Marilyn."

"Alice? It's Shirley. How are you?"

"Still in *heaven*. I'm just leaving for the hospital to visit Jennifer and baby Alice."

"Well, listen, just tell me, have you spoken with Polly in the last few days?"

"Um, no, actually. I tried to call her several times to tell her about the baby, but I've always gotten a busy signal. Why? Is something wrong?"

"I don't know. Hugh just called. He can't reach her, either."

"Well, damn! That's weird. Have you talked to her son?"

Shirley snorted. "Yeah, like *he* would know."

"I think Polly was going there for Thanksgiving . . ."

"Yeah, and to Carolyn's after that. Hugh says he saw Polly briefly Thanksgiving night."

"*Briefly.*"

"Yeah. I'm not sure what that means. I asked if they had a fight, and he said they had a *something*."

"Oh-oh. Sounds worse than a fight."

Shirley clutched the phone tight. "But even if they did have a fight, or broke up, or *something*, Polly wouldn't do anything *rash*, would she?"

"Of course not. Polly's sensible, optimistic—"

"But you *know* how the holidays can make you crazy. I mean, it's hard to be alone at Christmas, and her son and his wife aren't exactly loving, and if she and Hugh broke off—"

"I'm going over to her house."

"Wait, Alice. Let me see what Hugh says after he talks with Carolyn."

"You can call me on my cell phone. I'm driving over there now."

* * *

"Shirley?" Hugh's voice was taut with concern. "I spoke with Carolyn. She said Polly was very emotional on Thanksgiving. Made a bit of a scene and stormed from the house without taking a bite of her Thanksgiving meal, Carolyn said. She's been trying to phone her without any success."

"I spoke with Alice. She hasn't talked with her, either. She's driving over to Polly's house right now. Listen, Hugh, I don't want to pry, but . . . did you and Polly break up?"

"No, no, no," Hugh insisted. "Nothing like that." He hesitated. "Well, maybe it was something like that. I mean, not on my part. We had . . . a misunderstanding, Shirley. I don't want to say more without talking to Polly about it first. It's kind of a sensitive matter."

The hair on the back of Shirley's neck stood on end. "Oh, God! I'm going over there."

"I'll meet you there."

"She keeps a key hidden in a metal box behind the drainpipe next to the garage."

"I know."

"I'll check in with Marilyn from my cell phone."

"Marilyn? Listen, have you talked with Polly in the last few days?"

"No . . ." Marilyn's voice trailed off as she turned her head from the phone. "It's Shirley, Mother." Her voice was clear again. "Why? You sound worried."

"I *am* worried. Hugh phoned and he hasn't been able to get hold of her, and he saw her *briefly* on Thanksgiving night, and Carolyn said Polly was *emotional* and Hugh said he and Polly had a *something*. He wouldn't give any details."

"Oh, dear. That sounds bad. Have you—okay, Mother. Shirley, Mother says hello."

"Tell Ruth I say hello."

"Mother, Shirley says hello. Have you spoken with anyone else?"

"I called Alice. She's been trying to reach her, and so has Carolyn."

"I think I'll drive over there," Marilyn said.

"I'm on my way right now. And Hugh is, too."

"Yes, but I think I live closer to her than you do. What?" After a pause, Marilyn said, "Mother wants me to tell you it's always darkest before the silver lining."

Heat broke out over Polly's body, so intense it made her stomach heave as she lay twisted in her disgustingly damp and tangled sheets. With weak arms, she fought to shove the covers away. The movement made her stomach roil—desperately she flung her head over the side of the bed and barfed violently into the lobster pot sitting on the floor. How did that get there?

Her head was thick with heat and nightmarish blips of sound and color. Orange, purple, worms, swollen masses of—she barfed again. This time only a thin stream of liquid trailed out, burning her mouth as it came.

Collapsing back among her pillows, she touched her forehead with a shaking hand. She was sick. Really sick. Flu, probably. She'd been wallowing in her bed like an overwrought sow for—how long? She couldn't figure it out. She remembered coming home from Hugh's, weeping hysterically and shaking with cold, or with cold and emotion. She'd wept—she'd *howled*—she'd been so out of control she'd scared herself. She'd drunk some brandy, but vomited it all up immediately.

She *hated* vomiting, but it did clear her head momentarily. Her memory flashed vivid bits, out of sequence. She must have pulled herself together enough to get herself to bed, because she could remember morning sunshine streaming in through the windows and Roy

Orbison sitting by her on the bed, whining pitifully. Dutifully, she'd risen, wrapped her robe around her (when had she put on her nightgown?), and gone downstairs. The kitchen door had a dog flap, so she didn't have to worry about putting Roy Orbison out. She'd filled his food bowl to overflowing, grabbed the lobster pot, and staggered back up to bed.

Now she was *cold*, so cold her skin was covered in goose bumps. Chills rippled up and down her body like icy fingers on piano keys. She grabbed for the covers, the movement stirring up a rolling ocean in her stomach. She clutched the blanket to her chin.

"Where's a damn hot flash when you need one?" she whined.

Her voice came out in a croak.

Great, she had laryngitis, too.

Roy Orbison thought she'd called him. With a giant leap, he landed on the bed. The impact of his weight made the bed rock. Oh, God, she was so dizzy! She needed to get to the bathroom, but she felt too sick to move. Roy licked her arm. She managed a feeble pat on his head. Good old loyal companion.

Speaking of companions, why had none of her friends called? How much time had gone by? One day? Two? Well, Faye was in California, visiting her daughter. But why hadn't Marilyn phoned, or Alice or Shirley? Not to mention Hugh. She had been sure he would phone her to apologize, to explain, to—to *something*! He was a gentleman, after all; he wasn't a monster. She could understand how he would dump her in order to be with that lovely young woman. Men did it all the time. She hated it that he'd betrayed her, but she was astounded that he hadn't phoned to somehow attempt to make her feel better about it.

She was so thirsty! Her throat burned. She could actually feel her esophagus drying out like a sponge left in the sun. Out of the corner of her eye, she saw a can of ginger ale on her bedside table. Feebly, she reached out for it, brought it to her parched lips, and discovered it was already empty. When had she drunk it? For that matter, when had she brought it upstairs?

"Oh, boo hoo," she cried helplessly, as tears slid down her face. How did her body manage to produce moisture everywhere except where she needed it?

Next to her, Roy Orbison suddenly sat up. He cocked his head. Then he leapt off the bed and skittered out of the room. She heard his nails clicking busily as he went down the stairs.

Probably he was going to eat again. All Roy's best ideas involved eating. Polly sank into her pillows, a blubbery, pathetic mass of nausea and discomfort. In a moment, she'd get herself to the bathroom, and then she'd phone someone . . .

She heard voices. Several voices, all talking at once. Oh good, now she was hallucinating.

The voices got louder. Steps sounded on the stairs. Who . . . ? A burglar? Maybe someone was coming to murder her. She felt so sick she almost didn't think she'd mind.

"Polly!"

Alice exploded into the room, followed by Shirley, Marilyn, Ruth, and Hugh. Waves of cold air swept in with them, making Polly shiver. They radiated health, energy, and good humor as they gathered around her. She was aware of how she must appear, with her hair clumped with sweat and sticking out all over, her nose red, her eyes puffy, her lips chapped, her breath foul.

"Polly!" Shirley sank onto the bed, touching her cold hand to Polly's hot forehead.

"I'll empty this." Marilyn grabbed the lobster pot and disappeared into the bathroom.

Alice was fixing something on the bedside table. "Polly, you moron, you left the phone off the hook."

"Polly." Hugh peered over Shirley's shoulder. He was so handsome, his blue eyes so full of concern! "Polly, that woman was my niece."

"Oh, honey," Ruth cried, "you're sick."

"Oh," Polly sighed, closing her eyes. "I'm so glad."

28

I AM *NOT* NERVOUS, FAYE ASSURED HERSELF AS SHE waited for her guest to arrive. I'm an independent, intelligent woman, and if necessary, I can be stubborn. Or even *rude*.

To remind her guest that she was a professional artist—something Faye had almost forgotten after her husband's death, something she'd almost *lost*—she remained in the clothes she'd pulled on this morning: jeans with an elastic waist, a white cotton tank top, and a long, loose blue denim shirt, everything spotted here and there with ruby and celadon oils from painting Ruth's portrait. Her long hair was pulled back in a clip. Her nails, which she'd grown long during the past year when she wasn't painting, were clipped short again, the way she liked them when she was working. She wore no makeup. Now, at the last moment, Faye rushed upstairs and put on a touch of blusher and lipstick.

As always, a pause in front of a mirror led to a confrontation with her inner nag, who sounded very much like Joan Rivers. *For God's sake, look at you! You've gained back the weight you lost! Your skin is blotchy! Haven't you ever heard of exfoliation? And why are your eyes so puffy?*

"Stop it!" she scolded herself, and ripping her attention away from the mirror, she went back down the stairs—slowly, so she wouldn't fall—and into the kitchen to turn the burner on under the teakettle.

She took out the flowered Limoges teapot that had belonged to her grandmother and filled it with loose leaves of Earl Grey. Running her hands over the rounded belly of the pot, she admired its classical lines, delicate painted flowers, and brilliant gilding. All her life she'd intended to pass this tea set down to Laura.

During her visit to San Francisco this Thanksgiving, Faye had realized that Laura would never use this pot. Would never *want* to use this pot. The life Laura and Lars lived was so different from Faye's. Streamlined. Urban. Modern. And, it seemed to Faye, centered around electronic equipment. Lars and Laura were always on the computer or cell phone. Megan, at four, spent what to Faye were inappropriate amounts of time in front of the computer and television. Or else she was shipped off to the expensive, elite neighborhood preschool, while her little brother, only six months old, dawdled in a playpen at the accompanying nursery. Lars worked endless hours, and Laura also worked, in her own way, keeping to a rigorous exercise routine with her trainer at the local health club, supervising the live-in housekeeper/baby-sitter, attending committee meetings for the chicest charities, and planning cocktail and dinner parties for Lars's partners and potential clients.

It amazed Faye how different Laura was in San Francisco from the way she'd been just three short years ago, when Megan was still an infant. Laura had been depressed and overwhelmed with the responsibilities of motherhood. Now, somehow, she'd found herself; she'd entered that kind of "I am woman, hear me roar" phase that Faye could remember from her early days as a young mother. Laura had had her thick, long hair, for so many years tumbling to her shoulders, sheared into a kind of skullcap that made her eyes huge. She had lost more weight than Faye considered healthy, and racing around in her tight, rather athletic-looking clothing, she resembled a young boy, or an elf.

And she was radiantly happy.

The children were thriving, Lars looked at Laura with adoration, they were all having great fun—and their lives were so *different* from Faye's!

They loved California. They'd never return to the East Coast.

As Faye flew home from her visit, she'd leaned her head against the window of the huge humming plane, considering all this, trying to come to terms with the truth of it, struggling not to feel rejected, or disappointed, or solitary. Or, admitting she *was* solitary, but capable of making this phase of her life into one she not merely survived, but actually enjoyed. After all, she had her friends, she had a beau, and now, again, thanks to Ruth, she had her work.

The thought of Ruth's portrait, waiting for her in the little bedroom/studio, lifted Faye's spirits. The picture was finished; Faye had had it framed, and was keeping it until Christmas, when Ruth would present it to Marilyn.

It was a good portrait.

Somehow, as if a spell had been lifted, Faye was painting again. Really working.

Just before Faye left for San Francisco, while she was getting ready to take apart the little scene she'd set up, her attention had been captured by the way the light fell on the birds' nests in Ruth's portrait. The scratchy texture of the nests and the subtle, varied hues of the dried grasses challenged her. An image appeared in her mind— a still life of the nests, juxtaposed with fresh flowers. Daffodils? No. Something autumnal. Mums? Perhaps a sheaf of bright mums, lying on their side, their fluffy petals silky against the crisp grass of the nests—that would be fun to try to capture. During her stay in California, the thought of that still life nestled against her heart like a gold locket.

So that was what she was returning to: her work. It had always been part of who she was, why she lived, and now it had regained its place in her life. This year, she hadn't bothered to put up a tree in the kitchen. The little blue spruce in the living room was much smaller than any she'd ever had before. Since she'd been home, she'd been absolutely *high*, full of energy, eager to get to work every day, obsessed with thoughts of building a real studio in her back garden, so interested in her work that she considered Christmas a kind of interruption.

Three days ago, Carolyn Sperry had phoned and asked if she could meet with Faye. Regarding a *business proposal,* she had added, mysteriously.

Of course, Faye, always polite, had agreed, but she'd thought, *Egad! Now what?* She knew Carolyn wanted Aubrey to date Polly, but would she be brazen enough to offer Faye money to stop seeing her father? What else could she mean by a business proposition?

As Faye set out the teacups, cream and sugar bowls, and silver spoons on the tray, she saw that her hands were shaking.

"I liked it better last year," Alice mused thoughtfully, as she reclined on a sofa in the lounge of The Haven, cuddling her namesake in her arms. She drove out almost every day, to take care of baby Alice so Jennifer could take a bath or a nap.

Shirley, kneeling on the floor amid a crackling muddle of wrapping paper, paused to study the Christmas tree. "I know. Me, too. It's bigger than last year's tree, so all the ornaments are there, but it still lacks something."

"Maybe we should hang some tinsel?" With the tip of

her finger, Alice pushed back the blanket around the baby just a millimeter, so she could see all of her smooth, curving cheek.

Shirley watched Alice gaze adoringly upon her granddaughter. "Maybe some pacifiers and booties?" she teased.

"Maybe," Alice cooed.

"Oh, Alice!" Shirley laughed.

Alice looked up. "What?" She focused. "No, hey, I heard you. I mean it. What if we hung little bits on the tree that symbolized what we're celebrating this Christmas? Pacifiers would be *cute*! And some lacy tags from Havenly Yours. And since Marilyn went to Scotland, she could hang bagpipes, or little Loch Ness Monsters . . ."

"Are you nuts? You know Marilyn broke it off with Ian because of her mother. That's certainly nothing to celebrate, and as for me—I could hang, um, let me see, what have I achieved this year—oh, *I* know! A broken heart!"

Alice's face fell. "That's not *all* you've achie—"

Shirley waved her hands. "I'm sorry, Alice, forgive me for being such a pill." Pushing aside a roll of wrapping paper, Shirley lay back on the floor, stretching, closing her eyes.

"You're not a pill." Alice said everything in a light, breathy voice, so she wouldn't wake the infant in her arms. "But you're not at 'The End,' either. You're just kind of at a station, waiting for a train."

"I don't know." Shirley allowed herself to be honest. "It's been over three months, Alice, since Justin hit the road."

"Since you righteously kicked his nasty ol' ass out of here," corrected Alice.

"Whatever. Since I've been with a man." Self-pity struck her. She sat up, as if she could physically move away from it, grabbed a present, centered it on a square of paper covered with dancing reindeer, and grabbed the scissors. "I wish I could be the kind of woman who doesn't need a man!"

"Well, you are, in many ways." Alice leaned sideways, stretched out an arm, and grabbed her cup of tea from the table. "I mean, you're professionally and financially self-sufficient. It's not like you lack meaning in your life."

"I know. I know." Shirley measured a length of scarlet ribbon and snipped. "Still . . ."

"Still, you're happier with a man around." The baby squirmed and squinched up her face. Alice loosened the blanket around little Alice's feet and retucked it.

"Yes, who isn't?" Shirley said, defensively.

"I'm not arguing."

"That's a first," Shirley muttered under her breath.

Alice just smiled. "All right, we've named the problem. What can we do about it?"

"I wish I knew!" She reached for another box.

"Let's see." Alice tapped her lower lip with one long, red nail. "If I met Gideon at the symphony, and Polly met Hugh at the doctor's, and Marilyn met Ian while traveling, then how . . ."

"Sounds like there's a light-bulb joke in there," Shirley chuckled.

Alice brightened. "I know! Remember last year? We all found one single man for Faye to date."

"Yes, and remember last year? When none of them worked out? Faye met Aubrey at our open house, by accident."

"Hm." Alice subsided against the sofa. "You're right. Well, then, let's think of places where you could meet a guy."

Shirley set a present under the tree. "Not here, because mostly women come here."

"Okay, how about a bookstore?"

"Right. I'll just lounge around the auto repair section."

"That's not a bad idea."

"Actually," Shirley said, as she cut along another roll of paper, "I'm kind of off books in general, after Justin."

"Understood. What kinds of clubs could you join? Or maybe you could take some courses. Remember, you met Justin when you took that business management seminar."

"That might work. But not until after the first of the year. So that's another month without getting laid."

Alice pointed a finger at Shirley. "Is that all you want? Think about it. Remember how old you are. Men your age, our age, aren't going to be as lusty as younger men."

"So I'll date younger men."

"I don't think that's smart. You seem to get in trouble with younger men. Besides, Shirley, men are already, naturally, *psychologically* younger than women. You were dating Justin, who was fifty, which was sort of like dating someone, oh, forty-two, but if you date someone sixty-three, he'll be fifty-five."

"Maybe psychologically or intellectually, but sexually, to date a man who's fifty, I need to date a man who's forty." Confused, Shirley threw up her hands. "Look. I'll date anyone any age, but first I have to *meet* someone, and I don't seem to be doing that!"

Alice leaned her head against the sofa and closed her eyes. "We're two creative, intelligent women. We ought to be able to find a solution. I mean, even a hundred years ago, women answered ads as mail-order brides, so—" She sat up, swung around, set her feet on the floor, and faced Shirley. "I've got it. We'll sign you up on an online dating service. Match.com or something like that."

Shirley looked at Alice. "Hmmmm."

"It's brilliant!" Alice said. "Tell me it's not."

Thoughtfully, Shirley twirled a strand of hair. "I'm not so sure about *brilliant*, but it could be fun . . ."

"Let's go try it out now!" Alice said, getting to her feet.

"But I'm not through wrapping—"

"Oh, you can do that later! Come on!" Alice clopped away across the parquet floor, and in her arms, little Alice made kissy movements with her mouth as she slept.

"Your house is really lovely," Carolyn told Faye as she settled on the sofa by the fire. Carolyn was clad in a snug-fitting camel pantsuit that set off her sleek blond hair. She looked chic, young, and terrifying.

"Thank you." Faye finished the tea ritual and handed Carolyn a cup of steaming Earl Grey. She felt like a hippo entertaining a gazelle. Leaning back in her chair, she aimed for a pose of relaxed confidence, but even though Carolyn had seemed friendly so far, Faye knew that if she tried to lift her cup off its saucer, everything would chatter like teeth in the Arctic.

"Delicious." Carolyn sipped her tea, and with steady hands, returned the wafer-thin cup to its saucer. "Faye, I'll get right to the point. I think the Christmas card you sent us is absolutely beautiful. And when I was here for your Halloween party, I saw your paintings. Aubrey told me you did wonderful work, but I had no idea. Your paintings are exceptional."

"Thank you." Faye's infinite relief sparked off a hot flash.

"Sperry Paper is hitting hard times," Carolyn continued. "We've got so much competition these days. We produce premier-quality, personal stationery, but we're looking for ways to branch out. I'd like to put out a line of note cards, with your paintings reproduced on the front. Some of what you've already done would work well for what I have in mind. But I'm hoping you wouldn't be averse to creating a few scenes especially for our purposes. Holiday scenes, for example, and occasion scenes. Birthdays. Anniversaries. That sort of thing."

Faye was stunned. If she'd been standing, she would have fallen down. As it was, she was overwhelmed, her brain short-circuited with shock.

Apparently Carolyn was used to causing this sort of response. "I've mentioned it to Father, by the way, and he thinks it's an excellent idea." When Faye still didn't speak, Carolyn shifted on the sofa, crossing one sleek leg over the other. Her hand fiddled with the heavy gold chain around her neck—the only sign that she might be nervous herself. "I realize I haven't been what you might consider welcoming over the past few months. I apologize. My father's been very happy since he's been dating you, and I want you to know I'll stop trying to match him up with Polly. I can be stubborn and I like to have my own way, but I know when it's time to quit."

"I don't know what to say," Faye admitted. *Deep breaths,* she reminded herself.

Carolyn's cell phone rang. She reached into her handsome leather briefcase and shut it off. "I don't want you to feel pressured about this. Obviously, this business arrangement stands completely apart from your relationship with my father."

Faye finally managed to speak. "I'm so glad. I like your father very much. And I'd like to be your friend, too—" She noticed Carolyn's slight flinch. "—although I realize, what with your baby and running your business, you don't have much time for friendships."

Carolyn smiled. "Sometimes I can be a wicked, cold bitch, I know."

"That's all right," Faye assured her. "I've met worse. And I like your idea about the note cards. I've just started painting again. When my husband died, I—lost interest for a while. But now, well—would you like to come up to my studio to see the still life I've set up? And I've got some old paintings stored there as well. You might want to look through them, to see if you like something, to give me an idea of the sort of thing you've got in mind."

"I'd love to see them." Carolyn stood up, eager.

Faye stood up, too, and when she set her cup and saucer on the table, her hands were as steady as if she were holding a brush.

29

MARILYN WAS DREAMING. IT WAS THANKSGIVING, OR perhaps Christmas—some holiday. She was at a party with her Hot Flash friends, and all their acquaintances, and lots of other people, too. Glamorous men and women laughed and drank Champagne. Marilyn's mother clutched her arm tightly, afraid of getting lost in the crowd. Suddenly, they were all called in to dinner. Marilyn found her place card next to Ruth's at a table with a few strangers in a room annexed to the main room. Slices of turkey lay on her plate, but nothing else. Marilyn sneaked a look around the corner of the door into the other room, where her friends sat at a long table laden with bowls and platters of delicious, aromatic food: creamed onions, chestnut stuffing, garlic mashed potatoes, cranberry sauce.

"Could I have some mashed potatoes, please?" Marilyn whimpered.

No one even noticed her.

Marilyn woke up with a start. It was seven in the morning. She could hear Ruth fumbling around in the bathroom. She covered her eyes with her arm, letting the dream sift back into the recesses of her brain.

"Okay, now," she said aloud. "That was just pathetic."

Tying her striped bathrobe around her, she headed

into the kitchen to start breakfast. She liked coffee; Ruth liked tea.

Cold rain streaked the windows, and even in this well-insulated building, she could hear the wind moan. Flicking on the television, she curled up in a chair and waited for the Weather Channel to give the local forecast. She never used to watch TV in the morning, or during the day at all, and only rarely watched it in the evening. She had so many research articles to read, or students' papers to grade. But Ruth liked to have the television on all the time, and now that Marilyn was on sabbatical, she had no papers to grade or committee reports to read. She was supposed to be doing her research, but going to her lab made her squeamish these days, afraid she'd run into Faraday. She'd seen him several times since he broke off with her, and he'd always been polite, but clearly it was uncomfortable for them both.

"Good morning, dear!" Ruth toddled into the living room, clean, clothed, and fragrant with lavender cologne. She pecked a kiss on Marilyn's cheek, then went into the kitchen to pour a cup of tea. "What's on the schedule for today?" Ruth stirred milk into her very strong tea and added a teaspoon of sugar.

"I was thinking we'd get our tree." Marilyn put a couple of eggs on to boil. "But it's going to rain all day, perhaps turn to snow. Maybe we'd better wait until tomorrow."

"If it snows later on, we could get it then. It's always fun to choose Christmas trees in the snow." Ruth dipped her spoon into the sugar bowl.

"You've already put your sugar in," Marilyn told her.

Ruth giggled. "Oh, did I? I guess I have a sweet heart."

"Sweet tooth," Marilyn murmured as she popped bread into the toaster.

They settled down at the table, their eggs in their little cups, the clever egg-slicing device next to Ruth's plate. It made Marilyn smile to watch her mother attend to the opening of her egg. It was a moment of pleasure and concentration for Ruth as she carefully fit the aluminum ring over the top of the egg and snipped the shell, then neatly lifted off the top bit of egg, revealing the shimmering yellow yolk inside the solid white.

"Perfection!" Ruth said, as she did every morning. She sprinkled salt and pepper on the egg, dipped in her spoon, and nearly purred with pleasure.

This is a moment in a life, Marilyn told herself. *This is a good moment in a life that deserves lots of good moments.*

She ate her own egg without much noticing its flavor. All food seemed bland these days. All life seemed bland—bleak.

Mentally, Marilyn slapped herself. "So, Mom," she said brightly, "let's go to the Museum of Science!" Her mother loved going there.

"Well, dear, actually, I was thinking I'd like to stop in at the local Senior Citizens' Center." Ruth dipped a tip of her whole-wheat toast into the eggshell, soaking up every last bit of buttery yolk.

Marilyn stared. "The local Senior Citizens' Center—is there such a thing?"

"Oh, yes. On Hawthorne Street. Open every day from nine to five. Sometimes in the evenings, too, if they have a speaker."

"How did you find out about this?" Perhaps Ruth had been scammed by a telemarketer when Marilyn was out . . .

"It was in the *Boston Globe*. There was an article about it last week. It looks like fun. They've got bingo, and arts and crafts, and dances, and programs."

"Well, great!" Marilyn felt oddly rejected. She felt all snarly inside. Here she'd changed her life in order to take care of her mother, and her mother had made other plans.

Ruth peered over her glasses at Marilyn. "You'd better get dressed, sweetheart. It's rather late in the morning to be in your robe. You don't want to acquire slovenly rabbits at this age."

"You're right, of course." Marilyn set her dishes in the sink and went off to get dressed for the day, which suddenly loomed emptily before her.

In her bedroom, she listlessly pulled on trousers and a sweater, vaguely aware her Hot Flash friends would scream at the mismatched colors, but unable to give a damn. What would she do with herself after she dropped her mother at the Senior Citizens' Center? How much time would she have? An hour? Two? Three? She allowed a mild surge of resentment to surface before reminding herself it didn't really matter—she didn't care whether she went in to the lab or not. Her work seemed so unimportant these days.

She forced herself to move forward. "Okay, Mother. Let's get our coats on."

She held Ruth's coat for her, then pulled on her own, choosing the ugly, puffy down one her friends hated, because she was in such an ugly, puffy mood. Ruth gathered up her purse and gloves, Marilyn locked the door, and together they took the elevator down to the lobby.

"You wait here," Marilyn instructed her mother. "I'll bring the car around, then come in and get you."

"I can walk to the car myself, honey," Ruth objected.

"Of course you can, but I'd feel better if you'd wait for me. The rain's turning to ice."

"All right, dear," Ruth said agreeably.

Marilyn ran through the bitter wind to her car in the condo lot. It was one of those bleak, gray days when clouds drained the world of color. In her hurry to get inside the car, she hit her shoulder, *hard*.

"Damn!" She dropped her head onto the steering wheel. Deep breaths, she told herself. Take deep fucking breaths! Get your act together, Marilyn. You're not the only woman making sacrifices on this planet. Think of Shirley—she's carrying on without Justin.

When she'd regained a bit of self-control, she drove around to the front of the building. Just where she needed to park the car, at the end of the sidewalk leading from the condo, a taxi was stopped, its exhaust spiraling up through the rain like smoke from a chimney. A man stepped out of the cab, pulled up the hood of his raincoat, took the two suitcases the driver handed him, and ran for the condo. He disappeared inside.

Marilyn waited until the taxi drove away, then pulled up and parked in the empty space. She switched on her hazard lights and turn indicator, then ran through the streaming rain.

In the lobby, Ruth stood dry and perky with her red-and-green striped Christmas muffler, matching cap, and mittens. She was chatting with the man in the raincoat, her face bright and animated. In contrast, Marilyn felt drenched and soggy.

"Ready to go, Mother?" Marilyn asked, straining to sound cheerful.

"Not just yet, dear," Ruth said. "Look who's here."

The man in the raincoat turned.

Marilyn's knees went weak.

"Ian?"

"Hello, Marilyn." Ian was smiling from ear to ear.

"What are you doing here?" Her brain couldn't assimilate this new information. It was like trying to fit a cookie cutter in a jigsaw space.

"I've just come from Boston University," Ian told her. "I'm taking a position there."

"You are?" Marilyn felt herself stagger backward. She put a hand out against the wall to stabilize herself.

"I didn't want to tell you until I knew for sure." Ian put his hands on Marilyn's shoulders, steadying her. "I'm moving here. And while I didn't envision asking you in exactly such a time and place, once again, I'm asking you to marry me."

"Oh, Ian!" Marilyn's heart flowered like a poinsettia.

From behind Ian's shoulders, Ruth said, "There's always light at the end of a prayer."

30

Steam wreathed the heads of the Hot Flash Club as they lounged in the fragrant Jacuzzi.

Alice's tense muscles were melting like butter in the soothing warmth. "Shirley, this was a brilliant idea."

"Thanks! I thought we could all use a little relaxation time."

Shirley had invited them for Christmas Eve lunch at her condo. She'd surprised them with a beautifully served salad of field greens and chopped vegetables, and a concoction of mixed fruits. Sparkling water was the only beverage, and dessert was, instead of food, a nice long soak in the Jacuzzi.

Faye patted her bulging belly. "I really appreciate this, Shirley. I've been eating so much—you know how it gets during the holidays—everything's so rich. People drop off gifts of chocolates or homemade fudge or—"

"Pecans!" Polly chirped. "Those wonderful salted, candied pecans!"

"I made a *bûche de Noël*," Alice told them. "Needless to say, I ate half the icing while I put the thing together."

Marilyn looked surprised. "A *bûche de Noël*? That's pretty ambitious."

Alice stretched her limbs like a contented cat. "I've really got the Christmas spirit this year."

"Yeah, you should see her tree," Shirley said enthusiastically. "It touches the ceiling. And the *presents*! It's like Santa's workshop in her living room."

Alice grinned. She didn't feel the slightest bit abashed. "Well, a baby needs so much! And I got quite a few little goodies for Jennifer—you know how emotional young mothers are."

"Oh, and old nonmothers aren't?" Shirley teased.

"I got you a few things, too," Alice assured her. She told the others, "Shirley's spending tonight with us. I didn't like the thought of her being alone on Christmas Eve and Christmas Day."

"Plus," Shirley added enthusiastically, "while the turkey's roasting and Gideon's watching football, I'm going to access my site on match.com and show Alice all my prospective suitors."

"How many do you have?" Polly asked.

"Twenty-two!" Shirley giggled. "I don't know when I've had so much fun!"

"Speaking of beaux . . ." Marilyn pulled up the strap on her bathing suit. "Ruth has a man in her life!"

"How wonderful! Where did she meet him?" Faye asked.

"At the Senior Citizens' Center. His name is Ernest Eberhart. He's just her age, and very cute. And wait till you hear how they met! They were in line to go into the cafeteria, and Ernest was in front of Ruth. He was using a walker, and he turned to Mother and asked her to pull his pants up."

The other women gasped in surprise.

"Well, you see," Marilyn explained, "he'd just gotten out of the hospital, and he'd lost weight during an operation, so his pants were loose. This was his first time out in public with a walker. He was afraid that if he took his hands off the walker, he'd lose his balance and fall. So he asked Ruth to just hitch up his pants."

"What did she do?" Polly asked.

"She reached over and yanked up his pants with both hands. Then she said, 'This is the first time any man has ever asked me to pull his pants *up*.' "

They all shrieked with laughter.

"The saucy thing!" Faye chuckled.

"That Ruth is my role model," Shirley said.

"Well, Ruth and Ernest and their group are pretty impressive for their age." Marilyn laughed. "Ruth told me a story, and it's *true*. Ernest's best friend, Harold—I haven't met Harold yet, but my mother has—anyway, Ernest's friend Harold went to the doctor this week. He's eighty-six and hasn't been feeling up to snuff. The doctor told him he has cancer, and has only a year or so to live. 'In that case,' Harold said, 'I want a prescription for Viagra.' "

"Good for him!" Alice cheered.

Shirley looked thoughtful. "What's that saying? It's better to travel hopefully than it is to arrive."

"Speaking of traveling," Marilyn looked at Polly and Faye. "When do you leave?"

"We're flying down to Florida tomorrow morning," Faye said. "Aubrey and me, Polly and Hugh."

"The guy who dreamed up this Christmas Getaway Cruise was a genius," Polly added. "When I dropped off my presents to Amy, David, and Jehoshaphat yesterday morning, I was in such a hurry I didn't have time to feel rejected by them."

"At least Carolyn's changed, don't you think, Polly?" Faye asked.

"Oh, absolutely," Polly agreed. She told the others, "Carolyn and her family—everyone except Aubrey— left for London yesterday. And the evening before, Carolyn gave a dinner party. She invited Faye and seated her next to Aubrey. She told me to bring Hugh, and she placed us next to each other."

"So your Thanksgiving temper tantrum worked!" Shirley said.

Polly objected, "I wouldn't call it a *temper tantrum* . . ."

"You're right," Shirley agreed. "That makes it seem irrational. I just meant you stood up for yourself and what you wanted. Sometimes that's hard to do."

"Sometimes it's hardest to do with members of your own family," Marilyn added.

"Speaking of families," Faye said, "it was such a good idea, Shirley, to have that Christmas party for the families of the employees of The Haven. Everyone enjoyed it so much."

"I think I enjoyed it most of all," Shirley said. "I had so much fun buying presents for all those little kids— and when they saw the tree! And opened their presents! They were genuinely thrilled. All those darling faces." She patted her chest. "Makes me tear up."

"This time last year," Faye said in a musing tone of voice, "you wanted it to be a Dream Come True Christmas."

"I still do," Shirley admitted. "I suppose I always will."

"You're an incorrigible optimist," Alice declared.

"But sometimes you're right," Marilyn told Shirley, smiling. "I'm living proof of that."

"Have you and Ian found a house yet?" Faye asked.

Marilyn shook her head. "Oh, with Christmas and all, we've had to put the search on hold. We'll have more time after the first of the year."

"How does Ruth like Ian?" Polly asked.

"She adores him. But she still insists she'll only live with us as long as she has a private apartment. She says we need our privacy and she needs hers."

Alice said, "Lots of places have mother-in-law apartments these days."

Marilyn nodded. "Good thing. There are about thirty-eight million women over fifty in the United States today. I don't know how many of their mothers are alive and kicking, but it's got to be quite a few. Fathers, too. Anyway, if Ian and I find a house we like that doesn't have one, we can always build an apartment on."

"Have you decided on a wedding date?" Shirley asked.

Marilyn smiled dreamily. "Not yet. Don't worry. I wouldn't dream of getting married without all of you in attendance!"

Alice waved her fingers. "Prunes!"

Shirley nodded. "Right. Time to get out."

The five women climbed out of the Jacuzzi, went into the locker room, took quick showers, then pulled on their warm winter clothing. They'd entered the Jacuzzi separately, and now as they dressed together, they noticed they were all wearing the same thing: hot pink sweatshirts printed across the bust with the logo "Havenly Yours," given to the five by the employees of The Haven and Havenly Yours.

"Look!" Shirley called. "Someone should take our picture!"

"No camera!" Faye faked a pout.

"That's all right," Alice said. "We'll wear these again, in the new year, when someone else is around to get all five of us together." She glanced at her watch. "Oh-oh, it's late! I've got to run."

Shirley said, "You go ahead, Alice. I've got to get some stuff from my apartment. I'll be at your place soon."

"Merry Christmas, everyone," Faye said as she tucked her hair into a red wool fedora decorated with a green sprig of holly.

"Merry Christmas!" the others chorused.

They pulled on caps, and gloves, and mufflers, and

coats. They hugged and kissed, and grabbed up their purses. Chattering and laughing, they rushed out of The Haven to their cars and their busy lives.

And snowflakes drifted down around them like snippets of celestial lace.

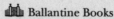